Murder

in Ordinary

Time

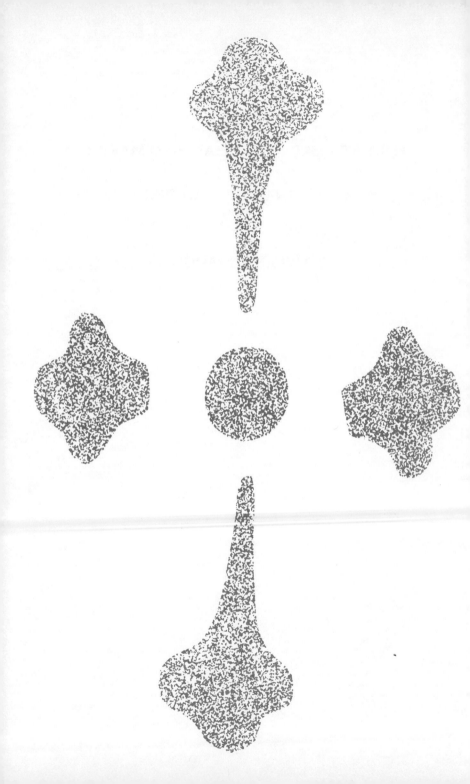

Murder in ordinary time

Sister Carol Anne O'Marie

DELACORTE PRESS

PUBLISHED BY
DELACORTE PRESS
BANTAM DOUBLEDAY DELL PUBLISHING GROUP, INC.
666 FIFTH AVENUE
NEW YORK, NEW YORK 10103

LIBRARY OF CONGRESS CATALOGING-IN-PUBLICATION DATA

O'MARIE, CAROL ANNE.
    MURDER IN ORDINARY TIME / CAROL ANNE O'MARIE.
        p.   cm.
    ISBN 0-385-30226-6 (hc) : $18.00
    I. TITLE.
    PS3565.M347M87   1991
    813'.54—dc20   91-20455
                                           CIP

BOOK DESIGN BY DIANE STEVENSON/SNAP-HAUS GRAPHICS

MANUFACTURED IN THE UNITED STATES OF AMERICA

PUBLISHED SIMULTANEOUSLY IN CANADA

OCTOBER 1991

10 9 8 7 6 5 4 3 2 1

RRH

DEDICATION

In gratitude to those who have helped me with my Sister Mary Helen mysteries, especially Rosalie Kelly, the Pendragons, and Sister Mary Williams for their critiques, Violet Lane, my "before-computer" typist, assorted members of the San Francisco Police Department for their technical advice, and Sister Maureen Lyons, my faithful research assistant.

Murder
in Ordinary
Time

—

January 10
TUESDAY OF THE FIRST
WEEK OF ORDINARY TIME

Sister Mary Helen had a case of the blahs! Sitting alone in her small, cold basement office, she stared into space. These are not your ordinary Monday-morning blahs, she thought, dumping a stack of Christmas cards into the wastepaper basket. This is serious. The cards hit the bottom with a metallic thud.

Furthermore, today wasn't even Monday. It was Tuesday, the first Tuesday in Ordinary Time.

Ordinary Time! Ugh! That was one of the few liturgical reforms set in motion by the Second Vatican Council that she totally opposed. Ordinary Time, indeed! Some liturgist with a sense of humor, which was rare in itself, had called it a "season without a reason."

Why, in the old days—good grief, she was beginning to sound like a seventy-six-year-old—or was it seventy-eight? No matter, the point was that years ago the thirty-four Sundays of the year belonging to no particular feast were attached to a holy day. In winter they were called the Sundays after Epiphany; in summer, the Sundays after Pentecost. That way you could root these aimless winter months in a celebration.

From somewhere down the empty corridor, a door

slammed. Mary Helen jumped. Pushing up her bifocals, which had slipped down her nose, she stared out the narrow slit of a window set high on the wall.

Even the weather was downright dull. The fog just hung there. It didn't tumble and roll in with any pizzazz or burn off like magic, leaving behind a sparkling winter sky. No, it just sat there all day long, gray and drizzly, wrapping San Francisco in gloom.

And the college itself was no help with its gray-green lawns and borders of black, bare trees and pruned rose-bushes. Now that all the students were on semester break and just a skeleton crew on hand, Mount St. Francis College seemed like a ghost college, high on a lonely hill, with the City below hidden in the overcast.

Good night, nurse! Mary Helen shook herself. Maybe what I have is a case of the winter blahs. What had they called it in the *San Francisco Chronicle*? SAD, Seasonal Affective Disorder. The morning paper said that the disease was accompanied by a carbohydrate craving.

Actually, right this minute she'd love to bite into a thick, soft slice of sourdough bread, its brown crust crunchy and chewy, smothered in butter. Yum! Mary Helen checked the buttons on her white blouse to see if they were pouching. They were. She tugged at her navy blue suit skirt, which was beginning to ride up.

Actually, her craving was most likely caused by her having given serious thought to starting a New Year's diet. The very word *diet* always made her hungry.

"Good morning, Sister. It's I." The outer office door shut with a cheerful bang.

Even if Mary Helen hadn't recognized the voice or the staccato click of the high heels, she still would have known it was Shirley. Her secretary was probably one of the few people left alive who said "It is I" instead of "It is me."

"What in the world are you doing sitting here in the dark?" Reaching around the doorjamb, Shirley flipped on the fluorescent lights. With a pop they lit up the room, making Shirley's silvery white hair shine. "Is that better?"

Mary Helen blinked at the sudden brightness. Shirley stood in the doorway wearing a two-piece scarlet dress, a large paisley scarf around her neck. To Mary Helen's constant amazement, her secretary's earrings and shoes always matched her outfits perfectly. And, sure enough, she had done it again.

"Are you all right?" Shirley looked concerned.

Before Sister Mary Helen had a chance to answer, the phone rang, its shrill, insistent *br-ring* echoing in the deserted building.

"I'll get it." Quickly, Shirley moved to her own desk, leaving only the faint odor of her perfume wafting through the air.

White Linen! Mary Helen recognized the scent. Bernadette Harney had given her some White Linen dusting powder for Christmas.

The intercom crackled. "It's Bernadette Harney for you, Sister. Line one."

"Speak of the devil," Mary Helen said.

"Pardon me, Sister?" Her secretary sounded puzzled, and it was no wonder. Mary Helen realized she had been thinking, not speaking.

"Never mind, Shirley," she said. It wasn't worth explaining. "Did Bernadette mention what she wants?"

"No, just that it was a 'personal matter.'"

Personal? That was odd. Usually, Bernadette's calls were business. In fact, since Bernadette Harney had become the president of Mount St. Francis's Alumnae Association, almost all Mary Helen's dealings with her touched on alumnae business. The old nun was glad, since Bernadette Lally—Mary Helen's friend Sister Eileen still called her by her maiden name—was easy to do business with.

"A true Mount St. Francis girl," Sister Therese proudly dubbed Bernadette. And Mary Helen knew that, from Therese, this was no small compliment. As a matter of fact, it would probably be easier to achieve a Nobel prize than to wrest that honorable title from Therese's lips.

"Good morning, Bernadette. What can I do for you?" she asked, hoping she sounded a lot more helpful than she felt.

—

"What is it, Sister? You are all flushed." Shirley dusted a few Christmas tree needles off the edge of Sister Mary Helen's desk and put a stack of mail in their place. "Is something wrong?"

"Not wrong, really." Mary Helen's head was reeling. "It's just that Bernadette asked me to do her a favor."

"Oh?" Shirley didn't say anything more. She just stood there. Behind her oversize glasses, her green eyes looked both curious and sympathetic. It was the sympathy that always undid Mary Helen.

"As a matter of fact, Bernadette asked me if I would be on TV. The noon news, to be precise." Mary Helen pronounced the words deliberately, as if hearing them aloud would make the request seem like nothing out of the ordinary.

Shirley frowned, but was too polite to say "Why you?"

"You remember her daughter, Danielle?" Mary Helen started to explain.

"Class of eighty-six, wasn't she?" Shirley knew very well she was, but not being a know-it-all was part of her charm.

"Yes, I guess. Bernadette tells me that Danielle has a brand-new job helping to produce the noon news on Channel Five. What with the Tony Costa trial coming up, and my part in the—what did the media call it?—the Holy Hill murders, well, Danielle thought a short interview with me would make a good show."

"When?" Shirley always went straight to the point.

"Day after tomorrow."

"Why didn't Danielle call you herself?"

"I suppose she was afraid that I'd turn her down. She knew I'd never say no to her mother."

"That kid's smarter than I figured," Shirley remarked. "Don't worry, Sister, whatever you say, you'll be a welcome relief to all the hype about the 49ers and the Super Bowl." She turned on her high heel, leaving Sister Mary Helen to figure out how she was going to break the news to the rest of the nuns.

⌐

At lunchtime, Mary Helen spotted her friend Sister Eileen in the Sisters' dining room. Alone at a corner table, Eileen was huddled over a bowl of steaming soup, reading.

Hooray! Mary Helen thought, choosing a grilled cheese sandwich for herself. This would give her the chance to tell Eileen about Thursday's interview before the other Sisters came in for lunch. Test the waters, so to speak.

When Mary Helen approached the table, Eileen was so absorbed in her book that she scarcely looked up.

"Busy morning." Mary Helen sighed for effect and sat down.

Eileen grunted.

"I received a very unusual request this morning." Mary Helen pulled the grilled sandwich apart and put a couple of pickle chips on the oozing cheese.

Another grunt, but this time, at least, Eileen glanced up at her.

"Bernadette Harney wants me to be interviewed on the noon news." Mary Helen watched Eileen's bushy gray eyebrows arch.

"Good for you," her friend said.

Crossing her fingers under the table, Mary Helen wished away the question she was sure was coming, although she could tell by the look on Eileen's face that her wishing was in vain.

"And will they be asking you about the college and the wonderful work of the Alumnae Association?" Sister Eileen's eyes lit up and her pudgy, round face wrinkled into a smile.

For a split second Mary Helen toyed with the idea of feigning deafness. The ploy never failed for Sister Therese.

"No, not that." She bit into her sandwich and chewed slowly, leaving Eileen to wait for her answer. No one, especially Eileen, would expect her to speak with her mouth full.

"What, then?" Eileen's gray eyes narrowed.

Patting the sides of her mouth with her paper napkin, Mary Helen muttered, "You remember Tony Costa?"

Eileen grimaced. "Glory be to God! Who could ever forget him? But what has that to do with you?" Her voice rose a tone and a bit of the brogue began to slip in, as it always did when she was agitated. "Oh, no! When is this interview?"

"Oh, yes. Thursday." Mary Helen took another bite.

"Poor, dear Cecilia—wait until she hears about this!" Eileen nodded toward the door. "And here she comes now."

Sister Mary Helen turned and watched the college president enter the dining room. Tall, with rimless glasses and a poker face, Sister Cecilia gave the illusion of being unflappable. But having flapped her several times in the recent past, Mary Helen knew it was just that—an illusion.

"I suppose I should tell her about the interview." Mary Helen shrugged. "Forewarned is forearmed, as they say."

"You *suppose* you ought to tell her? Of course you should! And the quicker the better, if you ask me," Eileen added for good measure.

Mary Helen knew that her old friend was trying to sound more aghast than she really was. If the truth were told, she was sure that Eileen enjoyed having the college pot stirred occasionally. And who could blame her? Without a little excitement, life in the ivory tower could be deadly dull. Or, at their ages, just plain deadly. And she also knew, from over fifty years of friendship, that Eileen might fuss a little, but that in the end she could always be counted on for support.

"By the way, what are you reading?" Mary Helen

asked, stalling. At least she'd give Cecilia time to find a place at a table.

Eileen held up the green and white paperback. "It was a Christmas gift from one of my library staff entitled *So You Think You're Irish?*" She popped open the book. " 'Trivia that every knowledgeable Irish person should know,' " she read. Leaning forward, she patted Sister Mary Helen's hand. "But enough procrastinating, old dear. I am quite sure that Cecilia will understand."

"What makes you so sure?"

"Is it your fault if people keep dying all around you and the media wants to ask you about it?"

"You're right." Mary Helen rose from the table with more bravado than she felt. "By the way, see if that little book can answer this question: Why do you Irish always answer a question with a question?"

Eileen winked. "Oh, do we now?" she said, then quickly returned to her reading.

January 12
THURSDAY OF THE FIRST WEEK OF ORDINARY TIME

Sister Mary Helen awoke with a start. Opening one eye, she checked the luminous dial on her clock. Five minutes to six! Her alarm was set for six. Intending to savor every extra second in bed, she snuggled down under the covers, closed her eyes, and tried to block out the morning sounds.

Impossible! From somewhere down the hall the plumbing gurgled. The basement furnace hummed. It must have rained during the night, since she heard a steady drip, drip from the gutter and, farther away, the swish of tires on the wet pavement. An insistent wind rustled the eucalyptus leaves. Even wet they sounded like dry bones. Maybe one of those winter storms that piled up along the coast every January was finally deciding to blow in and clear up the gloom.

A mechanical whine and the thud of metal against metal reminded her that Thursday was garbage day. Perhaps the Sunset Scavengers emptying the cans was what had awakened her. At any rate, she was awake now and there was nothing that was going to save her from facing the day.

Breakfast was a little strained, especially after Sister Anne had prayed aloud at the early morning Mass for the success of Sister Mary Helen's television appearance. With a few pious words, the young nun had dashed any hope Mary Helen had that it might have slipped some of the Sisters' minds.

"You'd think she'd have better sense," she had hissed at Eileen.

"You'd think somebody would," Eileen had hissed back.

—

By nine-thirty, however, when Mary Helen met Eileen by the convent's green Nova, she was resigned to her fate, even if it was dredging up some unpleasant college history.

"What will be, will be," she said, handing Eileen the car keys.

"That is very true, my friend, if not very original." Eileen revved up the motor.

Mary Helen tried not to cringe. She should be grateful. After all, Eileen had been kind enough to offer to drop her at Channel 5 so she wouldn't have to hunt for a parking place. And Eileen had signed out the convent car.

With a roar, the Nova started down the curved driveway. Barely glancing sideways, Eileen merged onto busy Turk Street, then made a wide left turn in front of the old Presentation Sisters Motherhouse. Between St. Elizabeth's Home for Unwed Mothers and the Sears, Roebuck store, Mary Helen discreetly shielded her eyes. She didn't want to hurt Eileen's feelings, but she felt sure that they were about to hit the two men next to them who were riding double on a Yamaha.

I should be grateful to Eileen for going out of her way, she reminded herself as they wound up the Masonic Avenue hill, passed the Muni carbarn, shot over Bush Street onto Divisadero. Wondering why Eileen had taken this route, Mary Helen tried to admire the three-story Victorians to get her mind off Eileen's driving. Even the dreary weather couldn't dull the charm or the splendor of the brick mansions on Pacific Heights.

When Eileen careened onto Broadway, Mary Helen held her breath. Shooting up and down its tree-lined hills, the car narrowly missed Jaguars, Mercedeses, and BMWs. She waved to a couple of nuns shivering on the corner by St. Bridget's Church before Eileen raced into the Broadway Tunnel, then down into an already crowded Chinatown.

Even if Eileen had not chosen the most efficient way, it was surely the most colorful. Breathing easier, Mary Helen tried to enjoy the ornate pagoda lampposts and the open carts of exotic fruit and fish that lined the narrow sidewalks and alleys of Chinatown. She noticed that preparations were under way for the upcoming celebration of Chinese New Year.

As they drove past what was left of the nightclubs on the old Barbary Coast, she thought they looked worn and tired in the gray morning light. I should be grateful, Mary Helen repeated, closing her eyes as they approached the off-ramp of the Bay Bridge jammed with late-morning commuters. At the moment, however, all she was grateful for was that she, not Eileen, usually did the driving.

Cleverly circling the block, Eileen slid the car to a stop in front of a smoky black building with an enormous brass 5 by the entrance. The dazzling red and pink prim-roses planted in the window boxes fought to give the place a touch of color. But today even the weather was against them.

"Ring me when you want to be picked up," Eileen called as Mary Helen gratefully got out of the car. Totally unaware of the havoc she was wreaking, Eileen merged into the traffic to the sound of brakes squealing all around her.

Watching the green Nova disappear, Mary Helen realized that she hadn't given a moment's worry to her upcoming interview since leaving the college. If the truth were known, she had been too busy worrying about an imminent accident. It is an ill wind that turns none to good, she thought. That was an expression Eileen always used, although never in reference to her own driving. Somehow it fit.

"Yoo-hoo! Sister!"

Mary Helen recognized Bernadette Harney's voice. Like it or not, there was no possible way out of the interview now.

Turning to the Channel 5 building entrance, she spotted Bernadette coming down the sidewalk toward her. Actually, it would have been difficult to miss her. Not only did her beautiful chestnut hair set her apart, but Bernadette was wrapped in a full-length lynx coat.

"Follow me, Sister." The long, feathery fur waving like pampas grass, Bernadette ushered her past the line of people waiting to be in the audience for the morning talk show. "Danielle will meet us upstairs," she explained.

Once inside the building, they stopped briefly at the front desk filled with buttons, phones, and lists. A uniformed guard with one wandering eye checked their names. A wandering eye would be a handy thing for a security guard, Mary Helen thought as she followed Bernadette through the turnstile. The crook could never be quite certain where he was looking. The elevator whisked them to the fourth floor with such a lurch that Mary Helen was sure her stomach had stayed behind on the ground floor. She wished she were there with it.

When the elevator doors opened, Bernadette brought her over to a frazzled, red-faced Danielle.

"Hi, Sister. Thanks, Mom." Without another word, the young woman led Mary Helen up a circular staircase, through a maze of milling people and narrow hallways that opened into congested rooms. The whole place crackled with urgency, and Danielle moved so quickly that Mary Helen hardly had time to wonder what had become of Bernadette. In fact, it was all she could do to keep one eye on Danielle's slim back and the other on the cartons, ground cords, and people popping out of doorways.

Falling flat, even before opening her mouth, was not the way she wanted to prepare for her upcoming interview. What questions would they ask her, anyway? She hoped she would have the opportunity to talk with someone before she went on camera.

Stopping suddenly, Danielle pointed to an open door and gave Mary Helen a harried smile. "You can wait here in the greenroom, Sister. Help yourself to something to eat. I'm sorry I can't stay with you, but someone will come for you when it's time to go on the air. Just try to relax."

Relax, indeed! Nevertheless, feeling as if she had just been granted a stay of execution, Mary Helen surveyed the crowded room. As far as she could tell, nothing about it was green—not the walls, not the worn, peach-colored couches, not even the round buffet table. A television set, tuned to Channel 5, of course, blared from the center of one wall. Everyone in the room seemed to be ignoring it. Two women sitting on the couch smiled nervously at each other while an older man hunched forward in his chair, his elbows on his knees, and twirled his hat. A bearded fellow with his head back, eyes closed and mouth open, was sound asleep. A handsome young man with blond hair stood in the corner talking on the phone.

Helping herself to a cup of coffee and a bran muffin, Mary Helen took the one vacant seat. Balancing the muffin on the arm of her chair, she rummaged through her pocketbook with her free hand until she found the murder mystery she had brought to read, just in case she did have to wait. With all these people eyeing her, she was relieved that she had slid the paperback with its gory cover into her plastic prayerbook jacket. What they didn't know wouldn't hurt them.

Sitting beside her, a plump, friendly-looking woman with champagne-colored hair fixed in a bouffant, smiled.

"How-do." Mary Helen smiled back, returning her mystery to her pocketbook and blowing on the scalding coffee.

"Hello! I'm Mrs. Potter," the other woman introduced herself. "I'm Dolly Thomas's tutor. You know Dolly Thomas, of course," Mrs. Potter said, naming a couple of films Mary Helen had never even heard of, let alone seen.

"Which one is she?" Mary Helen kept her voice low. She didn't want to embarrass the child. Or herself either, for that matter.

"Dolly? She's still in makeup." Mrs. Potter glanced

at her jeweled watch. "She's going to be on that new talk show this morning."

Just then a short woman in an even shorter skirt appeared in the doorway. She thrust out one hip and put her hand on it.

A high school cheerleader straight out of a 1970s yearbook, Mary Helen thought. That's what the woman reminded her of—an aging cheerleader. The only things missing were the pompoms and, of course, the blush of youth.

"Is she still in there?" the woman snapped at Mrs. Potter.

Mrs. Potter nodded. "That's Mrs. Thomas," she mouthed to Mary Helen. "Who is definitely not a dolly," she added when the woman had left the room.

"And who are all these others?" Mary Helen asked, glancing around. She was really curious now. Were they all part of Dolly's retinue?

Before Mrs. Potter could answer, a slim, young woman in a Gypsy skirt sashayed through the door, clipboard in hand. "I'm Cindy." She smiled as she approached Mary Helen. "Sign here, please."

Adjusting her bifocals on the bridge of her nose, Mary Helen tried to read the paper—it looked like some sort of release form—but she was too distracted. There was so much activity in the greenroom! Two tall, gangly technicians, still in earphones, had come in, laughing and joking about some foul-up. They waited for the caterer and his assistant to set out salad and French rolls for a midmorning snack, then helped themselves to the food. The handsome young man was still talking on the phone in the corner of the room. He appeared to be speaking with his agent, in quite a loud voice, Mary Helen thought.

"That's the TV car salesman, the one who wears those ten-gallon hats." Mrs. Potter nudged her and nodded toward a man seated at the far end of the room.

"Makeup for the morning cooking show guests," a delicate young man with hennaed hair announced from a side door. He didn't seem to be addressing anyone in particular, yet the two suburban matrons sitting opposite Mary Helen heaved themselves up from the couch and followed him out of the room.

"They are almost ready for you on the set, Sister. Please sign," Cindy urged.

Sister Mary Helen signed the paper, still not sure what it was. This place was so confusing. It's a miracle that anyone can concentrate, she marveled. And it's no wonder so many TV personalities are young. All these goings-on would drive an older person crazy.

Cindy had just disappeared when a breathless Danielle rushed in. "We're ready for you now, Sister Mary Helen," she announced.

The greenroom became unusually quiet. Mary Helen rose. The others must have wondered who she was too. Now they knew.

Taking a deep breath, she fought down her nervousness. After all, it was only going to be a five-minute interview on the noon news, she told herself. There's nothing to it. Hardly anyone watches the noon news, anyway. And so what if they do? What could possibly go wrong?

She followed Danielle Harney down the low-ceilinged and cluttered hallway. If nothing can possibly go wrong, she wondered, trying to relax the tightness across her shoulders, then why do I suddenly feel like a condemned prisoner being escorted to the gallows?

Compared to the greenroom, the set for the noon news was calm. Not only because there were fewer people —in fact, there were almost as many—but because all of their attention was focused on the raised desk along the side wall and the three familiar faces behind it.

When Mary Helen arrived, Christina Kelly, Channel 5's leading investigative reporter, was smiling into the camera. She looked older and much tinier in person than she did on the evening news. Her straight dark hair was cut to make a parenthesis around her delicate features. In fact, in person, everything about Christina Kelly was tiny and delicate, almost fragile. She was not at all like one would expect a tough investigative reporter to look. Perhaps that is the secret of her success, Mary Helen thought. One would expect this petite woman to cover society teas and art shows and not to tackle slumlords or prostitute rings or corrupt city fathers.

At the moment, Christina Kelly was rehearsing yet another story on the 49ers, who had won their league and were already gathering in Miami for the Super Bowl.

"That's great, Chris. Thanks." A voice, like the voice of God, boomed out of the ceiling and through the studio.

"That's the producer checking sound," Danielle explained, pointing to a speaker high on the wall. "You can sit over here." She steered Mary Helen across a floor covered with taped x's and thick coiled cords. They ducked behind three large cameras to reach a row of folding metal chairs.

"There will be two, no, three stories before our first commercial break." Danielle fumbled through some papers. "Then an in-depth report on stress, which Wendy Hartgrave will give. Then the weather. You're after the four-alarm fire in the Tenderloin district. Ray Kerns will do that segment. Then we'll take another commercial break and Christina will interview you. Over there." Pushing a straggly piece of hair back from her forehead, Danielle pointed to a small set off to one side with a couple of chairs grouped around a coffee table.

"Someone will tell you when to go on. Until then, just sit back and relax."

Sister Mary Helen sat on the metal chair that Danielle had indicated, but she could not possibly relax. There was far too much activity.

Monitors blared. Lights of all sizes in conch-red casings hung from bars on the ceiling and focused on the news desk. They removed any shadows and made the panoramic sweep of the City behind the desk look amazingly real.

A thin young girl with a green backpack walked rather clumsily behind the news desk. "Not behind. Go in front," a woman's voice shouted at her. The girl cringed and quickly retraced her steps, carefully avoiding a woman who appeared from behind the scenes with a large brush and ran it across anchorman Ray Kerns's bald crown. Could that young girl be Dolly Thomas? Mary Helen wondered. She wished she could ask someone, but she'd been left completely on her own.

Behind the desk, anchorwoman Wendy Hartgrave sat in what Sister Mary Helen remembered as Christina Kelly's usual chair and a makeup woman powdered her almost perfect profile. Only the hint of an uptilted chin spoiled it. Mary Helen feared that time and age would join forces to give poor Wendy a slightly witchlike look.

The two technicians she had seen eating in the greenroom had come back to the set and were getting ready to go to work. The older man, the one with a gray mustache and rimless glasses, looked to Mary Helen as though he should be wearing a white medical coat. If she hadn't known better, she would have pegged him for a gynecologist; he had that look about him, one that would be hard to explain to anyone except another woman.

The second fellow appeared to be at least twenty years younger with a mop of shiny black hair that nearly covered his eyes. Or maybe his eyes were set too high on his sallow face? Whichever, they were difficult to see.

Mary Helen watched the men talk briefly, then step behind two enormous cameras. A third fellow, bald on top but with a ponytail and a full beard, was already behind the pedestal of camera three.

A slender figure in a black polo shirt and Reeboks— was it a man or woman? Mary Helen wondered—darted around the set, a battery sticking out of the back jeans pocket. It wasn't until the frizzy-haired person turned around to face her that Mary Helen could see it was, indeed, a woman.

"I'm Betty Hughes, the floor manager," the woman said, coming toward her. "I'll come get you when it's time." She smiled a quick smile. "Just relax."

That word again! She would try.

In the semidarkness, she spotted Bernadette Harney's lynx coat and when her eyes adjusted, could make out Bernadette leaning against a wooden set. There was no mistaking the look of motherly pride on her face while she watched Danielle.

As far as Sister Mary Helen could tell, all that Danielle seemed to be doing was flipping through tattered papers on a clipboard and nervously chewing on the end of her pencil. But the old nun had learned long ago never to underestimate or question the pride mothers take in their offspring.

Next to Bernadette, the youngster who she thought might be Dolly Thomas slouched against the wall. From what Mary Helen could see behind the straight blond hair partially covering her face, she seemed to be pouting. Perhaps it was because the voice in the control room had shouted at her earlier.

"Hi, Sister. I'm Douglas Wayne." The deep, theatrical voice startled her. Its owner, a square-shouldered man with a full head of styled and blow-dried hair, bent over her. "I understand you're to be on our noon news."

He extended his hand, which Sister Mary Helen shook, unable to miss the diamond and onyx cuff links that stuck out from the sleeves of his cashmere jacket.

Dressed the way he was, he had to be important. Mary Helen knew that his title would be the next thing out of his mouth. Mr. Wayne did not disappoint her.

"I'm the controller here at Channel Five," he said, straightening his shirt cuffs.

Although Mary Helen had no idea where a controller ranked, she tried to appear duly impressed. "Well, I am very happy to meet you," she said.

In the background, she heard Wendy Hartgrave announcing something about "continued low, dense fog." The weather! They were getting closer to her spot. Mr. Wayne hadn't moved. He must be expecting her to say something.

"This is fascinating," she offered for lack of a

brighter comment. "So much going on. In your job you must meet so many interesting people."

Clasping his hands behind his back, Mr. Wayne cleared his throat and surveyed the room. "I suppose it is fascinating the first time you see it," he said with a studied nonchalance. "We get so used to it, it becomes just a job. We almost forget it's TV."

In the awkward silence that followed, Mary Helen fought down the urge to reply, "Baloney!"

Instead, remembering the sullen youngster standing by Bernadette, she asked, "By any chance, is that girl Dolly Thomas?"

Squinting, Wayne followed her pointing finger. "Don't I wish." He straightened his cuffs again. "That's my daughter, Cheryl. She started college last fall and is home on semester break. I brought her to work with me in hopes that we might get a little closer." He winked. "Actually it was my wife's idea."

Adjusting her glasses, Mary Helen looked from the girl to Wayne. Although it was difficult to see in the semi-darkness, there was a slight family resemblance. Maybe it was the cleft in her chin or the full lips. Did she have his full lips or was she simply wearing braces? No matter, the girl looked entirely too young to be in college, even if she was only a freshman. But then again, even the college girls' mothers were beginning to look younger these days.

Before she had a chance to ponder that phenomenon, everything in the studio changed. The lights went up. The floor manager stretched. The cameramen came out from behind their cameras. Christina took off her glasses. Ray Kerns blew his nose and Wendy ran a comb through her curly red hair. They all seemed to be talking at once over the voice of a woman on the monitor who was chatting happily about fiber in her cereal.

"Look what I found on the chair just before we went on." Christina's voice rose above the rest. She held up a heaping plate of cookies loosely wrapped in cellophane and tied with a bright red bow.

"Who are these cookies from?" she asked, pushing back one that was slipping out of the wrappings. Looking around, she undid the package.

"Doesn't it say on the card?" Ray asked, putting his handkerchief back in his pocket and adjusting his striped tie.

Christina held up the tag. "I can't read it without my glasses."

Wendy snatched the note. "I guess that's what happens when you get old," she muttered.

Everyone laughed. Canned laughter, Mary Helen thought, listening to Wendy read aloud.

" 'A Happy New Year to all of you! From an admirer. Enjoy!' "

"Take a cookie," Betty, the floor manager, ordered. "Then get that damn package off the desk. It's almost time to go back on the air."

"Not me." Wendy pushed the paper plate down the desk. "I'm allergic to chocolate. Besides, I'm on a diet." She patted her nonexistent tummy.

If that doesn't beat all, Mary Helen thought, betting that the woman's waist must be no bigger than twenty inches around. With her thumb in the measuring tape besides.

Watching Ray Kerns break a cookie in two and pop one whole piece into his mouth, she half hoped they would pass her the plate. It was nearly twelve-twenty, well past her usual lunch hour.

"Yuck!" Christina said when she bit into hers. "Raisins!"

Maybe I'm just as lucky they didn't offer me one, Mary Helen thought, watching Christina wrinkle up her nose. Her stomach growled in protest, but she was sure no one heard it. They all seemed to be listening to Christina, who was chewing as quickly as she could while muttering something about "hating raisins," and "didn't Wendy say these were chocolate chips," and "not wearing my glasses."

Almost at once the set dimmed and the lights focused on the news desk. The crew went back into action.

"Early this morning a four-alarm fire burned out of control in the Tenderloin district," Ray Kerns began.

Mary Helen stiffened. She was next. As soon as Ray finished, Betty moved her to the table and chairs at the side set and adjusted a small mike around her neck.

"Just relax, Sister." Christina took the chair across from her. "I'll ask you a few simple question about your connection with the Holy Hill murders." She patted Mary Helen's cold hand. "I promise not to put you on the spot."

Sister Mary Helen took a deep breath, ran her fingers through her short gray feather-cut hair, adjusted the jacket of her navy suit, hoping the buttons down the front of her blouse didn't pouch, and tried to look relaxed. She always enjoyed watching Christina Kelly on the news. The woman was mature and intelligent and Mary Helen found her in-depth reports both interesting and provocative. She had especially enjoyed the latest Kelly report on the plight of homeless women in San

Francisco. On the television screen, there was something warm and homey about Christina Kelly.

Fortunately, she was the same way in person. The cinnamon-brown eyes studied Mary Helen kindly. At last, she could feel herself begin to relax.

Hot lights focused on the two of them. Three cameras zoomed in. Christina sat up straight. As the newswoman adjusted the small mike around her neck, Mary Helen caught a familiar, almost nutty odor. Was it Christina's hair spray? Maybe it was her hand lotion.

"We have a special treat this noon," Mary Helen silently read along with the words on the TelePrompter as Wendy Hartgrave began her introduction.

Betty Hughes held up three fingers, then two, then one, then pointed at Christina. This was the real thing! Mary Helen concentrated on Christina's face, hoping not to catch a glimpse of her own in the monitor.

Christina's cheeks blazed under the spotlights. Even the heavy makeup did not hide the flush that was, by now, almost a violent pink.

"Now, Sister"—Christina turned toward her—"let me ask you a few questions about your involvement in . . ."

Smiling, Sister Mary Helen waited for the woman to continue. To her surprise, Christina said nothing, only gulped noisily, as if something had caught in her throat.

Suddenly, Christina's head twisted wildly from side to side, her cinnamon eyes wide, terrified, searching, pleading. Both hands tore at the collar of her blouse, ripping the skin on her neck. Frantically, she gasped for air. With a sickening jolt, her spine straightened, jerking back her head. Her whole body convulsed, then, still trembling, lurched forward. With a horrible thud Christina Kelly's head hit the coffee table.

"Christina!" Mary Helen shouted, bending over the still body. It was only then that she recognized the odor emanating from the anchorwoman. It wasn't hair spray or hand lotion at all. It was the piercing smell of bitter almond, the unmistakable odor of cyanide.

—

"Are you watching the noon news?" the anxious voice on the phone asked.

Inspector Kate Murphy recognized it immediately. But, even for her mother-in-law, the question seemed a bit bizarre.

"No, I'm at work," she answered, then felt foolish. Of course Mrs. Bassetti knew where she was. That was the number she had dialed.

"Then, you didn't see it?" Kate knew by the tremor that Mrs. B was unusually upset.

"See what?" she asked, trying not to imagine the worst.

"Your friend Sister Mary Helen was on the TV with Christina Kelly and she just dropped over dead!"

Kate's heart did a somersault. "*Who* dropped dead, Mrs. B?"

"Christina Kelly, of course!" Her mother-in-law's voice trilled even higher. "And don't call me Mrs. B. Sweet Mother of God! You're nearly ready to deliver my first grandchild. Can't you at least call me Loretta?"

"Are you sure she dropped dead, Loretta?" Kate indulged the woman's latest quirk.

Across from her, Kate's partner, Inspector Dennis Gallagher, picked up his phone on the first ring. She figured from his dark scowl and the way he began loosening his necktie, that he was receiving the same news.

Leave it to Mrs. B—Loretta, Kate mentally corrected herself—to scoop even a television station in contacting Homicide. The woman was incredible.

"It's that old nun again," Gallagher shouted the moment Kate put down the receiver. "Another goddamn corpse!"

He slapped his palm on the desktop. Kate watched the cloud of cigar ashes rise. "She's like a . . . like a . . ." Gallagher blustered, trying, no doubt, to think of an epithet bad enough, yet not too bad, to pin on a nun. "Like some modern-day Typhoid Mary!"

He grabbed his jacket from the back of his chair. "Let's step on it, Murphy, before she has the whole of Channel Five littered with bodies."

Almost before he had started, Gallagher stopped. "Here, let me give you a hand," he offered, avoiding her eyes.

"I'm perfectly capable, Denny." Kate lowered her feet. When the call came, she had had them propped up on the open bottom drawer of her desk. Some of the books she had read on pregnancy said it was better to walk, some said it was better to elevate your feet. Kate did both, just to be sure.

Trying not to look awkward, she pushed herself up from the swivel chair. The one thing she knew was that it was better not to sit too long.

Gallagher had already snatched the navy blue wool jacket from the back of her chair. It barely fit over her one-size-fits-all jumper. Jack had given them both to her for Christmas. Dear, sweet Jack! She could hardly wait to

26

get home to him tonight and have him rub her aching feet.

—

"Jeez, Katie-girl, when are you going to call it quits?" As soon as he turned the key in the ignition, Gallagher began his familiar tirade.

Kate was grateful he had waited until they had left the Homicide Detail to launch into his lecture. She didn't want to give the other inspectors a chance to join in. And she was certain that they would. To a man, they wanted her to go on maternity leave. And she would, too, a full two weeks before she was due. But, right now, Kate wasn't ready to go. "I'm just fine, thanks," she told them every time they asked, and they must have asked her at least fifty times a day. Actually, their concern was much more nerve-racking than their teasing had ever been.

"I've told you a million times, Denny, I'll go on leave in plenty of time to have this baby and I intend to take the entire six months' maternity leave." Kate struggled with the seat belt.

"Well, if I was chief, you'd go, all right. And right away! Look at you," he fumed. "You practically need a hydraulic lift to get you in and out of the car.

"A woman in your condition should be ashamed of herself, running around with a gun in her purse. Isn't it just my luck, too? Stuck, not only with a killer nun, but a pregnant partner." He took his eyes off the road just long enough to glare at her over the tops of his glasses. "Who ever heard of such a thing? And me only a few years from retirement. It's not right, Kate. Not only do I have to worry about killers, but I have to worry about miscarriages. It's no wonder I'm going bald."

Dennis Gallagher had been bald for as long as Kate could remember, so she just ignored him. The baby moved in her womb. She rested her hand on her abdomen. Such a nice baby, who didn't kick, really, just sort of glided.

Gallagher continued grumbling to himself, but he was predictable. Soon, she knew, he would bring up her father. The two policemen had been longtime friends.

Hardly listening, Kate gazed out the car window. The city streets were abloom with pregnant women. Where, she wondered, had they all been before?

"And what would your dear father say?" she heard him ask. "If I know old Mick Murphy he's rolling over in his grave right now. It's crazy, Kate. You should be home knitting those little things, those booties. Or singing to your plants. Or cooking, like my wife. Everytime she got pregnant she'd cook up a storm. Just like some TV gourmet."

So that was how Denny had begun his finely developed paunch. It could be traced back to the Gallaghers' five children.

"That was a long time ago, of course," he said, "but some things don't change, Katie-girl." He softened. Kate realized that he was about to use the pitch hardest to resist.

"I'd never forgive myself if anything happened to you or the baby and it worries me, goddammit!"

"I wouldn't be here, Denny, if I was afraid anything would happen to the baby. Or even if I thought my being here jeopardized your safety. You both mean too much to me."

Kate leaned sideways and patted his hand. It was cold and tense as he gripped the wheel. Siren blaring, the unmarked car shot up the Sansome Street hill. Cars pulled quickly to the curbs, or at least as close to a curb as the double-parked delivery trucks would allow.

As Gallagher wove in and out of traffic, Kate could feel the baby flutter, then leap into high gear. Kate was starving. She had just finished lunch when Mrs. B—oops, Loretta—had called, and yet here she was, hungry again.

Rummaging through her purse, she found a plastic bag of carrot sticks. She would rather have stopped for a juicy hamburger, oozing with mayonnaise and catsup and pickle relish, but she had already gained thirty pounds with a full month left to go. Someone has to be counting wrong, she thought. It seems as if I've been pregnant for at least two years. As they zipped by Jovanelo's Italian restaurant, she offered Gallagher a carrot stick.

"See what I mean?" he started again, recharged after his brief pause. "What kind of a thing is this? One cop offering another cop a carrot? A cup of coffee? Yeah. A doughnut? Okay. A cigarette? Sure. But a carrot stick?

"Kate, it's unnatural. Bad enough you go by your maiden name, while anyone with an eye in his head can see you are definitely no maiden, but then to stay on active duty until you are damned near ready to deliver? Which it looks to me like you are already."

"I told you, I still have a month until my due date and first babies are notoriously late."

"Are you sure about the date?" Gallagher glared at her over his glasses.

Kate glared back.

"You wouldn't be the first one who made a mistake, you know." He careened around a corner. "And what if we're on a case and you go into labor? Then what do we do? I tell you, Kate, this whole thing is a helluva mess and it worries me."

So *that* was it! Only as they pulled up in front of Channel 5, did Kate realize what was really worrying Gallagher. It was the very last thing he mentioned, of course.

Her partner was afraid that her trip to the delivery room would end up being some sort of a cliff-hanger. He was scared to death that they might not make it to the hospital on time and that he would end up helping with the birth.

The very thought of it made him turn white. And, frankly, Kate didn't feel too happy with the prospect either.

—

The television studio was unnaturally silent, as though a movie had been stopped in midframe, leaving all the actors standing frozen in time. The only sound was the cheery voice of the woman on the monitor babbling, once again, about the fiber in her cereal.

A lot of good it did Christina Kelly, Mary Helen thought numbly. She felt the woman's pulse for the second time, unable to believe it was really still. "She's gone," Sister Mary Helen whispered to the stunned onlookers, "gone home."

"*In paradisum deducant te angeli . . .*" Instinctively, the comforting tones of the ancient Latin chant floated into her consciousness. "*Chorus angelorum te suscipiat . . .*" she prayed. "May the angels lead thee into paradise, may the martyrs welcome thee and take thee to the holy city. . . . May the choir of angels welcome thee. . . ."

The moment Sister Mary Helen saw Kate Murphy's

head of red hair, a feeling of relief washed over her. "Thank You, Lord," she shot a prayer heavenward. "Thank You so much for sending someone I know."

The expression on Inspector Gallagher's face, however, gave her a moment's pause. Then again, the devil you know is better than the devil you don't. She rushed forward to greet the pair.

"I'm so glad it's you." Mary Helen grabbed both Kate's hands and squeezed. She actually wanted to give her a big hug, but she knew that the eyes of everyone in the studio were focused on them. Better not to let the others know that she and the Homicide inspector were dear friends.

"I'm not so glad it's you," Kate said under her breath. "How in the world do you manage?"

Pretending not to hear, Mary Helen turned toward Gallagher. "And I'm glad it's you, too, Inspector."

Gallagher nodded politely, although Mary Helen would swear that the look on his face could easily have soured milk.

"It was cyanide," she blurted out. "It must have been in the cookies."

Kate Murphy frowned. "Are you sure, Sister?"

Mary Helen nodded.

"Pardon me, S'ter," Gallagher stepped forward. His expression hadn't changed, but now his face was crimson. "How the hell, excuse me, heck, do you know? The medical examiner and the lab boys aren't even here yet. They're pros and it'll take them a little time to—"

With a wave of her hand, Mary Helen interrupted. She knew exactly where Gallagher was headed. "I know, because a cookie was the last thing she ate. And anyone who reads as many murder mysteries as I do knows that cyanide works fast and smells like bitter almonds. Just smell for yourself, Inspector." Mary Helen pointed toward poor Christina.

The anchorwoman's thin body, unnaturally twisted, was slumped forward, her head resting on the coffee table. Her baby-fine brown hair had parted in the back to expose her long, thin neck.

Loosening his tie, Gallagher glared. "I hope you also read enough of them books to tell everybody not to touch anything."

"Absolutely, Inspector." Sister Mary Helen studied the toes of her pumps, hoping she looked properly deferential. "All I did was touch poor Christina's wrist to see if she had a pulse. . . . And the phone to call you," she added.

All at once, the TV studio swarmed with men holding cameras and notepads and black cases. The SFPD swung into action. Flashes popped, one officer paced off the room while another dusted for fingerprints, and a third man bagged what was left of the fatal plate of cookies. A couple of pimply-faced attendants wheeled in the gurney.

"I'm going to have to ask you all to remain in this room for a while," Gallagher's voice boomed above the hubbub. "Inspector Murphy and I will want to talk to you one by one, in there." He pointed toward the control room and then motioned for Douglas Wayne to follow him.

Sister Mary Helen took advantage of the confusion to ask Kate if she could call the convent. Please, God, she hoped the nuns weren't watching the news. Dropping her two dimes into the pay phone in the hall, she heard the dull ring.

Sister Therese, arthritis or no, was Mount St. Francis convent's champion phone answerer. Mary Helen swore she could get it on the third ring from anyplace in the entire building. At the moment, Therese's voice was the last voice she wanted to hear.

"One, two, three," she counted. When Sister Eileen answered, Mary Helen was relieved. Eileen had beaten Therese. This, however, could mean only one thing. The convent was in a tumult.

"I saw it." Her friend's voice was thick with the brogue. "How are you?"

"Fine, I guess." Mary Helen hadn't really thought about herself until Eileen asked. All at once, her hands began to tremble. She clutched the receiver, trying to stop. Her knees went watery. Holding on to the wall with one hand, she sank into the folding chair below the pay phone.

"Are the other nuns in an uproar?" she asked.

"Is the Pope a Catholic?" Eileen asked back. "Now, you'll ring me when you are ready to come home, won't you, old dear?" She added, "I promise that I'll beat Therese to the phone."

"Thanks for sticking with me." Mary Helen could feel the tears stinging her eyes.

Eileen cleared her throat. "They have an old saying back home," she began.

Mary Helen should have known. Eileen had an "old saying" from "back home" to fit almost every prickly situation. Sometimes Mary Helen suspected that she made them up as she went along.

"In for a penny, in for a pound," she said as cheerfully as she could.

Hanging up the receiver, Mary Helen had the uneasy

feeling that this particular situation was going to turn out to cost both her and her friend at least a pound and a half.

Back in the studio, even the TV monitor was turned off. Sitting down, Mary Helen closed her eyes. Had this really happened or was she dreaming? Just twenty minutes ago her biggest worry was what kind of appearance she would make on television. How quickly everything had changed. One moment Christina Kelly was alive, smiling, asking her a question, and the next, she was gone.

Crazily, a snippet of poetry caught in her mind. "For brief as water falling will be death, and brief as flower falling, or a leaf . . ." The rest escaped her.

From somewhere she heard the sound of crying, a tiny high sound like a lost kitten's. Opening her eyes, Mary Helen surveyed the room. Against the wall Bernadette Harney hugged Danielle close, gently rocking her daughter back and forth.

Next to them, Cheryl Wayne sat on the floor, her tattered green backpack in a lump beside her. Limp blond hair nearly covered the girl's face. *She* was the frightened kitten, sobbing into a wad of tissue. And why not, Mary Helen thought, the poor kid! First a death, then the police taking her father into the control room.

Betty Hughes sat dejectedly on the edge of the news desk platform. Elbows on her knees, she buried her face in her hands. From behind the desk, Wendy Hartgrave stared ahead blankly, all the color drained from her face. Still seated beside her, Ray Kerns twisted and untwisted his striped tie. "Why Chris?" he asked no one in particular. "Everyone loved Chris. Who in the world would want to kill her?"

MURÐER IN ORÐINARY TIME

The three cameramen stood mutely behind their cameras, obviously stunned.

To be quite frank, in Mary Helen's opinion, everyone in the studio appeared to be stunned. And why not? Someone had come in, probably while the studio was standing open and unattended, and left a mysterious package of cookies. "A Happy New Year to all of you!" the tag had read. Any one of them could have been the victim. Perhaps somebody had noticed a stranger, a person who did not belong.

Now that she was feeling a little less wobbly, Mary Helen sidled over to the bald cameraman with the ponytail and beard. "How long is this studio left open before you come in to do the noon news?" she asked in a whisper. She was only trying to help Kate in the investigation, of course, but from past experience she knew how Inspector Gallagher felt about her help. There was no sense getting on his nerves.

At first, Mary Helen thought that the man had not heard her. She was just about to repeat the question a little louder when he spoke.

"No time a'tall," he said with a cowboy twang. "Betty, there, she's got the keys and her and me opened up the doors about eleven-thirty so as we could set up. This studio is locked up tight. I was with her when she opened up and it looked to me like nobody, not even the janitor, had been here since last night."

"Did you see anyone come in who didn't belong?" she asked, eager to identify the stranger.

Slowly, the cameraman shook his head. "No, ma'am, everybody what came in, belonged in."

Sister Mary Helen returned to her chair. Without warning a sharp, unsettling pain shot through the bottom of her stomach and sent a twinge of fear wiggling up to her brain. It lodged there and made her feel chilled all over. If the studio was locked up tight and no one else entered it except those who belonged, then one of the people who was already in this room, one of these people looking so very ordinary and so very stunned, one of them is a shrewd and cunning murderer.

JANUARY 13
FRIDAY OF THE FIRST WEEK OF ORDINARY TIME FEAST OF SAINT HILARY, BISHOP AND DOCTOR

Sister Mary Helen had deliberately overslept. Or was that a contradiction in terms, she wondered, pulling her electric blanket up under her nose.

"Why don't you stay in bed in the morning?" Sister Cecilia, the college president, had urged her last night. "You look very, very tired."

Mary Helen had been touched. For all-business Cecilia, using "very" twice was tantamount to being maudlin.

At any rate, she had not needed anyone to second the motion. She knew she was tired; sad tired, shocked tired. Although she still hadn't totally accepted that Christina Kelly was dead. . . .

The subconscious is a funny thing, she mused, wriggling to get comfortable; it lets you comprehend only as much of reality as you can bear. And Mary Helen knew she was not ready yet for the full impact of what had happened. She wasn't even sure that she was ready to face the day.

As she lay there in the semidarkness, all she could see through her bedroom window was sky; bruised-looking sky with the wind hurling black and gray clouds across it. A lone gull, like a slash of white paint, squawked and wheeled in the dullness.

It's bound to storm soon, Mary Helen thought, deliberately distracting herself. A good, healthy downpour would clear the City of all this gloom. Maybe a full-blown storm would even clear the air in the convent.

Not that the convent air was gloomy. *Tense* would be more the word. The nuns had been kind enough when she finally arrived home last night, and genuinely sympathetic. But Sister Mary Helen couldn't help feeling from Sister Therese and some of her cohorts that, somehow, she was being held to blame for what had happened.

It was nothing she could put her finger on, really. It was their occasional "humphs," the exaggerated "Oh, reallys?" or the sudden dart of the eyes followed by silence.

A gentle tap, tap, tapping on the door interrupted her thoughts. Even as the door opened a crack, Mary Helen could smell the delicious aroma of fresh, hot coffee.

"Are you awake?" Sister Anne entered the room, pushing the bedroom door shut behind her with her foot. In one hand, the young nun held a steaming cup and in the other, a homemade yeast roll.

"Ramon sends his love," she said, handing Mary Helen the freshly baked bread. "He wants to know how you are."

Mary Helen groaned. Even Ramon, the college's pastry cook, had seen the noon news. "I thought no one ever watched TV at noon," she said, blowing on the hot coffee.

"It's on the front page of the *Chronicle*," Anne admitted, "along with the 49ers. And the Tony Costa murder trial has dropped to page two."

Closing her eyes, Mary Helen tried not to imagine the looks and "humphs" that must have gone on at breakfast in the Sisters' dining room.

Well, at least, the college was still on Christmas break. Thank God for small favors! Sister Therese would have had a field day if the "girls" had been subject to yet another Holy Hill murder. Mary Helen could hear her wondering aloud, "Whatever will the girls think? And their parents? Oh, dear!"

Despite Therese's horror, Mary Helen secretly harbored the opinion that for the most part the girls, some of their parents, and even Sister Therese herself, took a morbid delight in being part of all the excitement. It certainly was a conversation stopper.

"I didn't want to wake you." Anne's purple-rimmed glasses magnified the size of her hazel eyes. "But Eileen said I should. Inspector Gallagher called already this morning. Eileen took the message. He wants you at Channel Five by ten-thirty."

"What time is it now?" Mary Helen squinted at the alarm clock and was surprised to see that she had slept until nine-thirty.

"Eileen took the green Nova out to get some gas. She said to tell you that she would meet you by the front door at ten."

"Front door?" Mary Helen frowned. "Why the front door?" The moment she saw the expression on Sister Anne's face, she wished she hadn't asked.

"It's the reporters." Anne peeked out a corner of the bedroom window. "They've staked out the back door figuring you'll go from there to the garage. Channel Five has offered a ten-thousand-dollar reward to anyone leading them to the . . . to the person who did this."

She turned back toward Mary Helen. "Oh, by the way." Her eyes seemed to widen. "Eileen told me to remind you that today is Friday the thirteenth. So, she said for you to be extra careful and don't be counting on your good luck, because today you haven't any."

Before Anne could say another word, Sister Mary Helen turned on the bathwater full force. Drought or no drought, she could not listen to another word.

―

Kate Murphy was finally dressed. Putting on her shoes was getting to be a real chore. Since she could no longer see or reach her feet, tennis shoes were out. It was impossible to tie the laces.

"I feel like an astronaut," she called out, lumbering down the narrow staircase toward the lighted kitchen. She was afraid she looked like one, too, in the sturdy denim maternity dress Mrs. Bassetti—oops, Loretta—had given her for Christmas. At least it's better than that frilly, little-girl pinafore look, Kate thought, feeling for the next step.

"Jack, are you there?" she called again, grateful that she had run up and down these same steps since childhood. They seemed to have disappeared from her sight at about the same time as her feet. No answer.

"Is that you, pal?" She hung on to the wooden banister. "Or shall I call a cop?"

A loud grunt assured her it was her husband in the kitchen. "Hi, hon," he said without looking up from the paper he was scribbling on, or from the open book that obviously dictated what he was scribbling.

"How'd you sleep?" Jack pushed a package of gingersnaps in her direction.

MURÐER IN ORÐINARY TIME

A policeman with whom Jack worked in Vice had told him about gingersnaps. Apparently, they had worked magic for his wife when she was pregnant. How they helped, Jack hadn't said. Maybe they just kept his wife chewing and quiet. Whatever, Kate figured the fellow was wasting his time in Vice. He should have been a cookie salesman judging by the supply of them that Jack had stored in the old-fashioned pantry.

"What are you up to?" Kate pushed the yellow box aside and carefully lowered herself into the wooden chair.

Jack held up the book: *What to Name the Baby, A Treasury of 15,000 Common and Uncommon Names.*

Inwardly, Kate groaned. Another book of baby names! She suspected that every time Jack passed a branch of the public library, he brought home a new book of names.

Already, they had copies of *The New Age of Babies' Names, New Treasury of Names for Baby,* and *The Best Baby Name Book in the Whole Wide World* piled on the kitchen table. Each one with a different due date, Kate had noticed. And now, *What to Name the Baby.* Would they ever decide? Maybe they'd choose a name by the time the gingersnaps were gone—in which case, Baby Bassetti would be nameless till kindergarten!

"Did you know that five centuries before Christ, Pythagoras worked out a science of numbers for naming a child?" Jack showed her the page.

Kate leaned forward and pretended to be interested. She owed it to him. She had awakened the poor guy three times during the night to rub the cramps in her calves.

"Each letter has a number value," he said. "By adding up the letters and finding a total, you find a key number."

Kate leaned over as far as she could. Jack was so busy adding numbers, however, that she suspected he really wouldn't notice whether or not she was interested. He was working on her name, Kathleen Mary Murphy. Each letter had a number over it.

"You add up to ninety," he announced. " 'Nine plus zero. You are a nine person. The number of justice and righteousness,' " he read from the numerologist's chart. " 'Those who have it as their key numeral will battle with their lives for what they believe to be right.'

"Which reminds me." Jack put down the book. "Denny was on the phone while you were in the shower. He said that if you aren't going to go on maternity leave today, which he thinks you should, then he'll meet you at Channel Five. He's already called everyone who was in the studio yesterday and asked them to meet you two there starting at eight-thirty."

Kate pushed herself up from the chair and poured a bowl of cereal. "You know, Jack, it's really strange. Eleven people in that room, yet not one of them saw anyone actually place that plate of cookies on the desk chair." She cut a banana into the flakes, then labored toward the cupboard for raisins.

Jack poured her a cup of decaffeinated coffee. "Someone saw something," he said, "they just don't know what they know. Maybe overnight one of them will have remembered."

For a few moments, the couple sat in silence. Jack reached around the pile of baby-name books and squeezed her hand. "Abigail," he whispered. "How does the name Abigail strike you? It means 'father's joy.' "

"What if it's a boy?" Kate mumbled through a mouthful of crunchy flakes. "Besides, there was a girl in my class named Abigail, Abigail Matthews, and she used to break the points on my color crayons on purpose."

"Scratch Abigail." Jack went back to his book, leaving Kate to wonder just exactly what the day would bring. Jack was right. Somebody had seen something, they just didn't realize it. Late last night the coroner had confirmed that the cookie Christina Kelly had eaten was indeed contaminated with cyanide. Poisoned cookies, even in a TV studio, don't just float in from nowhere. Another funny thing: According to the lab report, just one cookie on the plastic plate was laced with the poison. How could someone be sure which cookie Christina would take?

"The case is almost too close to an Agatha Christie mystery to be true." Kate wondered if her husband had heard her.

"Agatha," he said, flipping through *What to Name the Baby*. " 'Greek for the kind and good. Patron saint for protection against volcanoes and earthquakes.' "

"Stop that, Jack. You are driving me crazy!" Kate snapped. She regretted it the moment she saw the puzzled look in his hazel eyes. "Sorry," she said, blowing him a kiss.

"Me too," he said, catching it and planting it on his lips. "What did you say that got me started on Agatha?"

"This case is too much like something you see on that PBS mystery show," Kate said, afraid to mention Agatha Christie again, or Dorothy Sayers or even Rumpole of the Bailey.

Humming the theme music from the series, Jack tapped his pencil against the stack of baby books. "It seems to me you are overlooking something elementary here, my dear Watson." He pointed the eraser toward her.

"And what is that?"

"When you have eliminated the impossible, what remains, however improbable, must be true." He poured them each a fresh cup of decaf.

"Excellent, Holmes, excellent! But what in the world does it mean?" Kate cupped her mug to warm her hands.

"Damned if I know. But with our friend Sister Mary Helen in the TV studio looking on, I'm betting that the poison cookie–dropper doesn't have a snowball's chance in hell. In fact, if I had to choose between Miss Marple, Harriet What's-her-name, you know, Lord Peter Wimsey's ladyfriend, and Sister Mary Helen, I'd put my money on the old nun."

"Vane," Kate said, filling in the blank, "Harriet Vane."

"Harriet, Harriet." Jack began to thumb through the baby-name book. " 'Feminine form of Henry, ruler of the home.'

"Nah," Kate heard him mutter as she left the kitchen, "we've already got one lady-ruler around here. One's enough."

—

The news studio at Channel 5 looked exactly the same as when Sister Mary Helen had left it last night. Kate and Inspector Gallagher had kept the news employees and her there for several hours, asking them to describe what had happened over and over again, posing numerous questions. Twice, Mary Helen was asked to corroborate the two cameramen's stories that they were together in the greenroom eating before televising the noon news.

This morning, she dreaded going into the studio, the scene of the murder. Apparently, so did the night janitor, even after the police announced that they had finished with it. I don't blame him, she thought. I wouldn't be here either if I had any choice. His neglect of the room, however, had done nothing to brighten the scene.

Paper cups, half full of coffee, and overflowing ashtrays were still on the floor around the metal folding chairs or balancing on ledges. The cardboard boxes that had finally been brought in with pizza for dinner were spread open across the news desk, filling the room with the odor of cold pepperoni. The only thing that seemed to have changed was the pile of coffee grounds in soggy filters atop the papers in the wastebaskets. It had grown.

Talk about the morning after the night before! Mary Helen picked out a padded chair. Chances were that this was going to be a long sit. She chose the seat next to Betty Hughes, the floor manager.

Poor Betty looked as if she hadn't had much sleep, but had just rolled in and out of bed in the same black polo shirt she had been wearing yesterday. Her face was strained and, although she hadn't taken time to put on makeup, she had run a comb through her blond hair. Or at least, Mary Helen thought so. With that frizzy-style hairdo it was difficult to tell. Not that it mattered. They were hardly here for a fashion show.

"How-do?" Mary Helen said, careful that she didn't knock the steaming white cup in Betty's hand.

The woman nodded toward it. "Do you want some coffee, Sister? It's fresh, I think, and God knows it's strong enough to wake the dead."

As soon as the words left her mouth, Betty's face blanched and tears filled her eyes.

"I know what you mean." Mary Helen pretended not to have noticed. "My friend Sister Eileen always says that our coffee at Mount St. Francis would make a dead mouse trot."

Still pale, Betty forced a smile, grateful, no doubt, that Mary Helen had chosen to lighten the situation. She looked skeptical, however, that anyone really "always" said such a thing.

Mary Helen shrugged. "Well, I heard her say it once."

Betty's soft chuckle ricocheted through the dim, nearly deserted TV studio. In the stillness, the sound was jarring, like hiccuping in church or giggling at a funeral. The patrolman standing in front of the closed door down the hall turned to scowl at the women.

Only Sister Mary Helen, Betty, and he were visible in the studio. The policeman must be guarding the room where Kate and Inspector Gallagher were interrogating a suspect.

At the thought of being a suspect, Mary Helen felt her stomach give a sharp lurch.

Surely, Kate Murphy did not believe that she had poisoned Christina. And regardless of what else Gallagher thought about her, neither did he. Even if she were capable, she had no motive.

No one killed without a motive. Any mystery reader worth her salt knew that. And everyone liked Chris. Ray Kerns had said so yesterday. She had heard him say it and then ask, "Who in the world would want to kill her?"

Yet to her mind something didn't jibe. Christina Kelly had worked for years as Channel 5's investigative reporter. Having done a little research herself, Mary Helen was always impressed with the woman's in-depth probing. She remembered vividly Christina's clear and fearless exposés of several corrupt city politicians, a slumlord or two, a prostitute smuggling ring in Chinatown, and, most recently, the plight of homeless people.

With those stories under her belt, certainly someone, or a number of someones, were bound not to like her. What story was she working on currently? Was that the key? Or would someone in her own network want to kill her?

Sister Mary Helen searched her memory for the four reasons people murder. She had read them somewhere years ago. She recalled that they all began with the letter *L.* The only one that she could think of, under the pressure of the moment, was lunacy, and everyone present in the studio yesterday at noon had at least appeared to be perfectly sane.

Furthermore, there was the possibility that the poisoned cookies had not been intended just for Christina. Any one of them could just as easily have eaten a cookie and become the victim. If she had taken a cookie as she had wanted to, Kate and Gallagher might very well be investigating her demise. The prospect sent a shiver up Mary Helen's spine.

Not that she wasn't spiritually prepared to die. She surely was. God and she had been friends for so long that the thought of meeting Him face-to-face delighted her. Besides, He owed her a number of explanations.

But humanly speaking, she hoped to have a little more warning. She wanted to be able to clean out her desk and label the pile of photos that kept growing in the box in her trunk; or, at least, to throw away her worn-torn slippers.

What was that warning in the Gospel parable, the one about the wise virgins? "Watch, therefore, for you know neither the day nor the hour." Right then and there, she decided to dispose of the slippers, no matter how comfortable they were. Tonight she would start wearing the new ones Sister Anne had given her for Christmas. Far be it from me, she thought, to get caught short like the ten foolish gals that Saint Matthew had written about, at least not with something as easy to remedy as a pair of worn slippers.

Sister Mary Helen was so absorbed in her wool-gathering that she didn't hear Ray Kerns until he had joined Betty and her. Actually, the spicy tang of his after-shave lotion was what caught her attention.

Sitting next to them, Kerns blew on, then sipped, the cup of coffee in his hand. "This stuff tastes like hot lead," he said as if he knew.

The puffy, dark circles under his eyes showed that the City's favorite anchorman hadn't slept much, either. "I can't believe that Christina's dead." He leaned forward, elbows on his knees. "God, I loved that gal."

Watching large tears course down his pudgy cheeks, Mary Helen doubted that anyone would question his sincerity. In fact, everything about Ray Kerns positively exuded sincerity: the candid look in his large brown eyes, the truthful tenor of his voice, the fact that he was honestly balding, the unpretentious gray wool suit. Even the striped tie was straightforward. In poor taste, but straightforward. No wonder he was regarded as the most trusted newsman in the Bay Area.

"I was awake half the night trying to remember if

anything was different on the set." Kerns glanced from Mary Helen to Betty. "Honestly, I can't remember a thing out of the ordinary happening here yesterday. We were having a guest spot, but we have those all the time. Christina and Wendy switched chairs behind the desk, but we do that every time we have a guest spot."

Kerns was babbling. Mary Helen listened carefully, hoping that if he didn't notice anything unusual, she might.

"When I saw Christina pick up the plate of cookies from the chair, I just assumed that Doug's wife or her own mother had sent them," Kerns went on. "Or maybe that the new cameraman was trying to impress us."

"Does that happen often?" Mary Helen asked.

"Not often enough for him," Betty said. "Ray's always hungry."

"Ray," Mary Helen blurted out, "you ate a cookie." The mental picture of him devouring his cookie in two bites flashed through her mind. Obviously, not all the cookies on the plate had been poisoned or Ray, too, would be lying in the morgue.

Ray Kerns paled. The same possibility must have just occurred to him.

"I'll miss her too," Betty said, oblivious to the conversation going on around her. She wagged her head for emphasis. "Everyone loved her. Christina was a genuinely nice person. And there are few enough of those in this business." She gave a meaningful glance toward the studio entrance where Douglas Wayne's square shoulders nearly filled the doorway.

"Good morning, people," he said in his deep, theatrical voice.

Beside her, Mary Helen felt Betty stiffen. "Who did he expect, seals?" she muttered under her breath.

Wayne glanced at his watch, then straightened the cuffs of his shirt. "It's almost eleven o'clock. Cheryl and I were to be here at eleven."

Only then did Mary Helen notice Cheryl Wayne trailing behind her father.

"Go on in, pumpkin." Wayne moved aside so that his daughter could enter the room first.

From the way Cheryl glared at her father, Mary Helen figured that going into the studio was the last thing the youngster wanted to do. For a moment, she looked as if she was going to say something. Then, reluctantly, she stepped into the semidark room, looking even younger and more frightened than she had yesterday.

"Cup of coffee, pumpkin?" Her father offered her a paper cup. Tight-lipped, Cheryl shook her head.

Wayne shrugged. Apparently changing his mind, he poured his own back into the pot and took the chair next to Ray.

"How long have you been waiting?" he asked. Although his tone was matter-of-fact, as if he were asking about dinner reservations, his hands gave him away. Mary Helen watched him try to steady their trembling by pressing the tips of his fingers together to make five little church steeples. Was that why he had poured back the coffee? Was he afraid he wouldn't be able to keep it from spilling, or was he afraid that it, too, might be poisoned like the cookies?

Those cookies! Most puzzling. How many of them had contained cyanide? Mary Helen wondered, watching the very much alive Ray Kerns refill his cup. She would ask Kate Murphy as soon as it was her turn.

When no one answered, Wayne repeated his question. "How long have you guys been here?"

"About a half an hour," Betty said, staring down at the toes of her Reeboks. "I bet they'll call Sister Mary Helen next."

Almost as if some magic ear had heard, the closed door opened and out walked Wendy Hartgrave. The anchorwoman's face was drained of color, except for two bright spots on her cheeks, which were flushed and wet from crying.

"Crocodile tears," Betty hissed into Mary Helen's ear. "Wicked Wendy doesn't shed real tears."

Fumbling through her purse for a tissue, Wendy avoided making eye contact with anyone.

"Here, use mine." Wayne pulled out a monogrammed handkerchief from the breast pocket of his suit coat and offered it to her.

"Thank you, Doug," Wendy whispered, her ice-blue eyes darting flirtatiously to his face, then away.

"Can I get you anything, Wendy?" he asked. His voice dripped with concern. "A cup of coffee?"

"No, thanks." She closed her eyes and massaged her temples. "I have a terrific migraine and I can't seem to keep anything down."

Beside her, Mary Helen could hear Betty Hughes heave an exaggerated sigh. She was just about to ask Betty what her sigh meant when she heard her name.

"Sister Mary Helen, Inspector Gallagher will see you now," the patrolman on duty called out, then pushed open the door for her to enter.

Slowly, Mary Helen rose from her chair. She smoothed her skirt, adjusted her glasses, which had slipped down the bridge of her nose, and straightened her shoulders. Despite the brave facade, her stomach roiled. Why, she wondered, did she feel this sudden sense of dread?

After all, she was only going in to speak to Kate and Inspector Gallagher about a murder. Gallagher, she knew, would act disgruntled, but underneath, he was really nothing more than a lovable old teddy bear.

Why, then, did she feel as if she were being called before the judgment seat of God, to answer to a much more ferocious, exacting, and angry God than the one she knew and loved? Maybe there was something to Eileen's warning about Friday the thirteenth being unlucky. Perhaps her session would not be as easy as she imagined. Taking a deep breath, she set her jaw for battle, just in case.

As soon as Sister Mary Helen stepped over the threshold, Kate Murphy came across the room to meet her. "It's so good to see you, Sister," Kate said. Her official, police detective expression changed to a grin, and she gave Sister Mary Helen as much of a hug as Baby Bassetti would allow.

"Here's a seat for you, Sister." Kate motioned to a small wooden chair in the corner of what seemed to be a sound room. Or at least, Mary Helen assumed it was, since a counter with microphones on it ran along one wall. The space above it was filled with speakers and knobs next to complicated-looking dials.

When they were both seated, Kate seemed to relax completely. So much so that she turned over an empty wastepaper basket and, with a sigh, rested her feet on its bottom.

MURDER IN ORDINARY TIME

"How are you feeling, dear?" Sister Mary Helen asked, completely forgetting about Inspector Gallagher. Actually, aside from swollen ankles, she thought that Kate Murphy looked wonderful. Her blue eyes, the color of Wedgwood pottery, sparkled and her freckled face was full and glowing. Even her short auburn hair seemed bouncier and more full of life.

That's what Kate Murphy was—full of life and enjoying every minute of it!

"There will be a singing in your heart / There will be a rapture in your eyes." From somewhere that snippet of poetry jumped to her mind and it seemed to fit Kate perfectly. The two women beamed at each other.

Inspector Gallagher cleared his throat. "Pardon me, ladies." The edge in his voice brought them both back to reality. "This is a murder investigation." He explained with exaggerated patience. "M-U-R-D-E-R."

Mary Helen fervently hoped he wasn't going to spell out *investigation* too.

"Not a hoity-toity tea party."

Hoity-toity! She hadn't heard that expression in years.

"Yes, of course, Inspector." Mary Helen gave him her brightest smile. "You are absolutely right. We are investigating a murder and a puzzling one at that. I've been asking myself all night and all morning who on earth had a reason to murder a lovely, talented woman like Christina Kelly? And how did they manage to do it? Those cookies have been bothering me, Inspector."

Adjusting her bifocals, she frowned up at Inspector Gallagher. "There is something I need to ask you about the cookies."

One look at his flushed face and her instincts told

her not to say another word. Actually, she knew that the most prudent thing to do would be just to sit quietly and pretend she hadn't said anything at all. But prudence had never been her strong suit. Furthermore, she was anxious to get to the bottom of this murder. Damn the torpedoes, full speed ahead! she told herself.

"Were all the cookies poisoned, or were just one or two of them?" As soon as the words left her mouth, Mary Helen knew her instincts had been right on target.

Watching Gallagher's face grow even redder, all she could think of was one of those cartoon characters with smoke coming out of the ears, like Dagwood Bumstead's boss, Mr. Dithers. Mr. J. C. Dithers!

Inspector Gallagher loosened his tie and paced the floor of the small room for what seemed like minutes to Sister Mary Helen. Actually, it was probably only a few seconds, but it was long enough for him to grab control of his temper and for Sister Mary Helen to look innocently bewildered.

"Look, S'ter, I don't mean to be rude, here"—Gallagher perched one half of his ample backside on the wooden counter that ran along the wall, and leaned toward her with what she suspected was his most intimidating scowl—"but this is a murder. 'We' are not investigating it. Kate and me are. We are the professionals"—he nodded his head toward Kate—"hard as it may be to believe from appearances. So if you don't mind too much, her and me will be the ones asking the questions and you—you just give the answers. Okay? And just the answers you're sure of, the things you've seen or heard. Not what you think or what you feel, just the essential information. Am I making myself clear, S'ter?"

A little piqued by his attitude, Mary Helen bit her

tongue and nodded. She wanted to remind him of the old Saint-Exupéry saying that "what is essential is invisible to the eye. . . . Only with the heart . . . one can see rightly." But she thought better of it. In this case, perhaps prudence was the better part of valor.

"Really, Denny." Kate laughed. "Lighten up. You're beginning to sound like Sergeant Friday. 'Just the facts, ma'am. Just the facts.'

"Sister," Kate said, taking over the interrogation. "Is there anything that you can recall this morning that you didn't remember to tell us last night? Anything you saw that bothered you?"

Kate paused to give her time to think, although there really was no need. Mary Helen had been thinking of nothing else since it happened.

Still smarting from Inspector Gallagher's rebuke, Mary Helen simply shook her head. Nothing seemed out of the ordinary, but what did she know? It was the first time she had ever been in a television studio. People had moved around confidently, each one seeming to do his or her job. Of course, Bernadette Harney and Cheryl Wayne were onlookers. Surely, neither Bernadette nor Cheryl had a motive. Bernadette didn't even know Christina Kelly, and Cheryl was only a child.

That was the key to the whole thing, she knew, the motive. If a person had a strong enough reason to kill, he or she could always find the way. But what could the reason be? She barely knew the people, let alone their relationships to Christina or to one another. The one to ask about that would be Betty Hughes, Mary Helen thought, remembering the woman's sudden stiffening when Wayne appeared and her reference to "Wicked Wendy."

Although she had met Betty only once, Mary Helen could tell that she was the kind of a woman who didn't miss much. Maybe because of her job, she had become so much a part of the background that the others didn't realize she was even there. Or maybe the woman was just intuitive. Whichever, Mary Helen would put her money on Betty "to know more than her prayers," to borrow a phrase from Sister Eileen.

Inspector Gallagher, however, had told her quite clearly to stick to the facts and that she would. If he was so professional, let him figure out that, if he wanted to know about what really went on at Channel 5, Betty Hughes was the person to ask.

—

By five o'clock in the afternoon, Kate Murphy was exhausted. It had taken Denny and her all day to question the eleven people present in the television studio when Christina Kelly was murdered. As far as she was concerned, they were no farther ahead in their investigation than they'd been when they started.

"What do you think, Denny?" Kate asked, rummaging through her purse for her diminishing supply of carrot sticks. She was not only tired but famished.

Gallagher loosened his tie and unbuttoned the collar of his shirt. "The damn laundry puts too much starch in these things," he said, rubbing the angry red line across the back of his neck. "Never had this trouble before Mrs. G got liberated. But you'd be the wrong one to talk to about that."

"Right you are, fella." Kate pointed her carrot stick for emphasis. "What do you think about today, Denny?"

she asked again, then waited while he rifled his pockets searching for his cigar.

"If you really want to know, I think today was a colossal waste of time." He turned his jacket pockets inside out. Loose tobacco fell to the floor. "Damn," he said, scattering the specks around the carpet with his foot. "I must be out of cigars."

"Better for you and much better for me," Kate said, wondering if the liberated Mrs. G might have cleaned out his pockets to save them both from inhaling her husband's smoke. "But back to today," she said. "What do you think?"

"Well, not a one of them remembered anything different from last night. Not even your old nun friend."

"I think your blustering may have intimidated her," Kate said aloud. Momentarily anyway, she thought.

"Don't I wish!" Gallagher said.

Although he was too tired to go into a full-blown tirade, Kate knew that her partner couldn't let the opportunity pass without saying something.

"Why, the Pope himself, in full regalia with the entire College of Cardinals wearing their red hats, wouldn't intimidate her. I swear, Lucifer with a raging army of fallen angels breathing fire couldn't—"

"I get your point, Denny." Kate cut him off. "You don't think you scared her, do you?"

"Scared her? I'd like to scare the hell out of her. What is it they say? 'A good scare is worth more than good advice'?"

Kate frowned. "Who says that?"

"Who knows?" Gallagher shrugged.

"Nonetheless, I find it very unusual that Sister Mary

Helen didn't notice something, remember something, or at least have something to add. It just isn't like her."

"Not one of them noticed anything or remembered anything, Katie-girl. All we got from the whole bunch of them was what a nice, kind person the victim was; how no one disliked her; how she didn't have an enemy in the world. The cameraman with the beard thought that she was tops, the guy who thinks he's important—what's his name?"

"Douglas Wayne, the controller," Kate said.

"Yeah, Wayne, that floor manager, Betty Whatever, the anchorman, Kerns, and even that Wendy Hartgrave, who, if you ask me, could be a hot tamale. They all liked her."

Kate nodded. Gallagher was right. "What about Bernadette Harney?"

"The gal in the lynx? Here by coincidence, like Mary Helen. Take them both off the list, Kate, and I think that kid, too, Danielle, the one whose idea it was to get the old nun here. Although that ought to be a crime in itself." Gallagher stopped, waiting for Kate to react.

When she didn't, he went on. "I think we can also discount the other kid, the one with the braces, the controller's daughter, Cheryl. Both those kids were too torn up. Doesn't seem to me that either of them would have the stomach to murder someone, although in this day and age, when you hear about seven-year-olds pushing drugs and shooting one another, who knows what kids can do?

"And the other two cameramen, Michael Baker and Roger Schaffer—no opportunity. They were in the green-room eating until just before the show. Sister Mary Helen confirmed that."

"If we discount everyone who liked her and everyone who was here by coincidence, plus the two cameramen who were eating, we have just about eliminated our whole list of suspects." Kate counted on her fingers. "Never mind the just-about," she said, struggling to reach her one-size-fits-all sweater hanging over the back of her chair.

"Yet, Denny, the woman is dead, poisoned by one cyanide cookie with raisins planted in a plateful. That in itself is different." Kate began to twist a piece of her red hair around her finger, the unmistakable sign that she was thinking. "The preliminary lab report says one poisoned raisin cookie in a plateful of chocolate chips. Only one was poisoned, only one had raisins. How could you be sure to kill someone with one raisin cookie in a plateful of chocolate chips?"

"Yeah!" Gallagher brightened. "Anybody in his right mind would avoid the raisins like the plague and dive into the chocolate chips."

"Anyone but a health nut." Kate stared blankly at the wall of dials. "We are definitely missing something, Denny, since someone obviously did kill her."

"Damned if I can figure out who." Gallagher moved toward the doorway. "Come on, Kate. Let's knock off. I've got O'Connor looking into everyone's background. Maybe somebody has a shady past. He'll let us know if he stumbles across anything. Now let's get out of here. It's Friday and the freeways will be jammed with all those yahoos getting out of the City for the long weekend."

Kate had forgotten that Monday was a holiday. It was Martin Luther King's birthday and all the city offices and schools would be closed. Anyone who could would be heading for the snow. She wished she were one of them.

"By Tuesday, all the reports, including O'Connor's, should be in and we can start fresh." Gallagher ran his hand over his bald pate. "Maybe we'll stumble onto something we're missing. Hell, maybe somebody will call in over the weekend and confess." He switched off the bank of fluorescent lights.

Kate sat for a moment in the shadowy coolness of the small room. "You're right about it being a wasted day." She closed her eyes. The strong lights made them burn. "Maybe we've been searching in the wrong place," she said. "Let's not forget the fact that the victim was an investigative reporter. What story was it that Betty Hughes told us she thought Kelly was working on currently?" she asked, too tired to flip through her own notes.

"She said she thought it had something to do with Greek imports and exports, except she wasn't real sure. Seems she always played her stories real close to her chest. 'Because of her seniority, the producers gave her leeway,'" he read from his notebook.

"Don't you think it's funny, Denny, that Hughes was the only one we questioned who knew even that much?" Kate yawned.

"She's the floor manager. Maybe it's her job to know that kind of stuff."

"Maybe. And don't you find it strange, almost unbelievable, that no one had anything derogatory to say about the victim? When was the last time that happened?" She stared at Gallagher, who shrugged.

"Right," Kate said, "you can't remember. Christina Kelly was a very successful investigative reporter. On the way up, she must have made some enemies among her peers. Furthermore, when you work together, even the most saintly human being can get on your nerves."

"I wouldn't know," Gallagher said, then grinned. "The whole thing is goofy, if you ask me, Katie-girl. What can there be to investigate about Greek imports? Who kills for olives and cheese? And maybe those other guys were afraid to talk ill of the dead, or maybe they thought that if they said something bad about her, we'd think they did it."

He offered her his hand. "Look at the bright side, Katie-girl. At least we don't have a crowd of enemies to eliminate. When we find one, he or she will probably be the killer."

"You may have a point." Kate stood for a moment twisting a piece of hair around her index finger, then pushing it into a curl.

Her partner knew the sign. "Now what are you thinking?" he asked.

"It's silly, Denny, but if we believed everything we heard today, then the logical conclusion would be that no one wanted Christina Kelly dead. At least, no one who had the opportunity to do it."

"Maybe the woman damn well killed herself." Gallagher shut the office door and rattled the handle to make sure it was locked. "Time to knock off, Mangan," he called to the patrolman down the hallway.

"Killed herself? Now you're getting really desperate." Kate followed him to the elevator. "No one commits suicide by eating a poisoned cookie. There has to be a better explanation than that. There just has to be another logical conclusion."

January 16
MONDAY OF THE SECOND WEEK OF ORDINARY TIME MARTIN LUTHER KING, JR.'S BIRTHDAY

All weekend long, storms had piled up, one behind the other, off San Francisco's coast. January is notoriously the City's wettest month, and the shifting clouds threatening rain had managed only to keep the entire Bay Area covered in a dull, gloomy, winter-blah gray.

Wind, wailing like a portent of disaster, awakened Sister Mary Helen early on Monday morning. The sound made her feel restless and uneasy. After the eight o'clock Mass and breakfast, she stood for a long time staring out of her bedroom window, faintly annoyed by what she saw in the murky morning light.

The campus of Mount St. Francis College was littered with branches. Eucalyptuses, still swaying violently, hurled curly pieces of torn bark every which way. Towering pines creaked and the branches of the elms slapped and scraped against the convent windows. Screeching gulls, signaling a storm, flew across the darkening sky.

As Mary Helen brooded over another dreary Monday, the convent lights dimmed and the fire alarm gave a shrill *ding* before the electricity went out.

This is going to be some day, she thought, making

her way through the shadowy corridors to the Community Room.

Settling down on the overstuffed couch in front of the old-fashioned brick fireplace, Mary Helen was not surprised to see Sister Therese already there, busying herself trying to build a fire. Mary Helen knew better than to offer help.

After several attempts, Therese managed to set most of the paper wads aflame, and it looked to Mary Helen as though several pieces of kindling were beginning to smolder.

"There." Therese stepped back to admire the struggling blaze. "That should keep us warm and cozy." She bent forward to push the heavy oak log with an iron poker. Sparks exploding like fireworks on the Fourth of July peppered the hearth. Mercifully, none landed on the rug.

"I always say there is nothing like a roaring fire to lift the spirits," Therese said, dusting soot from her hands with a satisfied smile.

It would take more than that puny fire to lift my spirits, Mary Helen wanted to say; it would take at least a ten-ton crane. Instead she just nodded. After all, poor Therese was doing her best.

With all the electricity off and the phone line dead, Mount St. Francis convent was unusually still. Only the crackling sound of the fire licking at wood and paper and the keening of the wind outside filled the large Community Room. Sister Mary Helen stared at the flames, hypnotized by the red and blue and the sudden flashes of yellow and green when the funny papers caught fire.

"What we need is an honest-to-goodness rainstorm." Eileen's voice startled her. She hadn't even heard her friend enter the room. "Yes, old dear, a real sou'wester would clear the air once and for all." Eileen pulled back the window curtain for a better look outside.

"You're right about that," Mary Helen agreed, pushing herself up from the couch to join Eileen at the window. They both peered out toward the ocean, which, of course, was impossible to see. The sky was nearly black. In the far distance, lightning rippled across the darkness. Thunder rumbled.

"It can't be much longer now." Mary Helen returned to her seat on the couch.

Almost before she sat down, large raindrops began to hit against the glass pane. Quickly the drumming grew louder, more intense, until the rain pelted down in a blinding sheet driven against the glass pane by the force of the wind.

"Do you want to play two-handed pinochle?" Eileen raised her voice above the sounds of the wind and rain.

"That's no fun." Mary Helen shrugged. "Besides, where is everyone?" Except for Sister Therese, who was still stubbornly coaxing the fire, and two or three retired Sisters sitting companionably around a window crocheting in its dim light, the Community Room was empty.

"Believe it if you will, Sister Anne drove a whole carload downtown."

"Why on earth would anyone go downtown in this weather?"

"It's the sales." Eileen's gray eyes twinkled. "The Emporium, Macy's, Nordstrom, Neiman-Marcus are all having Martin Luther King Birthday sales. Anne says that the day has finally become a bona fide holiday, like Presidents' Day or Labor Day, since it can now boast its own sale."

MURDER IN ORDINARY TIME

Although she said nothing, Mary Helen could feel her face flush. She was trying not to look annoyed, but she must have failed, since Eileen added, "She was only joking, of course."

Mary Helen knew that, but Anne's joke, so close to the truth, had done nothing to improve her mood. In our crazy society, giving one's life for a noble cause did not make a holiday. It was having a sale that made a holiday.

The first reading from the Hebrews at the morning's liturgy had seemed so appropriate to Dr. King: One "taken from among men and made their representative before God to offer gifts and sacrifices for sins." And our society had plenty of those.

"How about a rousing game of Scrabble?" Eileen asked hopefully.

"I'll play with you," Therese spoke up, then hurried to the game cupboard before Eileen could change her mind.

Sister Mary Helen was delighted. In fact, it was the first good thing that had happened to her all morning. She detested Scrabble. She simply could not think of the words quickly enough, especially words that contained z or j or x, and these were the tiles she always pulled.

On the other hand, Sister Therese loved the game and Mary Helen had to admit that she was very good at it. Therese even knew a word that began with a q without the u following it. Some sort of ancient Chinese musical instrument, if Mary Helen remembered correctly.

Sister Therese was setting up the game board and tile holders on the card table near the window before her partner had even chosen a chair.

"You look as though you didn't sleep so well, old

65

dear." Eileen turned and looked Mary Helen full in the face, as if to double-check her own statement.

"Nobody sleeps well when it's windy." Mary Helen frowned. "Everyone knows that. It is a well-known scientific fact."

"Ah, and now you are a scientist." Eileen raised her bushy gray eyebrows and said no more. She didn't have to. Both of them knew that not the wind but Christina Kelly's murder was what was disturbing Mary Helen's sleep.

Still on the couch in front of the fire, Mary Helen brooded about the violence of the storm outside, about the violence of Martin Luther King's death, and about the violence she herself had witnessed last Thursday.

What could one lone individual do about so much violence? she wondered. Of course, she knew the answer. Nothing, really, except to be peaceful oneself. At this moment, Mary Helen did not feel very peaceful. If the truth were known, she was troubled. She had been since Friday evening. All weekend she had been unable to quell the gnawing of her conscience. Her feeling of guilt had built up like the storm outside, until it was ready to burst. She knew she should have told Kate and Inspector Gallagher to speak with Betty Hughes.

Difficult as it was to admit at her age, even to herself, it had been childish to withhold her hunch that the floor manager knew what was really going on in the studio because Inspector Gallagher had hurt her feelings. Human, perhaps, but childish nevertheless.

Listening to the wind lashing the rain against the windows, Mary Helen determined that the only thing to do, for her own peace of mind as well as to help apprehend lovely Christina Kelly's murderer, was to call and tell Kate Murphy her instincts about Betty Hughes.

Unfortunately, by the time phone service was restored, all Sister Mary Helen got was a loud, steady, unanswered ring at the Bassetti residence. Evidently Kate and Jack had both gone out.

Frustrated, she noticed the still-folded copy of this morning's *Chronicle* somebody had inadvertently left on the shelf in the phone booth. Mary Helen removed the rubber band and glanced at both halves of the folded front page.

The familiar face of Christina Kelly smiled up at her from one column just below the crease. BAY AREA MOURNS SLAIN TV ANCHOR the headline read. Tributes to Christina plus her funeral arrangements were set off by two-point lines.

"According to a San Francisco Police Department spokesman, there are still no suspects and no leads in the bizarre slaying," the article ended.

Maybe I can do something to change that, Mary Helen thought, jotting down the time and place of the funeral service. If I'm unable to contact Kate, perhaps I should talk to Betty Hughes myself. She is sure to be at Christina Kelly's funeral tomorrow.

—

"Why can't we just call your mother and tell her we'll be late?" Kate knelt on the living room couch peering out the front room window. The rain was blinding.

"It is pouring," she said, watching the wind roll a garbage can lid down Geary Boulevard. "I can hardly see the other side of the street."

"It'll let up soon, hon." Jack pulled an extra-large

yellow slicker from the hall closet and helped Kate into it. "You find an umbrella and I'll get the car."

"But Jack"—she tried to sound sensible and keep the annoyance out of her voice—"your mother is a reasonable woman. She wouldn't want us driving around in this downpour."

Jack stopped fumbling in his pockets for the car keys and stared at her in mock horror. "Are you speaking of the same Loretta Bassetti that I know? That sweet, gray-haired little old lady who can turn into a werewolf if her roast is overcooked? No, Kate, when it comes to being late for Sunday dinner, my mother is not reasonable. She is a killer."

"You're exaggerating." Kate reached way back in the closet for the now faded flowered umbrella that had been her own mother's. It had been so long since anyone had used it that she couldn't remember if all the spokes were still intact.

"Furthermore, pal"—she was not prepared to give up easily—"it is not Sunday. It's Monday and we can't be eating at two o'clock."

She checked her watch. "If we leave now we'll be there by two."

Her husband shrugged. "What do I know? She said, 'Come to dinner on Monday at two.' I said, 'Okay.' And I ask you, would you rather be wet or wasted? I wouldn't be surprised if the woman is Mafiosa. Besides, hon, I think the phone went out with the lights."

"Get the car, you wimp." Kate opened and closed the front door quickly so that the driving rain wouldn't get the hardwood floor in the hallway all wet. Peeping out the side window, she watched Jack pull the car up in front.

"Grab the banister," he shouted, jumping out of the car to help her down the front stairs.

Even though only one spoke of the umbrella was broken, by the time Kate and Jack reached the car both of them were drenched. Jack turned up the heat and the radio.

"Relax, hon," he said, patting her knee, but she couldn't. Rain drumming on the metal roof almost drowned out the music on KABL. She could feel the groaning wind buffeting the car, pushing it to the left.

Their tires hissed on the wet street and passing cars threw waves of water against them. The windshield wipers worked furiously against the downpour, yet several times they were blinded. Neither spoke, but the silence was not comfortable; it was tense.

"This had better be some dinner," Kate hissed finally, but Jack didn't seem to notice. His jaw was taut. He leaned forward, clutching the wheel with one hand and wiping the fog forming on the inside of the windshield with the other.

The signal was out at 43rd Avenue and Fulton. Cautiously, Jack edged his way blindly across the wide street and into Golden Gate Park. The park was deserted. A few ducks huddled close together in the reeds along the shore of North Lake as thunder rolled in the distance and rain sheeted onto the asphalt.

When Jack pulled up to the curb in front of Mama Bassetti's, Kate let out a deep breath. "No one cooks well enough to make this trip worth it," she muttered.

"You got that right, babe," he said, coming around to help her out of the car.

Kate started up the front steps before he had finished fumbling with the umbrella. "Hold on to the banister," Jack shouted. "Those damn stairs are slippery when they're wet."

"Come in out of the rain. You look like a drowned rat!" Loretta Bassetti stood at the top of the stairs with the front door opened, hands on her wide hips, beaming. "Quick, Kate, get inside, both of you." She had spotted her son. "Get those wet things off. Shame on you, Jackie, you should have more sense than to let your pregnant wife get wet. Kate, where are your galoshes? Come in and take off your shoes before you catch cold and something happens to my precious grandchild."

With each wet step up the slippery granite staircase, Kate could feel her Irish warm until her temper was beginning to bubble. Of all the mothers-in-law in the whole world, why did she have to be stuck with this one? The woman was absolutely unpredictable and positively infuriating. She was so bossy, so overbearing, that she made the proverbial Jewish mother look like a pushover. And if she dares to bring up my decision to go back to work in six months, I'll strangle her, she thought, gripping the banister.

Why in hell did you insist that we come out in this storm if you were so worried about your precious grandchild that you didn't want me to get wet? Kate wanted to shout, but she didn't have the chance. The moment she stepped inside, she knew Mama Bassetti's reason.

"Surprise!" a large gathering of familiar, smiling faces shouted. Mrs. Bassetti had planned Kate's first baby shower.

Feeling ashamed and beginning to form a puddle in the entryway, Kate handed her mother-in-law her slicker and gave her a hug.

"Come in, Jackie. Hurry!" Mrs. Bassetti shut the

front door and pushed back a lock of gray hair that, despite hair spray, refused to stay where the beautician had put it.

"Good boy! You did good." She smiled proudly at her only son. "I made you a sandwich, Jackie. It's in the kitchen. Fix us all a good drink. Then, *mangia* and go. This is for women only." Her cheeks flushed with excitement, she asked, "Are you surprised, Kate?"

"Thoroughly shocked, Loretta." Kate slipped out of her shoes and into the hand-knitted slippers Mama Bassetti handed her. Actually, Kate was more than shocked, she was overwhelmed.

From the looks of the Bassetti home, Mama and Jack's two sisters, Angela and Gina, had spent all week decorating and cooking. The front room ceiling was covered with pink and blue stork balloons. A baby doll wrapped in a blanket swung from each stork's long, narrow beak. Little lambs filled with pink roses and bachelor buttons, and miniature starched diapers holding candy and nuts, were on the end tables, the coffee table, the mantel and even on top of the television set.

The dining room table, all done up in pink and blue, was laden with enough food for three meals, while Mama Bassetti kept running into the kitchen for yet another casserole.

Wondering for a moment what had become of Jack, Kate surveyed the crowd. Her mother-in-law had managed to commandeer nearly every female member of both the Bassetti and Murphy clans into attending. Plus she had found several old college friends of Kate's whom she hadn't seen in months. And all this in a torrential rainstorm. The woman was phenomenal. Never mind a small family, Loretta Bassetti should be running a nation.

SISTER CAROL ANNE O'MARIE

—

When Kate finally settled down to open the gifts, she couldn't believe the number and the variety. She opened bibs and layettes, rattles and nipples, diapers, crib sheets, and a baby book. There was even a bottle of Nina Ricci bath oil for her. By the time she had finished, the mound of opened presents seemed to hold everything but the baby.

As if to remind her, the babe shifted in her womb. Kate put her hand on her abdomen and smiled. It won't be long now, kiddo, she thought, whatever your name is.

"I can't imagine why you didn't have an amniocentesis," Jack's sister Angela spoke up. "Then we'd know for sure if the newest Bassetti is going to be a girl or a boy. And your gifts wouldn't be so neuter." She pointed to the open boxes.

For the first time, Kate noticed that most of the presents she had received were a combination of pink and blue, a safe yellow or green, suitable for either sex.

Before she could answer, her mother-in-law did. "Shame on you, Angela. It is not safe to go fooling around with God's creation, messing up His work with needles. What if something should happen to the baby?"

"That's archaic, Ma. It is perfectly safe." Impatiently, Angela took a drag of her cigarette. "Why didn't you, Kate?"

Kate was relieved when Jack's aunt Dosie interrupted. "Never mind annio-whatnot. I can tell the sex with this." Grinning, she stood over Kate, letting a cork with a needle in it dangle from a long piece of thread. Some of the group joined in the fun.

"It's a boy. No, look. It's a girl." Intent on the needle, Dosie's hazel eyes followed its motion. "Yes. No. It's a . . ." Dosie seemed to be having trouble making the needle decide.

Not that it mattered to Kate, who had stopped listening. The sex of the baby was the least of her concerns. What she wanted was a normal, healthy infant. Many women who, like her, were having their first child in their mid-thirties, did take the test to detect genetic defects. But since for Jack and herself abortion was completely out of the question, she didn't want to know. There was nothing to be done with the information.

"God fits the burden to the back," her own mother used to say. Kate would wait. If something was wrong with their child, she would give God plenty of time to prepare her back and Jack's, too, for the burden. Right now, they were too happy to let anything spoil their anticipation.

"Never mind, Dosie." Mama Bassetti sidled up next to her sister with an enormous plate. The aroma of freshly baked oatmeal cookies filled the living room. "Maybe you're having trouble because it's twins, a boy and a girl," she said. "But now, *mangia.*"

Mrs. Bassetti offered the plate around the room. Kate took one and bit into the warm cookie filled with walnuts and chocolate chips and raisins.

Raisins. Hell! It had been such a nice afternoon. She hadn't thought about cookies and poisoned raisins and Christina Kelly's murder the entire time. Chewing hungrily, although after all she had eaten it didn't seem possible, Kate decided that she wasn't going to think about them now, either. Tomorrow would be time enough for that. Tomorrow she would be a cop. Today she was an expectant mother.

January 17

TUESDAY OF THE SECOND WEEK OF ORDINARY TIME FEAST OF SAINT ANTHONY, ABBOT

As quickly as it had come, the storm disappeared. During the night dry, polar air had stolen in from the Bay and had swept across the City, leaving it sparkling clear and brittlely cold.

After breakfast, Sister Mary Helen, the collar of her Aran knit sweater turned up around her ears, stood on the front steps of the college building drinking in the view. She felt as if she were the Abbot Anthony, whose feast they commemorated this morning, emerging from his hermitage in a tomb for a fresh look at the world.

The bright, hard sun deepened all the colors, turning the leaves of the tight-budded camellias to a dark forest green. The lavender-blue flowers on the heather plumes bordering the entryway shone even bluer, and the dandelions in the wet lawn were a gilded yellow. The day was so dazzling that she could define each glistening window of the houses on the hill leading to Sutro Tower.

Hands in her pockets, Mary Helen closed her eyes and breathed deeply, enjoying the crisp air. What a glorious morning! And yet, what a sad day it would prove to be for Christina Kelly's family and close friends. They would bury the poor woman this very morning.

MURDER IN ORDINARY TIME

With celebrities it was somehow easy to set them apart and to forget that they had mothers and fathers who loved them, and cousins and eccentric aunts and childhood friends, just like the rest of us. And that they, too, were friendly with the lady at the cleaners' and the checker at Safeway, and the paper boy.

The *Chronicle* had stated that the anchorwoman was widowed with a grown son and grandchildren and that her mother was still living. But in no way could facts give you the true picture. Were she and her son close? Mary Helen wondered. Did her mother depend on Christina for care? Would her grandchildren miss her terribly?

In a funk, Sister Mary Helen stared down at the spires of St. Ignatius Church. From its damp roof, vapor rose into the cloudless blue sky. In fact, smoke rose from every building of the University of San Francisco, making it look as if the entire campus were on fire.

From across her own campus, the sound of laughter and the bouncing of a ball carried on the air. A couple of students must have arrived to take advantage of the weather and enjoy an early game of tennis. The laughter rose again. Its rich sound fit in perfectly with such a splendid morning.

What didn't fit in at all was Christina Kelly's funeral, although Eileen claimed that sunshine at a funeral and rain at a wedding were good omens. Or was it the other way around? For the life of her, Mary Helen could not remember. Whichever, she felt sure that no amount of sunshine or rain would help to lighten the sadness of Christina's senseless death for her family and friends.

Sister Mary Helen checked her wristwatch. Eight-thirty. If she hurried, she had just enough time to stop by the alumnae office, check her mail and phone messages, and tell her secretary, Shirley, where she was going before she changed into her black-primarily-for-funerals suit. Then, she'd persuade Eileen to attend the services with her.

Mary Helen anticipated that convincing Eileen she should attend the funeral would be no easy task. In fact, the more she thought about it, the more she herself wondered if she should go. More than likely the church would be packed with celebrity watchers, the curious and the press. Actually, she had not met Christina either, except for those last few minutes before the woman's death.

On the other hand, through an accident of Providence, Mary Helen had been right next to the woman when she died. That fact alone linked them somehow. To bury the dead is one of the corporal works of mercy, she reminded herself, and although she personally did not like to attend funerals, she felt that praying with the bereaved family was the least she could do. Yes indeed, the more she thought about it, the more she knew that her place this morning was at the Greek Orthodox Cathedral of the Annunciation.

It stood to reason. She hadn't been able to contact Kate Murphy yet. And if the police were going to uncover Christina's murderer, someone had to talk to Betty Hughes. Actually, she had no choice. Her conclusion sounded a little shaky, even to her. She knew better than to try it on Eileen.

Hurrying across the campus, holding her collar up against the cold, Mary Helen hoped Eileen would be so confused by a Kelly being buried from a Greek cathedral that she would forget everything else. Or perhaps Eileen had been so absorbed in Scrabble that when the lights finally went on yesterday afternoon, she had just glanced at the front page and not read the entire article to discover that Christina Kelly's maiden name was Pappas.

There was just about as much chance of Eileen missing that as there was of Mary Helen losing those ten pounds she had resolved to shed for the tenth New Year in a row. Even Mary Helen wasn't counting on that much of a long shot.

—

An hour later, Sister Mary Helen and a reluctant Sister Eileen pulled the convent Nova in behind a long line of cars parked down the middle of Valencia Street.

"Are you sure we can park here?" Eileen glanced at the traffic streaming by on both sides of the busy street.

"Everyone else is." Mary Helen jerked on the hand brake.

"The world's worst reason," Eileen sniffed, and leaned in tight against the Nova, letting the traffic pass. "Don't forget to lock the door," she cautioned Mary Helen across the roof of the car.

"With all these Mercedeses and BMWs and Jaguars available, who would want to steal our old Nova?" Mary Helen fussed.

"Maybe there's no status among car thieves." Eileen watched for a break in the traffic, then dashed across the street to the church.

The Cathedral of the Annunciation looked strangely out of place on Valencia Street across from the wooden Levi Strauss Company building. Erected in 1850, the Levi Strauss building was now painted a trendy yellow and white. Mary Helen couldn't imagine what the conventional Mr. Stern, who had started the dry goods store, would think of the color. Undoubtedly, his enterprising brother-in-law Levi, who had hit upon the idea of selling canvas pants to miners, would be pleased.

Built from an old theater, the cathedral's flat, white front rose straight up from the sidewalk. Weeds pushed their way through the cracks. On one side was an empty building, on the other, the church parking lot. Two doors down was a small shop that claimed to be the "home of the largest selection of imported Greek food and wine in the Bay Area."

Two clearly used, unadorned wooden doors opened into a mosaic vestibule. Mary Helen blinked, waiting for her eyes to adjust to the dimness. To her surprise it was only a vestibule with a blue elevator in one corner and staircases on either end. Apparently, the cathedral proper was where the theater loges had been, on the second floor.

The two nuns started up the stairs. As they turned a corner, the sweet smell of incense and burning candles wafted down to meet them.

Another small vestibule on the second-floor landing was already crowded with people, all kinds of people, many with familiar faces. As the two nuns squeezed past television personalities, politicians, socialites, and business leaders, Mary Helen noted that most of the faces seemed a little ill at ease among the burning tapers and Byzantine Madonnas, and a little reluctant to enter the church. Only San Francisco's Greek mayor, shaking hands and clapping backs, seemed to be in his element.

"Hi, Sister."

At the sound of the greeting, Mary Helen turned. Betty Hughes stood behind her. With her were the three cameramen from Channel 5, who had traded in their jeans for three-piece suits. It took Mary Helen a moment to place them.

"See you afterwards," Betty whispered, following Ray Kerns, who led the foursome through the crowd.

Perfect, Mary Helen thought, passing a tender yet unsentimental icon known as "The Virgin Mary of the Sweet Kiss." The painting hung on the wall leading to the body of the cathedral. Perfect, Mary Helen repeated to herself. Meeting Betty in the vestibule could not have worked out better if she had planned it. Lord, You surely had Your hand in this one! She smiled at the Madonna and child. Their huge, dark eyes seemed to smile back.

Inside, the wooden benches were already crowded with mourners. Christina's open casket rested below the solea, a raised part of the floor in front of the inner sanctuary. Several women in black coats and black lace veils slid together to make room in a back pew for Sister Mary Helen and Sister Eileen.

Finally settled, Mary Helen looked around. The exquisite beauty of the interior took her breath away.

Beside her Eileen whispered, "It is glorious!" And that is exactly what the Cathedral of the Annunciation was—glorious. Its crystal chandeliers, luminous icons, ornate stained-glass windows, and altar gates of filigreed gold blended harmoniously to lift her spirit. All around them the walls glowed with small golden icons depicting the Passion of Christ, while larger ones portrayed the saints, such as George, frozen forever with his sword poised to kill the dragon of evil.

Ten flaming red lamps hung from golden chains in the sanctuary reminding all that this was a holy place. In fact, everything about the neo-Byzantine cathedral reminded the worshipers that they were in a holy place.

Everything, that is, except the casket bearing the body of a murdered woman and the dark-clad, stooped shoulders of her family members huddled together in the front pews.

On the wall behind the main altar, the red cloak of the Virgin Mary fell in rich folds around her outstretched hands. Her heart-shaped face had a look of melancholy as she reached to embrace the crucifix below her. A mother, like Christina's mother, Mary Helen thought, anguishing over the cruel death of her child.

"Look at the second icon to the left of the altar opening," Eileen whispered, interrupting her musing.

Mary Helen studied it, marveling at the skill of the iconographer who had painted the Angel Gabriel and the Virgin Mary, if she remembered correctly, with egg tempera on vinegar-soaked wood. The shadowless figures seemed neither flat nor spatial, but transparent, with a radiance that shone from behind.

"That particular icon always depicts the name of the church," Eileen explained.

Now Mary Helen marveled at her friend. She was correct. The second icon to the left of the altar portrayed the Annunciation. How in the world did Eileen know that? Or was she just a lucky guesser?

Sister Eileen must have noticed her surprise. "From now on, you will always know the name of any Greek Orthodox church you visit," she said, sounding, to Mary Helen's mind, very much like a third-grade teacher.

"You can take some people out of teaching, but you can't take teaching out of some people," Mary Helen whispered, parodying one of Eileen's own sayings from "back home," about Irishmen and the bogs.

Abruptly changing the subject, Eileen nodded her head to the left. "Isn't that Bernadette Harney?"

Sister Mary Helen surveyed the congregation. Sure enough, Bernadette with her chestnut hair and her horn-rimmed glasses stood against the wall next to her daughter, Danielle. Both of them looked very pale. Across the aisle, she spotted Douglas Wayne. His daughter, Cheryl, huddled between him and a petite woman with her glasses hanging from a chain. She must be his wife, Mary Helen figured, although in her opinion the two didn't look as if they went together, the way most husbands and wives did.

His clothes were sophisticated and tailored, while her outfit was full of ruffles and bows. Everything about his appearance was streamlined. She was, for lack of a better term, fluffy-looking. Even his hair cut was more stylish than her short, frosted bob.

To be honest, Mary Helen didn't know why she thought the woman was his wife, except that she had her arm around the girl's shoulder and was whispering something into her ear. Cheryl appeared to be weeping.

Wendy Hartgrave must be here somewhere. Mary Helen scanned the crowd looking for the thin nose and the upturned chin. She spotted Wendy toward the front next to Ray.

Her spirits rose. All the suspects were present. Certainly there would be time after the funeral service for a little chat with each of them. She'd make the time. And Kate Murphy and Inspector Gallagher could not possibly object. Why, they aren't even here, she gloated, scanning the crowd just to be sure. Surely, they will appreciate someone filling in for them.

A sudden quiet followed by a rustle of people moving, signaled the beginning of the funeral service. As the procession began and the congregation rose, Sister Mary Helen glanced up at the ceiling of the cathedral.

An enormous icon of Christ gazed down at the congregation with kindly eyes. The arched brows and narrow lips gave the sacred image a slightly amused, benevolent look, as though He viewed all He saw with tenderness and compassion. The thin fingers of His right hand were raised in blessing. Sister Mary Helen couldn't help but feel that at this moment Christina was there with Him and together they were blessing her undertaking.

—

With the deep, melancholy notes of the Kontakion, the memorial hymn, still echoing in her head, Sister Mary Helen followed the crowd downstairs into the cathedral hall.

At the end of the service, the priest had made an announcement. "After you have viewed the body, the family invites all here present to the hall to share in the Makaria, our traditional blessed luncheon, at which we celebrate the soul's joyful entrance into eternal life."

"Every nationality has its Irish wake," Eileen whispered.

"Christina's burial will take place tomorrow," the priest explained. "At the request of her family, it is to be private."

Although it was a beautiful day for a drive, Mary Helen was relieved that they would not have to make the trip to Colma. Colma, a few miles south of the City, is a small town of a dozen or more cemeteries where San Franciscans have buried their dead for more than a hundred years.

MURDER IN ORDINARY TIME

Mary Helen had winced when she first heard the town's unofficial motto, "It's great to be alive in Colma."

Not that she would have minded the ride, but she was afraid that after the trip to the cemetery, some of the people she needed to see would scatter. This arrangement was ideal. Surely everyone would stop in the hall for a cup of coffee, at least. She would just have to move quickly.

After the beauty of the cathedral, the downstairs hall was a disappointment. Not that it should have been. After all, it was just what it claimed to be, an ordinary church hall with a brown wooden floor, plain walls, and a stage hidden behind burnt-orange curtains, which, after years of service, looked more burnt than orange.

In front of the stage, tables covered with white cloths stood ready for the food. The aroma of freshly brewed coffee filled the room, which was swelling quickly with people. Caterers in black and white slipped in and out the door beside the stage carrying wicker baskets heaped with raised loaves of olive bread, platters of fresh fruit on skewers, and round plates of *spanikopita*, a spinach and cheese pie with tissue-thin crust brushed golden with butter. The tangy odors of oregano and lemon and garlic mingled with the coffee.

Almost forgetting her mission, Mary Helen stood with Eileen by her side, watching the caterers return again and again with earthenware bowls of green salad brimming with rich red cherry tomatoes, paper-thin cucumber slices, crumbly feta cheese, and luscious dark Greek olives. They carried in steaming silver chafing dishes of fish stew and deep-fried cod, and tray after tray with wedges of shiny baklava and honey rounds covered with powdered sugar.

"Traditionally, no meat is served at the funeral meal," Eileen whispered, leaving Mary Helen wondering, once again, how her friend had become so knowledgeable about Greek customs. She was just about to ask when one of the many caterers who were walking around the room with small, doily-covered trays, stopped to offer them a triangle-shaped *tiropita*. Mary Helen couldn't resist the golden brown pastry. Its fried cheese filling oozed onto the frilly white doily. Another waiter followed quickly with a tray of fluted glasses filled with white wine.

"Don't forget your diet." Eileen winked.

Mary Helen's mouth was too full to answer. She had just popped the last corner of the pastry into her mouth and was fighting the urge to look for another when she sensed a strong presence standing behind her.

Turning, she caught her breath. Even with the gray-streaked hair pulled severely back and twisted into a knot and the thickening waistline, the resemblance was uncanny. The woman looked exactly as Christina Kelly might have looked had she been allowed to live for another thirty years.

Surely she must be Christina's mother, Mary Helen thought, watching the woman set her lips into a thin, determined line. Like her daughter, she was slight, although her square shoulders, the lift of her chin, and the straightness of her back gave her the illusion of being much taller, much bigger. Her eyes, the same cinnamon-brown color as her daughter's, were flat and tearless, like those of someone who is "all cried out," with only the dark, almost purple shadows pressed under them to show where the tears had been.

"I am Eugenia Pappas," she said. Her accent was soft, melodious, like her native Greek. Her voice was composed, too composed, as if her sorrow was seeping out slowly and a cold, vengeful anger was taking its place.

An active anger seeking its prey. "Something to tear with sharp-tooth and claw." George Eliot's words popped into Mary Helen's mind.

"Thank you for coming, Sisters." Mrs. Pappas's words were stiff, formal. "It is a great honor to my family to have you here. In our church, too, we deeply respect religious women. When I saw the two nuns praying over my Christina's body, I felt as if God had sent you as a special gift to a grieving mother."

Embarrassed, yet deeply touched, Sister Mary Helen wriggled uncomfortably. She had been called many things in her life as a nun, but never "a special gift to a grieving mother."

Feeling her own eyes filling, she reached out to touch Mrs. Pappas's hands. "We are so sorry—" she began.

With a lift of her chin, Mrs. Pappas cut her off. "God has indeed sent you. Every gift is given for a reason. You must find the one who did this evil thing to my Christina."

A nervous shiver ran up Mary Helen's spine. There was a savageness in the woman's soft voice. The eyes like two polished stones narrowed and bored into Mary Helen.

"Whoever did this, he must be found and punished. My daughter's death must be avenged. God has sent you. He will help you."

Before Mary Helen could respond, a man in a well-tailored gray silk suit interrupted. Again, the family resemblance was striking. He was about the same age and nearly the same height as Christina and his eyes were the same cinnamon color.

"Mama," he said, his eyes darting from Mary Helen and Eileen to his mother and back again, "there is someone here to see you." He paused, giving the two nuns an apologetic smile.

"My son, Teddy."

"Thank you for coming." Teddy smiled again, then gently tried to turn his mother's shoulders. "Please, excuse us. Mama, it's Mrs. Hart. From the old neighborhood."

"You find who did this," Mrs. Pappas repeated, spitting out each short word.

"For God's sake, Mama!" her son hissed. "You are talking crazy."

With a stiff nod, she gave in to him and turned away to receive sympathy from her old neighbor.

Mary Helen stared at the woman's back, unable to believe what she had heard. Imagine, at my age, being thought of as the instrument of an avenging God! That was not the God she believed in and surely not the one she knew and loved.

Beside her, Eileen stood speechless. Few people could render both Eileen and herself speechless at the same time. Mrs. Pappas was what young Sister Anne would undoubtedly call a "tough broad." Quite frankly, Mary Helen felt as if she might just have spoken to the "Godmother."

"What are those Greek women warriors called?" Eileen said finally. "That old dear must surely be a direct descendant."

Mary Helen knew that eventually Eileen would think of something to say. Her next sentence proved that she had completely recovered.

"You don't really intend to find the murderer, do

you?" Her gray eyes narrowed into slits of suspicion. "That couldn't be why you were so insistent that we attend this service, could it? Glory be to God, don't tell me you are thinking of becoming involved in another murder investigation."

"Don't be silly!" Assuming an offended air, Mary Helen stared at her friend. She had no intention of telling her! Nor of admitting that when she came to the funeral service, she'd fully intended to gather information—for Kate and Inspector Gallagher, of course.

Everything had seemed to be going her way, at least until she'd met Mrs. Pappas. Now she was in a quandary. Something about Christina's mother seemed so sinister. That avenging-God thing must be making me overreact, Mary Helen thought. Little old ladies with soft accents and gray hair done up in knots are not supposed to be sinister. Yet she could not shake the uncanny feeling that finding one murderer could lead to another murder. I've been reading too many murder mysteries, she chided herself.

On the other hand, perhaps Eileen is right. I should not get involved in this one. Maybe the best thing for me to do is to go back to the convent where I belong, run my alumnae office, and leave Christina Kelly's murder investigation in police hands where it belongs.

"Are you ready to go home?" She turned to ask Eileen, but her companion was gone. Mary Helen spotted her edging through the crowded hall toward the dessert end of the table. Eileen was a sucker for sweets.

Getting something to eat here was probably a wise idea. Undoubtedly the kitchen would be closed by the time the two of them returned to Mount St. Francis. On the other hand, fruit and coffee were always available in the Sisters' dining room. This might be the perfect opportunity to start her diet.

"Hi, Sister." A familiar voice behind her cut off her vacillating. She turned. In one hand, Betty Hughes balanced a heaping plate of salad and fruit with a thick slice of bread teetering on the top. In the other hand, she carried a glass of wine.

"I've got the papse-lals," Betty said, raising up the glass. Mary Helen hadn't heard that expression since her brothers used to say it when they were dying for a drink. That was years ago; too many years to admit. She was going to get on famously with Betty Hughes.

"Why don't you get yourself a plate and join me?" Betty asked, snagging two metal chairs in the corner. "I'll save you a place."

Her decision about eating made and any hesitancy about becoming involved forgotten, Mary Helen hurried to fill a plate and join Betty on the reserved chairs.

"How are you feeling?" Betty asked when she returned.

"Still a little stunned," Mary Helen said before taking a tangy mouthful of cucumbers smothered in yogurt. "How about you?"

"I just cannot believe it either." Betty's deep-set eyes filled with tears. She blinked them back. "Chris was such a nice woman. You know the type, fair and kind to everyone. Even though she was a big noise at the network, she was real easy to work with. Not like some of those other yo-yos."

Betty rolled her eyes toward a small group chatting in the subdued tones people use at funerals or in the bank. Mary Helen recognized several of the group from Channel 5. Wendy Hartgrave's short, curly red hair bobbed as she spoke. Turning on one high heel, Wendy managed to twist her small waist and wiggle her slim hips to their best advantage. Douglas Wayne stood across from her, his eyes never missing a wiggle.

From Mary Helen's vantage point, Mr. Wayne looked absolutely smitten. That was the only word she could think of to describe that look. She had seen it often in the springtime when she taught the eighth grade. It was easy enough to recognize and so universal that Adam must surely have gazed that way at Eve.

Some eighteenth-century dramatist had captured it perfectly when he wrote, "Love and a red nose cannot be hid." She sincerely hoped that the fluffy-looking Mrs. Wayne with her glasses hanging from her chain was near-sighted.

Gazing around the room, Sister Mary Helen took a bite of her cookie, then dusted off the film of powdered sugar from her black funeral suit. Fortunately, Mrs. Wayne had her back to the group and was deep in conversation with her red-eyed daughter and the three cameramen from Channel 5.

"You see what I mean?" Betty Hughes must have been watching her watch the others. Mary Helen smiled. She was remembering an old children's book on good manners, the name of which escaped her. In the book there was always "a watch bird watching you."

"Yes, I see what you mean," she admitted, pausing to decide what she should say to keep Betty talking.

After all, Betty was the person that she'd come to the funeral to talk to. Mary Helen need not have worried.

"They are something, those two," Betty sneered. "And it isn't just innocent flirting either. She"—Betty spat out the pronoun with venom—"is all over him like a cheap suit. Actually, she's after anything in pants. Even poor Roger. Until she found out that Rog is gay."

Mary Helen frowned. "Who?" she asked.

"Roger Schaffer." Betty pointed to the technician who had reminded Mary Helen of a gynecologist.

"Rog and Michael Baker." Betty pointed again, this time toward the tall, gangly cameraman; the one with the shiny mop of black hair that nearly covered his eyes. "Camera one and camera two are an item," she said.

"Did either of them have a problem with Christina?" Mary Helen wondered aloud. Although she herself had vouched for seeing the two of them in the greenroom before the show, no one, however improbable, should be left out.

"You've got to be kidding!" Betty took another sip of her wine. "They are so involved with each other, they hardly know that any of the rest of us exist. You should have heard the scene over Roger between Michael and Wendy. Like something you'd hear on the afternoon talk shows." With a pleased smile, Betty scooped up a forkful of wafer-thin baklava.

Just as happy she had missed the scene, Mary Helen took a second look at Mrs. Wayne. Betty's gaze followed hers.

"Now, there is the gal I feel sorry for, Sister," she said. "Stuck with that pompous ass, excuse me, husband of hers. She's what you'd call the perfect, unsuspicious wife. The happy homemaker type. You know, cooks, sews, loves to vacuum. At least, that's the impression Doug always gives. He refers to her as 'the wife,' sometimes even as 'the little woman.' It's enough to make you gag."

Betty Hughes toyed with a black olive. "Poor

Daphne. That's her name. Everybody calls her "Daffy" for short, and maybe she is, but I can't help but feel sorry for her. She's so unsuspecting. She made each of us a personalized, needlepoint bookmark for Christmas, and she's always sending in treats for the crew. Tries to include each one's favorite."

She popped the olive into her mouth. "I'll bet you even money that while she is home making his dinner, he's out making it with Wendy. If I were going to kill somebody, I'd kill him or maybe her. Except that Wicked Wendy is brain dead already."

"I'm curious," Mary Helen said, "how did she come by that nickname?"

"By popular demand." Betty's mouth was set. "She's one of those women who likes to stir up trouble and manages to wherever she is. Always flirting, always needling. The last controller's wife made him quit and move the whole family to Seattle. The pay was not as good, but his chances of staying married improved.

"And you do remember how she was needling Christina about aging when Chris picked up the raisin cookie because she didn't have her glasses on, don't you?"

Sister Mary Helen remembered it vaguely. She had been too nervous about her upcoming interview to pay much attention to the chitchat that had been going on around her. Now that Betty mentioned it, however, she did remember that Christina had said something. What on earth was it? No time to stop and think about it now. Betty was on a roll. She must keep her talking. For Kate's sake, of course.

The caterer passed by offering a tray of white wine. Betty replaced her empty glass and helped herself to another. Good! *In vino veritas.* Or as Eileen always said, "Wine loosens the tongue." However, Betty's didn't seem to need too much help.

"What about Ray Kerns?" Mary Helen asked without even trying to cloak the question politely.

"Kerns?" Betty took a deep swallow from the fluted glass. "He's a love. Christina and he got along amazingly well."

Mentally, Mary Helen checked off her suspects. Only the third cameraman remained. "What about that one?" She pointed toward the technician with the cowboy twang.

"Joe Sousa?" Betty filled in the name. "He's an enigma. Talks like John Wayne with a ponytail and do you know where he was born and raised? Santa Clara!" Betty shrugged. "I don't know what his bag is. He's only been with the station a couple of weeks. Never says much about anything. What is it they say about still water?" She frowned, trying to remember.

"It runs deep," Mary Helen answered, making a note to talk to Mr. Sousa.

Betty took another swallow of wine and held out her empty glass to a passing caterer, who filled it. Mary Helen noticed that Betty was having a bit of trouble focusing her eyes. Perhaps she should suggest that Betty slow down a little. A loose tongue was one thing; potted was quite another, even if it was for a good cause. Yet time was running out. She still needed to ask about the cookies.

"When we talked before, Betty, you said a number of people brought in cookies."

"Cookies?" Betty's eyes were swimming. "Did you want some more cookies? These small white ones are delicious." She rose from the chair, holding its metal back to steady herself. "I'll get you some."

Frustrated and feeling a twinge of guilt, Mary Helen watched Betty Hughes make her unsteady way across the crowded room. Obviously, she would have to get back to the floor manager on another day.

Meanwhile, she must sort out the facts. Doug was smitten with Wicked Wendy. How did Wendy feel about him? And how much did his wife know? More often than not, the fluffy, happy homemaker type of woman had a steel rod for a spine. It was just more cleverly disguised.

Two of the cameramen were gay and the third one was an enigma. Ray Kerns was "a love" and Betty Hughes knew everyone's business. Then there was Mrs. Pappas. "Find him," she had said. Did she know that the killer was a him? And what had Christina said just before she died? Something about the cookie. Those cookies are the key. Who had sent them? Surely Betty would have a guess. Before the week was over, she must get back to Betty, but at the moment Sister Mary Helen's head was spinning with all she'd heard today.

She wished Kate Murphy were here so that they could talk. Why hadn't either she or Inspector Gallagher attended the service? Good night, nurse, there never seemed to be a policeman or -woman around when you needed one!

As the two Sisters stepped through the back door of the convent, Mary Helen heard the phone. Someone answered it on the third ring.

"It's for you, Sister Mary Helen," Sister Therese sniffed.

At times, that tone of voice made Mary Helen feel guilty, as though she had deliberately asked someone to phone her in order to snatch Therese away from some important business. At other times, the tone made her blood pressure rise. This was one of those other times.

"Hello," she growled at the unexpected caller.

"Sister Mary Helen? This is Ted Pappas, Christina's brother. Do you remember me?"

Of course she remembered him, a slightly built man in a gray silk suit who was anxious to get his mother away from her. She was aging, she was not stupid. Yet his phone voice was deeper and huskier than she remembered.

From the noise in the background, Mary Helen guessed that he was still at the cathedral hall, most likely at the pay phone. What was so urgent?

"I'd like to apologize for my mother," he said. "She was really upset today after the funeral service for my sister. I don't want you to feel any pressure about her asking you to find my sister's murderer. I overheard her saying something about God sending you to avenge her death. In her right mind, she wouldn't want you to even try to find the killer. It would be much too dangerous. That's what the police are for. Right, Sister?" There was a nervousness in his tone.

"Of course," Mary Helen answered. "And I understand perfectly, Mr. Pappas."

"Ted, call me Ted."

"Your mother had every right to be distraught, Ted. In fact, we all are upset about your sister's death. And as for finding Christina's murderer . . ." She crossed her fingers. "It is the farthest thing from my mind."

"Good!" Ted Pappas sounded relieved. "Like I said,

Sister, my mother would never forgive herself if anything happened to you. And I wouldn't, either. Killers are dangerous people. So just forget it, okay? The best thing you can do for us is to say a few prayers."

What was that all about? Mary Helen stared at the dead phone line. For the second time in less than an hour, she wished that she could talk to Kate Murphy. Why did Mary Helen feel that this time she should open their conversation with, "Ay, now the plot thickens"?

—

As it turned out, "My head is spinning" were the first words out of Sister Mary Helen's mouth.

By the time Sister Mary Helen had finished talking about Mrs. Pappas and Betty Hughes and the anchors and crew of Channel 5, and Kate had hung up the phone, her head was spinning, too. "How does that woman find out so much?" Kate put the telephone back on the nightstand. "And how did she know I was off work today?"

Jack sat on the edge of the bed rubbing her feet. "Beats me," he said. "Lucky guess, maybe."

The shades on the bedroom windows were still up. The sun sank into the Pacific, turning the sky into a study of lavender and pink and flaming orange. The fractured light bounced off the full-length mirror on the closet door and threw rainbows against the bedroom wall. With his thumbs Jack massaged the sore places between her toes. "By the way," he said, "why *are* you home, hon? When I left you this morning, you said you'd be up in a couple of minutes."

"I couldn't. I'm exhausted." Kate shifted the three pillows under her head. "I can't breathe. I can't get comfortable and, although you didn't seem to notice," she said, looking accusingly at her husband, "I did not sleep much last night. Furthermore, I can hardly fit into anything except your old 49er T-shirt, and it's much too cold for that and I'm getting sick and tired of the guys in the detail being so solicitous, so I decided to spend the day in bed."

"You called in sick?" Jack's hazel eyes widened. "I'll be damned. This must be an all-time first. What did Gallagher say?"

"Nothing. He acted as if he hardly heard me." Kate grinned. "But he called twice and dropped by on his lunch hour with a hamburger and a chocolate milkshake."

"Tough guy, just like we always suspected, right?"

A sudden cramp in her calf made Kate wince.

"What is it?" Jack's voice was concerned.

"Just a pain, pal." She pointed to the offending muscle. Jack rubbed.

"Did you get any sleep today?" he asked, checking her face to see if he was massaging the right place.

Kate shook her head. "Not much. I tried, but every time I started to doze off either I got a cramp, or my back started to hurt, or I felt as if I couldn't breathe, or I had to go to the bathroom.

"I got so desperate, I even read these baby-name books you brought home." Kate's hand groped through the flowered quilt covering her bed and she pulled out *Baby Names from Around the World.*

Her husband's face brightened. "Did you come up with anything?"

"I was leaning toward 'Doreen' for a girl until I read that it meant 'sullen.' Who needs a pouty kid?"

Jack shrugged. "I once knew a cute little girl named Robin."

Kate made a face. She hated birds' names for people. They were all right for babies, but several of the Robins she had known had grown up to look more like marsh hawks. "How about Jason for a boy?" she said.

This time it was Jack's turn to make a face. "Jason, Jason, get the basin," he said. "Not to worry, hon." He moved forward on the bed and put his hand on her abdomen. "We'll think of something. Baby B will have a name. I'll stop by the main branch of the library during lunch tomorrow."

Groaning, Kate put her hand on top of his. It was wonderful to have him home. All day long she had been lonely for him. She didn't know why, but today her emotions had been on a roller coaster. Out of the blue, she had felt elated, then just as unexpectedly, she plummeted, feeling tired and ugly.

She was assailed by doubts. Should she give up the Police Department and stay home permanently with the baby? Was she just being selfish to continue her career? The pregnant chief of police in some Texas city had written an article stating that motherhood and her career blended beautifully. Was that true?

And she had cried a few tears. Would Jack still love her if she could not lose all this fat? Of course he would; she soared again, feeling warm and cozy and nostalgic. Then came the plunge. She was unsure about motherhood, as if she could call it off now. Would she be a good mother? Or do good mothers stay at home? What if she didn't love her baby? Ridiculous. What mother wouldn't love her own baby?

But most painful of all, today she had been plagued with feelings of fear and anxiety about her child. Was her baby going to be all right?

Leaning forward, Jack kissed her on the forehead, the nose, the lips. His gentleness was too much for Kate. Her eyes filled with tears. Hugging him, she began to cry.

"What is it, hon?" he whispered. "Are you in pain?"

"I'm scared," she said.

"About having the baby?"

"Not that, yet. But about the baby. All day long, Baby B has only moved once, Jack. What if something is wrong? What if the little thing doesn't have enough nourishment or if the umbilical cord is wrapped around the baby's neck and is cutting off the breath? And I'm so big. Why am I so big? And I'm getting pink and blue streaks all over my stomach. Don't you dare look.

"Jack, what if something has happened to the baby? What if our baby is dead?" Kate buried her head in his shoulder and sobbed.

"Shush, shush, hon." Cooing softly, he rocked her back and forth in his arms. "It's all right. Whatever happens is all right, as long as we have each other."

Slowly, Kate's sobs began to subside. She fumbled underneath the quilt again, this time looking for the box of Kleenex to blow her nose, and leaned back against the pillows. Now even her eyes must be puffy.

"How often does the baby usually move during the day?" Although Jack was trying to sound calm and reasonable, Kate heard the concern in his voice.

Hiccuping, she thought about it. Actually, when she was at work, she was usually too busy to even notice. Once or twice a day perhaps, usually around mealtime.

Today the baby had kicked just before Gallagher arrived with her lunch. She was overreacting, she knew. Poor Jack! He sat there with worry in his eyes, patiently waiting for her answer.

She didn't have the humility to tell him that the whole outburst was probably nothing more than a bad case of hormones. Let him guess.

"I'm sure it's nothing, pal," she said, trying to act as if it were Jack who was unduly anxious. "Besides, my appointment with Dr. Maccabee was just last week. I know for sure that if anything was amiss he would have noticed." Playfully, she kissed her husband on the nose.

"What did he say?"

"Nothing, really. He just grunted and said that maybe I'm farther along than I think."

"Farther along? How far?" Jack's voice raised.

"He's crazy! I know exactly when it happened." Kate rolled her eyes and grabbed for a gingersnap. Nibbling it, she watched her husband rise from the bed and loosen his tie.

"Think I'll take a shower, then I'll get us some dinner," he said, grabbing his jogging suit from the closet.

With her eyes closed, Kate listened to the rhythmic beat of the water against the tile. At the top of his voice, Jack was singing "My Wild Irish Rose." He filled in "dumm, dumm, de, dumm," for the words he had forgotten. But Kate got the point.

She was behaving wildly, erratically. And she knew it. She had stayed home today because she was tired and had ended up more tired than she began. It was ridiculous.

No matter how she felt, tomorrow she was going

back to work. She would much prefer to deal with real horrors—even those dredged up by Sister Mary Helen—than to spend another day alone with the imaginary horrors she had conjured up for herself.

January 18
WEDNESDAY OF THE SECOND WEEK OF ORDINARY TIME EIGHTY-SECOND WEEK OF PRAYER FOR CHRISTIAN UNITY

Sister Mary Helen flipped on the television set. She watched the blackness open like a great eye onto Channel 5 and the noon news. Of course, the lead story was the burial service for Christina Kelly, their "beloved anchor," as Ray Kerns called her, "who is to be interred late this morning beside her husband at Holy Cross Cemetery in Colma."

"I thought it was supposed to be private." Sister Anne, sitting crosslegged on the floor in front of the set, reached for a piece of candy on the coffee table.

"It was," Mary Helen answered, determined not to follow suit. "I guess the studio considers filming at the gate and letting only the camera lens follow the cortege up the hill, private."

Secretly she was glad that they did. She wanted another look at Mrs. Pappas. As the first limousine passed the gate, the cameras zoomed in on her strong face. Mary Helen recognized the cold, angry set of her jaw. Beside her sat her son, his eyes puffy and red. Shadows hid the faces of several other passengers who were with them in the car.

A second limousine carried Nicholas Kelly, Christina's son, his wife, and their children. Or so the commentator announced. Assorted relatives and close personal friends followed in a long line of cars that were backed up on Old Mission Road.

Sister Mary Helen was especially happy to catch a glimpse of Kate Murphy and Inspector Gallagher standing beside the gray stone pillars of what had once been the entrance gate to Holy Cross Cemetery. Now the ornate gate with its gold crosses atop the pillars was used as an exit. Mary Helen spotted the two inspectors behind the camera crew. Thank goodness they were both on the job!

During the televised burial service, Sister Therese, entrenched in her favorite chair, gave one sniff, then a second. Finally, she pushed her glasses up to her forehead and dabbed her eyes with a white linen handkerchief, one of the last vestiges of her habit days.

"I will surely miss seeing that lovely woman on the news," she said, then looked at Mary Helen.

"As if it were my fault that she was poisoned," Mary Helen whispered to Eileen during the commercial break.

"You are making something out of nothing, old dear." Eileen patted her on the shoulder, "Therese had her glasses off. She had no idea who she was looking at."

Sister Mary Helen stared at the television screen, where the 49er quarterback was doing some fancy footwork with Beethoven's "Ode to Joy" thundering in the background.

Perhaps she was making more of Therese's look than

was necessary. Admittedly, her nerves were a little on edge. Whose wouldn't be? The last few days had seemed like scenes from a bad movie. The sooner the police caught Christina Kelly's murderer, the better. Why, she had just read in one of her murder mysteries that if the killer wasn't caught within the first few weeks, the case could go cold. Heaven forbid!

Right this moment Kate and Gallagher were at Holy Cross, no doubt checking out relatives and close friends. Too bad they couldn't bilocate. Somebody should be probing into other sources, whoever they were.

What was she thinking of? Of course! She knew another source without even probing. Betty Hughes. Mary Helen had planned to contact the woman before the week was over. Why wait? Why not give her a call this minute?

The nasal voice of the operator at Channel 5 informed her that Betty Hughes had called in sick.

There was lots of that going around.

"No, I am sorry but we cannot give out our employees' home phone numbers," she said, and added, "Will you hold, please?"

"No," Mary Helen shouted. But it was too late. She was thrown into the silent abyss called "hold." Mercifully, she wasn't forced to listen to canned music while she waited. After a moment, she hung up the receiver.

Thwarted, but far from defeated, she ran her finger down the two and one half columns of Hugheses in the phone book. There were no *Betty*s, one *B*, one *E*, and all sorts of *E* combinations. It took her five tries to discover that E. P. Hughes was the person she wanted.

Sister Mary Helen was so relieved to hear Betty's voice that at first she did not notice the edge to it.

"Betty," she began without even a "hello." "Am I glad to get you, finally! I was afraid I'd have to call every Hughes in the book. Is it possible for us to get together this afternoon?"

"Oh, hello, Sister." Betty paused as if she were uncertain of what to say. "You are quite a detective, aren't you?"

The question, hurled like a cup of cold water, gave Mary Helen a start. Was Betty annoyed with her? Had she awakened her? Maybe she really was ill. Or could the woman be embarrassed about having imbibed a bit too much wine yesterday?

"I'm sorry but I can't see you today, Sister."

"Tomorrow, perhaps?"

"No. I'm sorry, Sister. I don't mean to be rude, but I think I had better not see you again about what happened to Chris." Her voice trembled, ever so slightly.

It was then that Mary Helen recognized the tone. Betty Hughes was not annoyed or embarrassed at all. What she was, was plain scared stiff.

"What on earth happened, Betty? Just yesterday, you seemed perfectly happy to talk about Christina's death."

Betty's voice lowered to a stage whisper. "That was yesterday."

It sounded to Mary Helen as if Betty had her hands cupped around the mouthpiece, afraid someone might overhear.

Instinctively, Mary Helen whispered back, "Are you alone?"

"Yes, I think so. But who knows who's listening?"

"What on earth happened?"

"When I got home from the funeral yesterday, there

was a message on my answering machine. I'll let you hear it, Sister."

After an electronic screech, a strained voice began, "You got a big mouth, lady. A real big mouth. And if you don't shut it, I will. You get that? Mind your own business, lady, and tell that nun you were talking to to mind hers, too." The voice rose, shrieking obscenities. "Unless both of you want to end up looking like your friend Christina!"

A wicked, almost Halloween laugh, followed; a female laugh, high-pitched, nervous, close to hysteria. The sound made Mary Helen's scalp tingle, and her mouth went dry. Something bothered her about the voice on that tape. Yet she couldn't bear to ask Betty to play it again to find out what it was.

With clammy hands, she gripped the phone and took a deep breath before she spoke. At the moment, she figured the best thing to do was to keep her voice calm and to appear levelheaded. After all, there was nothing to be gained by both of them sounding terrified.

She managed to get her tongue around the words. "Do you have any idea whose voice that is?"

"None whatsoever."

"Maybe it is someone's idea of a prank, someone trying to frighten us."

"I thought the same thing, Sister, until this morning."

"What happened this morning?" Mary Helen asked, not sure she really wanted to know.

"About seven, while I was getting ready to go to work, my doorbell rang." Betty stopped and Mary Helen recognized the hollow sound of a swallow. "When I answered it, there was no one there, but I found a plastic sandwich bag with a large, poisoned cookie in it."

"How did you know it was poisoned?" Mary Helen wondered aloud.

"Because it was full of raisins!" Betty's voice rose. "As soon as I saw the thing, I began to shake." Betty swallowed again.

Mary Helen hoped that Betty was settling her nerves with a cup of tea, but she had her doubts.

"I was shaking so bad, I could hardly finish dressing. So I took a straight shot, called in sick, and here I am."

"Did you contact the police?"

After what Sister Mary Helen knew was another swallow, Betty grunted her "no."

"For heaven's sake, why not?"

"You heard the tape. 'Keep your mouth shut,' it said. So, I did. I am. I will."

Exasperated and almost afraid to ask, Mary Helen went on, "What did you do with the cookie?"

"I put the damn thing down the garbage disposal as fast as I could."

"And the plastic bag?"

"I flushed it."

Sister Mary Helen suppressed a groan. Not good for the plumbing and certainly not good for the investigation. "Did you see anyone when you went to the door?"

"Not a damn soul, pardon me, Sister." Betty gave a soft burp. "But it would have to have been the murderer, wouldn't it?"

"Not necessarily," Sister Mary Helen said, although she didn't really believe that. "Maybe it was that same prankster trying to give us a scare."

"Well, it sure as hell worked on me." Betty's speech was beginning to slur.

"Did you see any strange cars on the street when you opened your front door?"

"All the cars on my street are strange and so are the people in them," Betty said.

"Let me rephrase it. Did you see any unfamiliar cars?"

Mary Helen hoped that the long pause meant Betty was thinking and had not fallen asleep.

"It was still pretty dark outside, but I think I saw the back of a red car turning the corner. And then there was a small green Volkswagen."

"Could you recognize them again?"

When Betty didn't answer, Mary Helen continued. She was afraid Betty's papse-lals had gotten the best of her and that she wouldn't last much longer. "Are you sure you don't recognize the voice on the tape?" she asked. Something still bothered her about that voice. Something she couldn't put her finger on. She was hoping that Betty could.

Still no answer. She must be shaking her head no, Mary Helen figured, and tried another tack.

"Betty, there is something I've been meaning to ask you. Have you any idea what Christina was investigating?"

"Investigating?"

"You know, what story she was working on when she was . . ." Mary Helen paused, searching her vocabulary for a euphemism for *murdered*. When she couldn't find one, she just left the sentence dangling.

"In your position, I thought perhaps you would be privy to that information," she continued.

"My position?" This time the sound of swallowing, almost gulping, was unmistakable. "My position is simply crawling around on the floor keeping the 'personalities' from making complete asses of themselves."

"So you have no idea?"

"I didn't say that." Betty sounded insulted. "Chris always kept that kind of stuff to herself, but she did let me know, one day last week when we were having a cup of coffee together, that she was on to something in the City's import and export business. She thought it would be a kick if she ended up investigating somebody she knew, maybe even one of her own relatives." Betty gave a silly giggle.

"She didn't say anything more than that?" The image of Eugenia Pappas's face—cinnamon eyes tearless and hard as polished stones—flashed into Mary Helen's mind. The savageness of that voice echoed through her brain: "Whoever did this, he must be found and punished. My daughter's death must be avenged."

Did Eugenia Pappas suspect who had murdered her daughter? After the funeral, the cathedral hall was crowded. Had the murderer seen them talking? Was he afraid that Sister Mary Helen was getting too close? She shuddered, glad Eileen wasn't here to see it.

"Someone is walking on your grave" was always Sister Eileen's explanation for a shudder. And after Betty's mysterious phone call, maybe she wasn't too far from right.

Nonsense, old girl! Mary Helen tried to shake off a strange feeling of foreboding. The sensible thing to do would be to contact Christina's mother. Obviously there was no way to reach her today. Or, for that matter, tomorrow either. Everyone, especially the immediate families of victims, deserves the privacy to mourn. Mary Helen would respect that. But in the meantime, why not pursue her other options?

"Who were the people you said usually sent in cookies for the crew?" she asked.

Betty didn't seem to notice the quick change of subject. "Daffy Wayne and Chris's mother," she said, her speech slow. "You couldn't possibly suspect her of poisoning her own daughter."

"Of course not," Mary Helen said, knowing full well that in her present state, Betty wouldn't guess what she suspected.

Mary Helen searched her memory. Ray Kerns had mentioned a third person. He had suggested that maybe the new cameraman, the fellow with the cowboy twang, had brought in the cookies to impress them. Betty had called the man an enigma and said that his name was Joe Sousa. By his own admission, he and Betty had entered the news studio together. "Everybody what came in, belonged in," he said when Mary Helen questioned him about seeing any strangers on the set.

Perhaps he had baked the cookies. Why did she assume that it had to be a woman? Many of the world's most renowned chefs were men.

"Sister, are you still there?"

"Sorry," Sister Mary Helen pulled her thoughts back to the present. "I'm still here, Betty. I was just thinking."

"Good." Betty sounded as if she had a second wind. "Very important. Somebody needs to do that. Have you decided what we should do?"

"Off the top of my head, I think you should lie down for a while, until you've stopped shaking anyway. Then later this afternoon you should call Inspector Murphy at Homicide and tell her about the call and the cookie."

"What are you going to do?"

"I'm not sure, Betty, I'm still thinking."

After she'd hung up the phone, Sister Mary Helen sat in the dark telephone booth, puzzling. What was it about that voice that disturbed her? And what should she do next? Find out if anyone at the studio owned a red car or a green Volkswagen? Find out something about the new cameraman? See if any of the suspected cookie-bakers had access to one of the two cars Betty had spotted?

Probably the most sensible thing would be to take a stab at Daphne Wayne. After all, she had to start somewhere. And Mrs. Wayne seemed to be the most logical person to track down, and the easiest to find at home in the middle of the day.

Running her index finger down the short column of Waynes in the phone book, Mary Helen wondered what she would use as an excuse for calling. "Douglas Wayne" the listing read, and under it, "Kid's phone."

Of course! That was what she would do. Call Daphne Wayne and inquire about how her daughter was doing. When she had seen the poor kid yesterday, Cheryl had been very upset. A perfect opening!

She dialed the Waynes' number. After she got past the initial inquiries, she would worry about how to steer the conversation around to cookies and cars.

Mrs. Pollifax, Jessica Cain, Miss Marple, and all the other protagonists in her favorite mysteries seemed able to switch smoothly from any topic to the business of murder. Listening to the hollow ring of the phone, she wished she could remember exactly how they did it.

MURDER IN ORDINARY TIME

—

Kate Murphy stamped her feet to keep warm. Although the sky was cloudless and the noonday sun bright, the air had a nip in it. Standing by the stony entrance to Holy Cross Cemetery, she could feel the dampness soaking through the soles of her shoes and numbing her toes.

She shoved her hands deep into her coat pockets. Her fingertips were beginning to feel like miniature ice cubes. She should have worn mittens.

"You okay?" Inspector Gallagher's words came out with little puffs of smoke. He looked over the tops of his glasses, his blue eyes watery with the cold. Kate was surprised to see his look of concern.

"Yes, Denny, I'm fine. I'm just cold."

"Why the hell didn't you stay home?" he asked, reverting back to his old self. "Smartest thing you ever did, staying home yesterday. But I should have known I couldn't count on you, Murphy, to do something smart two days in a row. Were you afraid I couldn't handle this funeral detail without you?"

Kate just shrugged. Explaining to her partner why she had decided not to stay home with her anxiety would be much too complicated. "I suppose you would have asked O'Connor to fill in for me?" She wrinkled her nose.

"Speaking of the devil," Gallagher continued in a stage whisper, "I talked to O'Connor this morning and he found out about that cameraman, Joe Sousa, the guy with the ponytail and the western accent."

"Well, what did he learn?" Kate asked, not taking her eyes off the line of cars turning left and slowly snaking up the road toward the huge stucco mausoleum overlooking the rolling green lawns of the cemetery.

"Apparently the guy moved here a couple of months ago from Montana. Lives in an apartment on Sacramento Street."

"Where on Sacramento?"

"Just below Lafayette Park. Must be one of those flats that were converted into studios. Anyway, he did some free-lance work in photography until he landed this job at Channel Five.

"Born and raised right here—in Santa Clara. The second son of immigrant parents and, this will get you, he is related to, of all people, Tony Costa. A first cousin, to be exact."

"The same Tony Costa whose trial is coming up?" Kate felt her stomach jump.

"None other." Gallagher looked grim. "The same guy we arrested and, incidentally, are going to testify against in the Holy Hill murders."

"Small world," Kate said, trying to sound matter-of-fact. "How long has he been at Channel Five?"

"About two or three weeks." Gallagher fumbled in his pocket, pulled out the stub of a cigar, and stuck it into the corner of his mouth.

Tony Costa! Watching her partner search his pockets for a match, she tried to make sense of all the details of the case whirling through her mind.

"You okay?" Gallagher asked.

Kate nodded. She must have paled. And why not? Costa had been part of that screwy cult of Dom Sebastiao where young men had hoped that the medieval nobleman would be reincarnated and lead them to glory. They were willing to follow him and to kill anyone who stood in their way.

At the time, Sister Mary Helen had discovered that this was Costa's motivation. And now, another murder. On the same day that the old nun was to be interviewed about the case. A shiver of dread prickled the hairs on Kate's neck.

"Are you thinking the same thing I'm thinking?" Gallagher asked.

Trying to act noncommittal, Kate shrugged her shoulders. "That depends on what you're thinking, Denny."

"That it's possible, Katie-girl, that the Kelly woman was not the intended victim. That it was the old nun. And that this whole poison-cookie deal was intended to stop her from testifying. This Sousa character might be the one behind it, you know."

"Let's not jump to conclusions," Kate said with much more calmness than she felt. "Just because you're related to someone doesn't mean you would kill to protect him, for God's sake! For all we know, they were the kind of cousins who hardly know one another. I have nine or ten of that kind myself.

"Besides, Sousa's been at Channel Five for a couple of weeks and Sister Mary Helen was asked to be a guest just a few days before the murder. How could he have planned it? No. I say his being at the studio has to be nothing more than a coincidence."

"Okay, dammit, then maybe the guy saw it as his golden opportunity." Gallagher forgot his stage whisper. Several media reporters turned to scowl at him.

"I've been stewing about it all morning," he said more softly. "Something is wrong with this case. Has been from the start. My instincts tell me that something stinks here. First of all, everyone at the TV station says they loved this woman. That, in itself, is fishy. Nobody, not even Mother Teresa, has everyone loving them. And she's an investigative reporter besides. Don't tell me that everyone she investigated loved her, too. But suppose they did. Or at least, that they didn't hate her enough to kill her. Then, the one they intended to murder is still alive and vulnerable." Gallagher ran his hand over his bald crown. "And if that's the case, we're standing here freezing our tails off looking for a killer at the wrong place."

He pointed one finger at Kate. "What we should be doing, maybe, is watching your old friend."

Kate bristled. This was the part of the conversation that she had hoped to avoid. Whenever Mary Helen became a problem, Gallagher suddenly made it Kate's problem. "My old friend!" She glared at him. "She is our old friend, Inspector. Our responsibility and this whole mess is not my fault."

"Fault, smault," Gallagher growled. "It's nobody's fault, but how many times have I told you to tell that nun to lay off this investigating business? Huh, Kate? But no. She keeps right on. And see what happened?"

"Nothing happened."

"No? You call a murder nothing? And what if this Sousa guy gets to her? Goddammit, what if he kills an old nun?" Gallagher stuffed the cigar, still unlit, back in his pocket.

"Where did I go wrong? I ask you." He shook his head. "Me, just a couple of years from my pension with a pregnant partner who's touchy, and a killer stalking an old nun."

"Denny, I am not touchy and you are overreacting." Kate tried to quell the uneasiness that was beginning to take over. "Sousa, if he is the killer, is not stalking anyone. He was sitting in one of the cars that passed the gate. Don't tell me you didn't see him?"

"Yeah, I saw him," Gallagher admitted, "but that doesn't mean that as soon as this thing is over he won't beat it back to the City."

Kate grabbed on to one of the freezing bars of the iron cemetery gate and shivered. As much as she hated to admit it, she had to agree with her partner, at least about Christina Kelly. After interrogating all of the suspects, she, too, had the undeniable feeling that something did not jibe. As her partner had said, the victim had no real enemies at the studio; no one who had a reason to want her dead; no one who hated her badly enough to kill her. At least, no one that they had uncovered so far.

And if she remembered correctly, Betty Hughes, the floor manager, and Sousa, by their own admission, had been the first ones into the studio that day. In fact, they had unlocked the door.

Suppose Denny was right? Suppose Sister Mary Helen had been the intended victim and Sousa the murderer?

"Let's go." Kate's voice was hoarse.

"Go where?"

"The funeral procession is almost over." Kate pointed toward the last five cars signaling to make the turn into Holy Cross. "We don't seem to be getting anywhere here. If you really think that Sister Mary Helen is in some kind of danger, then I think that we had better drop by Mount St. Francis College and have a heart-to-heart with her about staying safe. When we are sure that we have duly impressed her, then we'd better drop by Lafayette Park and ask Sousa some questions."

"Hot damn, you are thinking what I'm thinking," Gallagher gloated down at her, "or you wouldn't give in so easy."

"I didn't say that." Kate turned on her flat heel. Even though she was inclined to agree with him, she had no intention of giving him that much satisfaction.

"Women," Gallagher grumbled, following Kate, who was waddling as quickly as she could across the busy boulevard to where their car was parked. "A guy can't live with them and some of us poor bozos just can't seem to live without them, either."

—

Daphne Wayne was a snap. Sister Mary Helen could not believe how easy it was to make a date with her. Not only was Daphne delighted to hear from her, but she invited Mary Helen over—immediately!

"I'm just making a fresh batch of cookies," she said. "They should be coming right out of the oven by the time you arrive."

Good Lord! Mary Helen sucked in a deep breath. Was it possible she was dealing with somebody right out of *Arsenic and Old Lace*? She fought down the urge to say, "Without raisins, I hope."

Daphne mistook her silence for indecision. "I don't know much about nuns"—her high-pitched voice was cheerful—"but I do know that they always travel in twos."

Oh, my! Mary Helen let it pass. For Daphne Wayne the Second Vatican Council and its reforms had come and gone, and even after twenty years she hadn't noticed the difference.

"So please feel free to bring a friend," she said. Then, with a lilting "Good-bye," she hung up.

For several seconds, Mary Helen sat in the phone booth staring at the dead receiver in her hand. With an uneasy feeling, she wondered exactly what else, and how much of it, had passed poor, cheerful Daphne.

Persuading Eileen to accompany her was a snap too. The whole arrangement had gone so smoothly; too smoothly. Mary Helen was apprehensive. Everything had worked out too simply. It was too pat. If she were as superstitious as Eileen was, she would be waiting for something, anything, to go awry.

"Where does this woman live?" Eileen asked as Mary Helen turned on to Park Presidio Boulevard. The street, located between 12th and 14th Avenues, should logically have been named 13th, but to satisfy those who considered the number bad luck, the avenue had been dubbed Park Presidio. In truth, the tree-lined thoroughfare did link Golden Gate Park to the Presidio, then cut into the park itself.

"The address is on Lakeshore Drive," Mary Helen said, entering Golden Gate Park. "From these directions" —she handed them to Eileen—"I'll bet that it's one of those large homes bordering Lake Merced."

Monday's storm had turned the park a lush green, and it smelled like wet earth and freshly washed leaves. Pine cones and bits of torn bark from the eucalyptus trees littered the road. Here and there a fallen tree waited to be cut up and carted away. Along South Drive violets had begun to bloom in the underbrush and a few rhododendrons, determined to peak ahead of season, blazed with clusters of hot-pink blossoms.

"Why is it that we are going to this woman's home in the middle of the morning for cookies, of all things?" Eileen asked. "I should think you would have had enough of cookies." Eileen pointed at the Sunset Boulevard sign and said, although there was only one way to go, "Left, here."

The wide, divided artery ran through the Sunset District, once known as the White Cliffs of Doelger, because of its rows of homes mass-produced by builder Henry Doelger. In contrast to the repetitious houses, the boulevard was like a park, bordered on either side by bike paths and walking paths, benches, a horse trail, and a series of clear plastic kiosks where residents could wait for the Muni bus.

"Why is it that we are going there?" Eileen repeated her question.

Sister Mary Helen was so absorbed in watching a skater on the bike path chew his gum in rhythm with whatever he was hearing on his Walkman headset, that she had almost forgotten the question.

"I told you, we are going to see how her daughter, Cheryl, is doing," she said, trying to get through the light signal on yellow. The squat woman with bushy white dandelion-fluff hair in the car ahead of them, however, was determined that they both should stop.

"That's what you told me. What I want to know is the real reason." Eileen glanced over at Mary Helen. "And they say that if you travel at the speed limit, you never need to stop on this boulevard."

"They, whoever 'they' are, exaggerate," Mary Helen

grumbled. Passing the rows and rows of flat-roofed, attached houses with their small front yards jammed together jowl to jowl, she wondered herself. Why *was* she going to Daphne Wayne's home?

Eileen waited patiently and silently for the answer, which surprised Mary Helen. She figured that Eileen was absorbed in checking the cross streets to see how close they were to their turn off. Some ingenious person had named them in alphabetical order.

Zipping by Noriega, Ortega, Pacheco, Quintara, Mary Helen tried to formulate an honest answer. When she finally did, her own audacity, her own rashness, brought her heart into her mouth. She was going to Daphne Wayne's home to find out if the woman was a murderer.

"There's the Sloat Boulevard overpass." Eileen pointed through the front windshield. "Won't we need to take a right turn?"

"Sure enough." Mary Helen signaled, relieved that they had arrived at Lake Merced so quickly. With any luck, Eileen would be so distracted by trying to find the correct house number that she would forget the question she had asked.

In her heart Mary Helen knew better. Her friend was like that bulldog in Oliver Wendell Holmes's old rhyme. "Small as he looks, the jaw that never yields, drags down the bellowing monarch of the fields."

And above all else, she was predictable. "Stop stalling," Eileen said when they had turned onto Lakeshore Drive. "We haven't much time. Tell me why we are here, and don't be giving me that old palaver about the daughter's health either. You are not fooling me for one minute, old dear." Her eyes narrowed. "We are here to find out if the Mrs. is the murderer, aren't we?"

Eileen turned to face Mary Helen, who nodded. "Just as I suspected!" Her gray eyes were opened wide. "Didn't you wonder why I left the library to come with you so willingly?" She didn't wait for an answer. "I thought that if she is, indeed, the murderer—in this case murderess—she would have second thoughts about doing away with you if I came along too.

"And did you say that the woman was serving us cookies?" Eileen's brogue thickened slightly.

Mary Helen nodded again.

"A young cousin of mine from back home had a saying about his aunt Bridie that seems to fit our situation perfectly."

"Oh?" Mary Helen pulled the Nova in front of a two-story blue house with white window-trim, a white-latticed balcony, and a white weather cock twirling on the roof. "And what is this saying?" she asked, wondering whether Eileen was about to make it up.

"The poor old darling seems to be one card short of a full deck!" Eileen put her hand on the door handle.

"Wait a minute," Mary Helen said. Before they went any farther, it seemed only fair to bring Eileen up-to-date on the whole affair. As briefly as she could, she told her friend about the cookie that Betty Hughes had found on her doorstep.

"Did she see anyone?" Eileen's gray eyes were wide.

"No one. Only a couple of cars; a green Volkswagen bug and a red car."

Eileen winced. "We had better be on the lookout, then. And before we go in, another old proverb comes to mind. One, I suggest, that we heed."

"And which one is that?" Mary Helen was curious. Two sayings in a row was unusual, even for Eileen.

"Be careful not to bite off more than you can chew!"

Laughing, the two nuns started up the freshly swept walkway. Eileen had just stopped to examine the neat row of pruned rosebushes, when the front door flew open.

"Be careful of the front steps. They can be slippery," Daphne called down in her unfailingly cheerful voice.

She must have been watching for us, Mary Helen thought. Had Daphne noticed them talking in the car?

Sister Eileen grabbed the banister and Mary Helen followed her example. Falling down was the last thing she wanted to do.

"It was very kind of you to invite us over, Mrs. Wayne," Eileen said, once the introductions had been properly made.

"Please, Sisters, just call me Daffy. And it was my pleasure. To tell you the truth, I am dying to talk to somebody about what happened. And Doug always seems to be so busy lately."

I'll bet, Mary Helen thought.

Following Daffy into the spacious living room, Mary Helen felt a sudden chill, as if she had walked from the sunshine into the shade. Not that the living room was dark. It wasn't. If anything, it was a light, airy room with a high ceiling, a bay window, dustless glass-topped tables, and gleaming white leather furniture. Even the plush rug was a mushroom white.

Perhaps it was the almondy smell from the baking cookies that wafted into the sterile room or the ill-at-ease way in which Daffy fussed with the collar of her pink ruffled blouse that had made Mary Helen shiver. At the moment, she could not pinpoint the reason.

"Why don't we go into the breakfast nook, Sisters," Daffy said. "It's my favorite room. When it's sunny, it gets the sun all day and there's always a beautiful view of the lake."

She steered Eileen and Mary Helen into the small room off the kitchen. The contrast between the living room with its Levolor blinds and single potted orchid, and the cozy breakfast nook, was as striking as the difference between Daphne Wayne and her husband.

The room was a mass of organdy curtains, dotted swiss ruffles, and cute knickknacks with ducks in bow ties holding bundles of straw flowers. The basic color was yellow—bright, cheerful, overpowering. Enough, Mary Helen thought, to jaundice even the most black-and-white point of view.

Daphne had set the table ahead of time, with delicate china cups and embroidered linen tea napkins. Mary Helen tried to remember the last time she had been served a starched linen tea napkin, but quite frankly she couldn't. Feeling almost sacrilegious, she unfolded it and put it in her lap.

Apparently, Eileen was not having any problem. "Aren't these lovely things." She flicked the napkin open and fingered the tiny embroidered rosettes with genuine appreciation. "They are so delicate, Daffy."

Sister Mary Helen noticed that Eileen hesitated on the name, no doubt finding it difficult to call a grown woman "Daffy." Mary Helen herself was finding it next to impossible.

"Did you do them yourself, dear, or are they an heirloom?" Eileen smiled at Daphne Wayne.

The woman actually blushed with pleasure. "I did them myself, Sister," she said. The sun caught one rim of her eyeglasses and made it sparkle. Her hazel eyes shone like two bright agates, the kind Mary Helen's younger brothers had used long ago to play marbles.

"I love to do fancywork, although no one really appreciates it anymore," Daphne said, moving toward the oven to scoop out a tray of golden macaroons.

At first their conversation was pleasant, but stiff and singularly unrevealing. Daphne talked politely, but with an air of cheerful detachment, about Christina Kelly's murder, Cheryl's upset, her husband's preoccupation with the studio, and the funeral. Sister Mary Helen couldn't help thinking that, like her embroidered linen tea napkins, no one much appreciated Daphne Wayne anymore, either.

Only after they'd eaten three or four chewy macaroons did Daphne begin to warm up, and then, only on the subject of Wendy Hartgrave. Although the change in her manner was not great, it was noticeable. Her back stiffened ever so slightly, her agate eyes hardened, and there was an edge to her cheerful voice.

"If I had to choose who in that studio would have been murdered, I think I would have picked Wendy," Daphne said, almost as if she wished she had been given the choice.

"Oh?" Mary Helen hoped to sound both puzzled and interested; not an easy combination to get into one single *Oh.*

"Yes indeed." Daphne bit into her fifth macaroon, obviously savoring its sweet coconut flavor. "That woman must be something!" she continued. "At every studio function, and Doug insists that I go to them all, the other women who work there are always mad at her for something or other. And the other wives don't care much for her either. Not that I blame them if she calls their husbands at home as often as she calls Doug. The poor guy is so tired when he gets home at night that I usually have his pitcher of martinis waiting for him in the refrigerator and his dinner nearly ready. You'd think she'd let him have an evening at home in peace and that her business could wait until morning."

"You mean your husband has to go back to the studio at night?" Mary Helen tried not to sound horrified.

Daphne rose from the table to take another batch of cookies from the oven. "You'll have to try these," she said, pulling out a square pan. " 'Heavenly brownies' they're called and they'll only take a few minutes to cool."

The kitchen and the breakfast nook were silent now, except for the slapping of Daphne's mules on the highly waxed linoleum floor. Watching her deftly cut brownies from the pan and set them on a plate to cool, Mary Helen wondered if anyone could possibly be that genuinely unsuspecting. In this day and age, could any woman be so trusting, so guileless, that she didn't even question her husband when he had phone calls from, and late night appointments with, a very attractive younger woman?

If Daphne Wayne's words were to be believed, not only was it possible but it was the case. Either she was that unsuspecting or this woman was as cunning as she was clever. Cooped up in her cozy kitchen, had she cheerfully mixed a batch of cookies, then deliberately laced at least one of them with one of the quickest and most deadly poisons known to mankind? Finally, had she carefully wrapped them in cellophane and tied them with a perky red bow?

Studying her more closely, Mary Helen wondered if

they had been spending the morning having tea and cookies with a saint or a psycho.

"Hi, Mom!" The back door to the kitchen burst open. Cheryl Wayne stopped abruptly when she saw the nuns. All the color drained from her face. Her brown eyes grew round and still with fear.

"Hi, pumpkin." Her mother looked up from the brownie pan long enough to brush a piece of blond stringy hair back from Cheryl's pale cheek, plant a kiss on it, and introduce her daughter to Sister Eileen.

"Want some cookies?" her mother asked.

Much to Mary Helen's surprise, the thin girl declined. It didn't seem natural. Young people are always hungry, she thought, especially college freshmen. The freshmen at Mount St. Francis College were reputed to eat anything that wasn't moving. Furthermore, how could anyone, young or old, resist the delicious smells that filled the room?

"Later, maybe?" her mother suggested hopefully. Shrugging her shoulders, Cheryl left the room.

"They stick in her braces," Daphne said. Settling down once again in the breakfast nook, she spoke softly. "Poor kid is still upset about the murder. Not that I blame her. It must have been an awful thing to see. And an awful shock. I'm glad she's still on semester break. I don't relish sending her back to school while she's so upset."

Daphne freshened their tea and brought over a plateful of warm brownies. "She's my baby, you know. Her two older brothers seemed so much tougher. Maybe it's because she's a girl that she's so much more sensitive. Doug says it's because I spoil her rotten and that what she really needs is a good, swift kick."

For the first time since Eileen's compliment about the tea napkins, color rose in Daphne Wayne's cheeks. If Mary Helen guessed correctly, this time it was the healthy flush of anger. Was this child the chink in the happy homemaker's armor?

"But I think she needs a little more of her father's attention and approval," Daffy continued. "He nearly has fits when Cheryl mentions that she wants to be a scientist. He thinks she should major in home economics, like I did."

Her color faded. "But I don't mean to give you the wrong impression. Doug is very good to us. He's a good father and he was great with the boys. He's very macho, you know. He just doesn't seem to know what to do with a little girl." She smiled a patient boys-will-be-boys smile.

Mary Helen could feel her blood pressure rise. "Boys will be boys, baloney," she wanted to shout, then to shake poor daffy Daphne and say, "From what I can see, a male chauvinist will be a male chauvinist for just about as long as you will let him be one."

Instead she filled her mouth with a brownie.

Unabashed, Daphne continued, "Cheryl has been wonderful. Running errands for me. Helping with the cleaning around the house. She finished the living room just before you came. Doug loves that living room. He picked out the furniture himself and he insists that it be vacuumed and dusted every day. She calls her father a neat-freak, to his face, and I'm afraid she's right." Daphne giggled at the disrespect.

Mary Helen was dumbfounded. She had no idea that such domineering husbands still existed, let alone such docile wives. It was like something right out of a Victorian novel.

"It's been wonderful to have her at home," Daphne said. "In fact she just came back from taking my old Volks bug to the garage for me. It needed an oil change."

A Volks bug! The words struck a gong in Mary Helen's mind. Betty Hughes had said that after the cookie delivery, a green Volkswagen bug turned the corner by her home. Could it have been Daphne's? Should she ask Daphne the color of her car?

Ridiculous! She calmed herself, sipping the herbal tea. First of all, in the state Betty was in when Mary Helen spoke to her, she was an unreliable witness at best. Second, there must be literally hundreds, maybe thousands, of green Volkswagen bugs in San Francisco. Even if Daphne's was green, the one that Betty saw could have belonged to anyone. Third, wouldn't it be too obvious for a well-known cookie baker to poison someone with, of all things, a cookie?

Lastly, and perhaps most important, Mary Helen was beginning to like Daphne Wayne. There was something about the woman, something Mary Helen couldn't quite put her finger on, that made her feel protective toward Daphne. She didn't want her to be the murderer.

Furthermore, there was no way on God's green acre that Sister Mary Helen could think of to introduce the color of Daphne Wayne's car into the conversation without sounding as if she were accusing her of something. If not murder, at least something. And if by some remote possibility Daphne was guilty, it would not be very prudent to point that out with dozens of innocent-looking cookies lurking about, especially since Mary Helen knew that any one of them could be fatal.

In the end, it was Eileen who saved the day. "A Volkswagen bug," she said with an innocent smile. "I love those grand old relics. You don't see too many of those around the City anymore. What color is yours?"

Daphne blinked and thought for a moment as though she could not quite remember. "It's green," she said finally. Then added in her cheerful, high-pitched voice, "A lovely shade of dark alligator green!"

Sister Mary Helen patted her mouth with the edge of the linen napkin, then set it on the table. A clear signal to all, she hoped, that it was time for them to go home.

"Sisters," Daphne said, bustling to the cupboard and pulling out a flowered plastic plate and some clear plastic wrap. "I insist you take some of these brownies home with you to the convent and some macaroons, too."

Mary Helen's stomach did a somersault. Don't be silly, she quelled her uneasiness. Nobody in her right mind would send poisoned cookies home to a convent full of nuns. But is Daphne Wayne in her right mind? a perverse little voice asked. Most certainly, Mary Helen answered protectively as she watched Daphne choose a piece of ribbon, pull the wrap up, and tie it together with a cheerful bow.

As sane as you or I, she repeated inwardly as Daphne took out the kitchen shears, opened them and, with a quick grating sound, pulled one sharp edge across the ends of the ribbon until they curled and twisted like giant bloodred corkscrews.

꠲

Kate Murphy checked her wristwatch, not once but twice. She could hardly believe that it was only five forty-five. Everything looked and felt like midnight, especially her tired feet.

MURDER IN ORDINARY TIME

Please let Jack be home, she thought, driving up Geary Boulevard toward their yellow peaked-roof house on the corner of 34th, and please let him remember that tonight is our Lamaze class and that it's his turn to cook. Three out of three was more than she should hope for, she realized, but maybe tonight she'd get lucky.

Along the boulevard streetlights and house lights and headlights shone through the swirling screen of fog that rolled down the avenues from the beach. Foghorns from outside the Golden Gate wailed their doleful warning. Like banshees, Kate thought, switching on her windshield wipers, banshees lamenting some poor lost sailor. The plaintive sound made her feel even more tired. And a little edgy.

Perhaps Denny was right. Perhaps it was time for her to start staying home. Today had been one of those "do-nothing" days that both she and her partner hated. They had muddled around and really gone nowhere. This morning's funeral service had produced nothing. Kate sighed.

Fearing that Sousa might get to Sister Mary Helen before they did, Kate and Gallagher had used the siren to rush to Mount St. Francis College. The old nun was also out.

"Sister Anne doesn't know where she is, but at least she says that she is with Sister Eileen," Kate had mulled aloud as the two inspectors started back to their car. "That's a relief."

"Why?" Gallagher had looked skeptical.

"Because there is safety in numbers, Denny."

"That depends on who you're counting." Unlocking the driver's side, Gallagher had looked across the roof of the car at her. "With those two, it's just as likely to be double trouble."

Kate had laughed, yet something warned her that there was an element of truth in Gallagher's joke. The frustrating part of it was that neither of them was able to do anything about the trouble until it happened.

Just in case, they had driven to Sousa's pink stucco apartment by Lafayette Park only to discover that, although a Yamaha registered to him was parked in front, the cameraman was not at home.

After lunch Betty Hughes had phoned. Kate had been in the ladies' room when the call came, so Gallagher had taken it.

"She sounds a little blotto," he said when Kate returned.

"What did she say?" Kate was so eager for a lead that she didn't care how the woman sounded.

"Something about a mysterious person leaving a poisoned cookie in a plastic bag on her doorstep, and running."

"Great!" Kate had grabbed for her coat. "Let's go pick it up."

"She disposed of it."

"Everything?" Kate groaned.

"The whole ball of wax. All we got is her word that the thing was poisoned, although it beats the hell out of me how she could tell."

"With all the crime shows clogging up the TV, you'd think that anyone would know enough to save the evidence." Kate sat down heavily in her swivel chair. "Unless she has some reason not to. Shall we pay Betty a visit, Denny?"

"Like I said, the woman sounds a little blotto. Let

me rephrase that: a lot blotto. When she called, I asked her what she was doing and she told me she had been in bed all day nursing a case of the jitters. God knows what else she was nursing. I told her to go back to bed and we'd get to her in the morning. I think we'll all be better off that way."

Reluctantly, Kate agreed, so they spent the rest of the day making phone calls, checking out a couple of rumors and doing the paperwork. Kate despised the paperwork part of her job.

Actually, the most exciting thing she did all afternoon was to pick her numbers in the Detail's Super Bowl pool. Everyone had picked the 49ers to win. Not to would have seemed too much like biting the hand that feeds you. Everyone, that is, except O'Connor, who had picked the opposition. For pure cussedness, Kate was sure.

She and Gallagher had parted a little after five with the promise that each of them would sleep on the case. They had stood in the Hall of Justice parking lot for several chilly minutes, assuring each other that things would look better in the morning. Although Kate did not admit it to Gallagher, she had her doubts.

When she drove up in front of her house, she was relieved to see the lights blazing. Jack had beat her home. With any luck at all, he had turned on the heat and started the dinner, so that, by now, the house would feel warm and smell delicious.

"Hi, pal," she called from the front door. When no one answered, she tried again. "Jack, are you there?"

No smells either, just the mutter of the television set in the living room drifting out into the hallway. Cautiously Kate entered the empty room. Her husband's jacket was thrown over the end of the couch. A half-filled bottle of beer sat on the table next to his favorite chair, and the *Chronicle,* folded to the Green Sheet, was on the floor beside it.

Kate strained for the sounds of Jack moving around upstairs, but there were none. This is crazy, she told herself, ignoring the tug of panic that cramped the muscles in her neck and shoulders. He's got to be here somewhere. Maybe he went down in the basement to get some wood for the fireplace.

Opening the door that led downstairs from the kitchen, Kate stared into the darkness below. "Jack," she called down the back stairs. "Are you there, pal?" Hearing her own voice echo in the blackness, she knew he would never be down there without a light. Or would he?

Kate leaned her forehead against the doorjamb. She could hear her heart beating and in the distance the foghorns keening, like mourners at a death.

This is crazy, she repeated, trying to calm herself. This business of always expecting the worst is nothing but a damn occupational hazard. Or is it being pregnant that is making me so jittery? Women have been having babies since time began, she calmed herself. They've survived, so will I.

"There must be a note here somewhere," she muttered, her words loud in the silent kitchen.

Kate was searching through the clutter on the sideboard when she heard a familiar whistle from outside, followed by the sound of her husband taking the front steps two at a time.

"You beat me!" he shouted, bringing a blast of cold air into the house with him. "I thought I'd be back with the dinner long before you got home, so I'd never have to admit that I forgot it was my turn to cook. Actually I was halfway through my beer before I remembered tonight's Lamaze. And we're in a hurry anyway." He set several paper bags on the kitchen table.

A rush of relief filled Kate. Without a word, she hugged her husband hard, then kissed him one, two, three times on the cheek.

"Whatever got into you, I like it." Jack pulled out a series of white paper cartons from the sacks. Each was filled with piping-hot Chinese food. *"Bon appétit* from the Superior Palace," he said, placing a fortune cookie beside each plate.

Kate had just emptied the last cashew and the last bite of chicken from the carton onto her plate when the phone rang.

"Who the hell can that be?" Jack shoved his chair back from the table. "Don't they know we're in a hurry tonight?"

"I'll get it," she said, walking slowly into the hallway. "Maybe it's Denny calling to tell me that he has had a bright idea about the Kelly homicide. We could sure use one."

"Hello," she said, fully expecting it to be her partner.

"Kate! Just the one I'm looking for." With a sinking feeling, Kate recognized her mother-in-law's voice. "I hope you aren't eating. But no, it's too early for you two to eat. What with both of you working, it's a wonder you ever get a decent meal. But what I called about is not how you eat, although I could say plenty about that, but about my neighbor's granddaughter. She's just married and now she's having a baby. You remember my neighbor, Mrs. O'Shea, God rest her?"

SISTER CAROL ANNE O'MARIE

For the first time, Kate had the opportunity to speak. "Yes, Loretta." She pronounced the name loudly for Jack's benefit. She heard him groan.

"What I called about is that I just got home from the girl's shower, Kate. And they were talking about names. And do you know what I liked about all the names that Mrs. O'Shea's granddaughter chose?"

"No, Loretta."

"They were all good, strong, old-fashioned Christian names. Saints you'd recognize like Catherine and Monica and Bernard. Nothing like Brandy or Tiffany or Kirk. You know, I've been thinking about names, Kate."

Kate felt a knot in her stomach and her back was beginning to ache. "So have we, Loretta."

Mrs. Bassetti went on as if she had not heard. "Do you remember the St. Gerard oil?"

How could I ever forget it, Kate wondered. Her mother-in-law had given her some when Kate had feared she was unable to conceive. Although she secretly suspected that the oil was pure superstition and neither Sisters Mary Helen nor Eileen had ever heard of it, shortly after she had used it, Kate was pregnant.

"Yes, Loretta," she said aloud.

"Well, maybe you should name my grandson Gerard. Like paying back a debt."

Kate was too tired to argue. "And if it's a girl?"

"I've thought of that. Gerardine!"

"What was that all about?" Jack asked when Kate returned to the kitchen. He put her plate of food, by now cold, into the microwave and cleared the table.

"Your mother is into the baby's name."

"What did she come up with?"

134

"Gerard."

He made a face and set the steaming plate before her. "That's my middle name," he said. "I wonder where she got it from in the first place?"

Kate had never told him about the oil and she had no intention of doing so now. Taking a large bite of cashew chicken, she shrugged.

"And for the girl? I heard you ask."

"Gerardine."

"That's not even a name." Jack frowned.

"That doesn't seem to bother your mother."

"Gerardine Bassetti! Out of the question." He began to gather up the dinner dishes. "That name wouldn't even fit across the top of that first-grade printing paper. Remember that stuff?"

She remembered. "Kathleen Murphy didn't fit so well either."

"My kid is having a real name, for God's sake." He closed the dishwasher door with a slam.

At the bang, Kate felt the baby give a sharp kick, as if to agree with Dad.

"Come on, hon. We don't want to miss the lecture on what to put into our Lamaze bag." Jack grabbed her hand to help her up from the chair.

Kate stared down at her ankles, which were beginning to look like the Pillsbury Doughboy's. In fact, so were her knees.

Jack must have noticed her looking. "It won't be long now, hon," he assured.

"It seems to me that I've been pregnant forever." She was feeling suddenly teary.

"The guys at work tell me that when we get to the

bag-packing class in Lamaze, we've almost reached the end." Jack stroked her hair. "It's almost over."

"I can't wait."

"Don't give up now," he said, as if she could. "We're getting close."

Kate's eyes burned and she squeezed them shut. Nothing else in her life seemed to be "getting close"—not any of the leads on the Kelly homicide, not even her baby's name. Why was she feeling so tired and frustrated? Maybe the doctor was right. Maybe she was closer to delivering than she thought. No! That couldn't be. She wasn't sure why she was feeling this way. But she knew that whatever the reason, those Doughboy ankles did not help at all.

JANUARY 19
THURSDAY OF THE
SECOND WEEK OF
ORDINARY TIME

The next day at breakfast, Sister Mary Helen was delighted to see that Sister Cecilia was still very much alive. If Daphne Wayne's brownies had been poisoned, the college president would surely be a goner by now. With her own eyes, Mary Helen had seen Cecilia gobble down at least six of them.

Eileen joined her at the table in the Sisters' dining room. "What's on the agenda for today?" She set down her tray, which held only dry toast and weak tea.

"Are you feeling all right?" Mary Helen asked, noticing not only the sparse breakfast but that Eileen's round, usually ruddy face was pasty, with purple shadows rimming her eyes.

"It's nothing I won't get over." Eileen cracked the unbuttered toast.

"You don't think it was from those cookies, do you?" Even posing the question made Mary Helen queasy.

"Of course it was those cookies!"

A sudden chill grabbed Sister Mary Helen. "Oh, no!" she said, rubbing her icy fingers together.

"Oh, yes." Eileen took a sip of tea. "I ate at least a

dozen of them. At my age, no one can do that and expect not to be sick. In fact, I don't remember being able to eat that heartily when I was half my age."

Mary Helen felt a warm wane of relief. "Thank God," she muttered.

"And that story of Father Adams's about the bubbling blood didn't help my stomach much either," Eileen went on.

Unlike Eileen, Mary Helen had enjoyed the priest's story. During his homily, he had mentioned reading an article about Saint Januarius keeping his appointment. According to popular belief, Januarius, an Italian bishop, was beheaded by the emperor Diocletian about the year 305.

He was born in Naples and somehow his relics found their way back home, where they are exposed three times a year. For the past four centuries, whenever a vial containing a solid red substance, reputed to be his blood, is exposed, it often liquefies, even bubbles and boils.

Devout Neapolitans consider this a miracle. The less pious consider it a sign of good luck. When the phenomenon doesn't happen on schedule, the devout and the impious often join forces to storm the cathedral, shouting, raving, and threatening the saint.

Mary Helen wasn't sure what Father Adams's point had been, but she always enjoyed the story. Most probably he had forgotten to prepare a homily. Regardless, in her mind's eye she visualized the frustrated Neapolitans reviling their saint. Sometimes, like this morning with everything at sixes and sevens, she would like to go into church herself and shout. She was sure that God wouldn't mind in the least. She had her doubts, however, about how Sister Therese and a few of the others might react.

By now the warmth had fully returned to Sister Mary Helen's hands and feet.

"And what's wrong with you?" Eileen asked, cracking yet another piece of dry bread. "First you look as pale as grim death and now you are all flushed."

Mary Helen could see the realization dawning in her friend's eyes.

"Oh, no! You thought my feeling ill meant that those cookies were poisoned." Eileen giggled. "If that were the case, by now Cecilia would be a dead duck! If you ask me, for Cecilia she's looking pretty chipper."

The pair glanced toward the stately white-haired president. Cecilia, her face like a frosty morn, to quote Eileen, sat alone at a table poring over the sheaf of papers piled next to her.

"She's a stomach of pure iron," Eileen commented, and lifted her cup to get the dregs of the tea. "She ate nearly as many brownies as I did cookies, and look at her —the picture of health."

After breakfast, Mary Helen started across the campus toward the convent. During the night, great shifting waves of fog had billowed in from the Golden Gate and covered the City. It was a cold fog, low to the ground, and drizzly.

The concrete walks were wet, and the shrubbery, flat-topped now from pruning, glistened. Mary Helen stooped to pick up a plastic cup that someone had dumped in the ivy, and made her way to the garbage can with it.

The cup hit bottom with an empty thud. Overhead a single gull with black-tipped wings shrieked and wheeled low toward the can, as if to protest her disposing of his treasure.

Beyond the college, the Buena Vista hills loomed like shadows. The fog had swallowed up row upon row of houses with only the three spiked orange and white arms atop Sutro Tower piercing the thick grayness. The scene was almost surrealistic, as if only Sister Mary Helen and the tower were left in a deserted world. The mournful bleating of a foghorn drifted in from the Gate, reinforcing the feeling of isolation.

Mary Helen shivered. Standing here alone, she felt uneasy. As a matter of fact, she had felt that way since Christina Kelly's murder. None of the pieces fit together. Betty receiving a threat—or so she claimed. Naive Daphne. Could she be smarter than she seemed? Joe Sousa. Perhaps he had baked the cookies? Mrs. Pappas. What was it that she knew and that her son didn't want her to tell? Perhaps the most puzzling thing was Christina Kelly herself, the woman everyone respected and admired. Why would anyone want to murder her? Unsettling! That's what it was, unsettling.

Nearing the convent, Mary Helen pulled herself up short. Enough of this. It's that blasted, dreary fog. Deliberately, she tried to emulate the feisty Neapolitans.

⟋

She would start by making a list. As usual, her first item would be "Make a list." That way, as soon as she finished, she could cross it off. Today, number two would be "Return Kate Murphy's call."

Before she reached her room, the phone rang.

"Hello, Sister," said the voice on the other end of the line when Mary Helen picked up the phone.

140

She recognized the voice immediately. Oh, good, Mary Helen thought. I can cross off number two.

"How are you, Sister?" Kate began.

Before Sister Mary Helen had the chance to answer, she rushed on. "Sorry we missed you yesterday."

"What exactly was it that you wanted?" Mary Helen was curious.

"Nothing really, Sister. Just to caution you to be very careful."

"Careful of what? Or should I say whom?"

"Nothing really, Sister. Just be cautious, and may I remind you once again not to get involved. That's our job."

When she hung up, Sister Mary Helen was more puzzled than ever by their rather one-sided conversation. Although Kate hadn't mentioned anything specific, she could sense the policewoman's uneasiness. It was almost as if Kate knew that hidden danger existed, but she hesitated to come out and call it by name.

—

"You sure beat around the bush," Gallagher said as soon as Kate hung up the phone.

"What did you want me to tell her, Denny?" She dropped into her swivel chair. "That Sousa is related to the murderer, Tony Costa, and although we have nothing to go on, we're afraid that it's Sister Mary Helen he's after? And by the way, we haven't been able to locate him. So have a nice day!"

"Well, to hear you talk, you'd think you two were chatting about a tea party." Gallagher mimicked her voice. " 'How are you, Sister? Do be cautious, Sister.' "

"It's a free country, Denny. We can't command her not to talk to people."

"Let's hope to God that she doesn't pick the wrong person, that's all. I ask you, Katie-girl, if you were the murderer and you saw her nosing around, asking all those questions, getting closer and closer, what would you do? You'd put your hands around her wrinkled little old neck and squeeze, that's what."

Kate closed her eyes. She didn't want to think about it.

Still grumbling, Gallagher helped her into a heavy tan wool sweater of Jack's. Her own coat no longer fit around her. Kate knew she didn't look very stylish, but at least she was warm.

"Where to?" she asked, feeling the babe in her womb give a sudden kick.

"While you were chitter-chattering with the nun, I called Betty Hughes. I told her that we'd meet her at Channel 5."

"What about Sousa? Shouldn't we locate him?"

Rubbing his hand over his bald pate, Gallagher gave her a complacent smile. "Stick with me, kiddo," he said. "I already located him."

"Where?"

"He's at work, where every upstanding citizen should be on a Thursday morning."

Still wondering what Kate Murphy had really called about, Sister Mary Helen arrived at the door of the alumnae office a few feet behind Shirley, her secretary.

"Hi, Sister," Shirley called cheerfully. After unlocking the door she flipped on the bank of fluorescent lights and the space heater.

The damp fog had left the basement office bone-cold. Both Mary Helen and Shirley took their places in front of the heater.

"I didn't expect you in so early, Sister." Shirley swished her magenta flared skirt back and forth to circulate the heat. Her dangling earrings, which matched her skirt perfectly, clinked gently as she moved.

"I've made a list." Mary Helen fished into the pocket of her Irish knit sweater for the paper. With a shiver, she flipped it open. "And I've already crossed off the first two items."

"This is going to be some morning," Shirley said, braving the ice-cold seat of her desk chair.

Straightforward Shirley made no bones about the fact that she hated Mary Helen's "list days." Nor was it any secret that on such days she referred to her boss as "The Gray Tornado." Never to her face, of course, but always close enough for Mary Helen to overhear.

Leaving her secretary to retrieve the messages on the answering machine, Sister Mary Helen went into her own office to plot her day. Item number three on her list was "Call Mrs. Pappas." Although Ted Pappas had meant to dissuade Mary Helen from contacting his mother, she didn't feel right about it. After all, the woman deserved the dignity of being heard, regardless of what her son was afraid she might say.

What's more, we older women must stick together, Mary Helen thought. Yet she hesitated to dial. The day after the daughter's funeral was too soon. The woman deserves time to mourn. Mary Helen crossed Mrs. Pappas off the top of her list and rewrote her at the bottom, wondering if she should call her tomorrow or wait until the weekend.

Her problem was solved when Shirley entered the office with a pink paper in her hand. "This is the only person on the answering machine who says to call back immediately." Her long, magenta fingernails clicked against the wood as she placed the slip of paper on Mary Helen's desktop. The urgent message was from Eugenia Pappas.

Mrs. Pappas picked up the phone on the second ring. "Hello," she said in her soft Greek accent.

From the sound of the voice, Sister Mary Helen had the uncanny feeling that the woman knew who was on the other end of the line even before she'd picked it up.

After Mary Helen had muttered her condolences, it was Mrs. Pappas who took command of the conversation and got right to the point. "Sister, will you be able to visit with me today?"

"Today?"

"If that is convenient for you, Sister. Shall we meet at noon at my daughter's home? We will have a light lunch. Please feel free to bring a companion with you."

Before Mary Helen could mentally figure out if both a car and a companion would be free, Mrs. Pappas was giving very precise directions to her daughter's home in the upscale Marin County island community of Belvedere. "We will talk there, Sister," she said, and hung up.

Sister Mary Helen sat back to catch her breath. That was one determined woman! Mrs. Pappas's direct approach had taken her by surprise, although it shouldn't have. It was the way that any strong woman, herself included, would approach the matter: head-on.

A line from a medieval Spanish drama pushed itself

into her mind; a line she hadn't thought of in years, yet it was so apropos: "He is a fool who thinks by force or skill, to turn the current of a woman's will." She, too, might just as well "go with the flow," to quote young Sister Anne, and call upon Mrs. Pappas as requested.

"Are you clearing up your desk already?" Shirley stood at the office door. "What about your list?"

"Something urgent has come up." Mary Helen placed the list under the pencil holder, which she centered on the blotter. "We will get to it tomorrow."

"Soon enough for me." Shirley let out an exaggerated sigh of relief. "Before you go, Sister, have you time to see Bernadette Harney? She's here and she only wants a minute."

"Of course," Mary Helen said, and it was a good thing that she did because Bernadette, holding a round tin in her hands, was right on Shirley's heels.

"Sister, I just stopped by to say thank you for helping out my Danielle." Behind her horn-rimmed glasses, Bernadette's hazel eyes filled with tears and her thin shoulders began to droop. "And to tell you how sorry I am about what happened."

Pushing herself up from her chair, Mary Helen moved quickly around her desk and gave Bernadette a hug. "You've no reason to be sorry." She patted Bernadette on the shoulder. "It wasn't your fault. It would have happened whether I was there or not."

"But if I hadn't asked you to go . . ." Bernadette fumbled through the compartments of her leather Fendi clutch bag until she found a tissue.

"Nonsense. You were just doing what any mother would do. Helping her child to succeed."

"And the sooner, the better," Bernadette said, much

to Sister Mary Helen's surprise. "Our three oldest have moved back in." Her eyes filled up all over again. "They all work, but they can't seem to afford to rent an apartment on their own. So now we have all four kids at home again and, as embarrassing as this is for a parent to say, they are driving John— You remember my husband, John?"

Mary Helen nodded that she did remember him well. As a matter of fact, Bernadette's John was always among the biggest bidders at the annual alumnae fundraising auction.

"They are driving John and me around the bend. And I thought that if Danielle, at least, could make it . . ." Bernadette removed her horn-rimmed glasses to wipe her eyes. "Anyway, Sister, thank you for trying to help. I brought you a batch of homemade cookies." She put the tin down on the desk.

Both women stared at it. Only then did Bernadette seem to realize the inappropriateness of her gift. "Cookies! How stupid of me! What was I thinking of? See? The kids are making me crazy," she wailed.

When Mary Helen pried off the lid, the delicious aroma of oatmeal cookies filled her small office. "Oh, how lovely," she said with as much gallantry as she could muster. "Thank you, Bernadette."

"Well, anyway, Sister, I hope you don't hate raisins, or something."

Mary Helen smiled. "No, I don't hate raisins." As soon as the words left her mouth, something—was it déjà vu?—tickled the back of her mind like an itch she could not reach to scratch. Like the voice on Betty Hughes's tape, there was something in these words that she should remember, something she should search her brain to find. But right now she did not have the time.

—

When Inspectors Kate Murphy and Dennis Gallagher arrived at Channel 5, Betty Hughes was standing behind the circular desk in the lobby waiting for them.

"They're here for me, Charlie," she told the guard on duty nervously, and he buzzed them through the turnstile without ever looking up from the control panel.

White-faced, Betty ushered the pair into the elevator and pushed the button. "Doug insisted that we use his office to talk," she said, leaning her head back against the elevator wall.

In addition to Betty's pasty-white face, Kate noticed the dark circles under her eyes. Her eyes were deep-set to begin with and the shadows gave them almost a grotesque look, as if someone had deliberately bored them even deeper into her skull.

"The wages of sin is death," Betty said to no one in particular. She held her stomach as the elevator leapt to the fourth floor.

Douglas Wayne's office turned out to be one of the three glassed-off cubicles amid hundreds of square feet of space divided into various sizes by green and white partitions.

Each space was decorated according to the taste of its occupant. Their tastes ran the gamut from 49er posters to pots of delicate African violets abloom in pink and purple, to a picture of a rhinoceros asking, "What is your contingency plan?"

An unnatural silence filled the place as Betty led the two police inspectors toward Wayne's cubicle. Most of the

Channel 5 staff either avoided their eyes or gave an uncomfortable smile and nod. Only the Asian woman behind the violets came out to shake hands with Kate. "If you want a job done right," she said with a wink, "send a woman."

The only indication that Wayne had any status was that his cubicle was in the southeast corner of the building and had a magnificent view of the Bay Bridge.

Kate stared out across the rooftops and the freeway on-ramp toward the bridge, its towers hazy against the dull gray sky. Yerba Buena Island, the connecting point between the San Francisco and the Oakland bridges, formed a black silhouette, ragged with eucalyptus trees. The bay itself was the color of graphite, flecked with whitecaps. Kate watched a ship cut its way through the water leaving two long white ruffles in its wake. From her place at the window, everything she saw—the ship, the traffic on the bridge, the cars on the on-ramp—seemed to be moving in slow motion.

The office proper gave away very little about Douglas Wayne as a person, except that he was extremely neat, almost fastidious. The glass-topped desk was dustless and, aside from the standard phone, a computer terminal, and a pair of binoculars shoved to one corner, it was empty. A white chalkboard hung behind the desk, the kind written on with marking pens so that there is no chalk dust.

A wooden shelf attached to the wall beside the desk held an economy-size bottle of aspirin, a smaller bottle of Tums, and a Christmas cactus, its narrow, fleshy stems aflame with fuchsia-colored blossoms. Kate guessed that the cactus was a woman's contribution.

As soon as they had shut the door and settled into the steel-rimmed chairs around Wayne's desk, Gallagher got right down to business. "Have you brought the tape?" he asked.

Without answering, Betty Hughes dropped the rectangular black disc into a recorder she was carrying and pushed all the appropriate buttons. The strained voice and high-pitched laughter filled the cubicle with its message. After screeching a string of obscenities, the tape ended suddenly as the phone was hung up. Kate rubbed at the goose bumps on her arms.

"What do you think of that?" Betty's face looked even paler, if that was possible.

"Sick," Gallagher said, "just plain sick."

"And when the doorbell rang and I saw the cookie" —Betty began to tremble—"I just panicked and got rid of it. You can see why, can't you?" Her eyes pleaded.

"I can see why," Kate said, and she could, too, provided that the tape-and-cookie story was true. Instinctively she wanted to believe Betty Hughes, yet several unanswered questions remained in her mind. Why had the mysterious caller picked Betty? What did she know, or what did the killer think she knew, that would make her a target?

Then there was the undeniable fact that Betty had been one of the first two people to enter the studio that morning. What if she had planted the plate with one fatal cookie on it, and now was faking the call to throw off the police? After all, they were working in the magic world of media where anyone could easily disguise a voice and tape a message.

And why had the caller mentioned Sister Mary Helen? "Tell that nun. . . . Unless you want to end up looking like your friend Christina." It was not so much the sinister words as the wild, demonic tone that echoed in Kate's mind and sent a shiver up her spine. Were Gallagher's suspicions correct? Could Mary Helen have been the intended victim? Kate didn't even want to imagine it.

"Can't you take a voiceprint?" Betty asked, interrupting her brooding.

"We'd have to take a voice sample of every person you know and maybe some you don't know to check it against." Gallagher ran his hand over his bald crown. "Unless, of course, you have some suggestions as to who that person might be." He pointed to the tape recorder.

Betty seemed to mull over the possibilities. Her sunken eyes narrowed. "Why don't you record Wendy Hartgrave's voice? She's the one woman who comes to my mind and she wouldn't be above this kind of trick."

"Did you and Wendy have some sort of altercation?" Kate asked, surprised at the amount of venom in the woman's voice.

Betty frowned. "Not really."

"There must be some sort of bad blood between you two," Gallagher said, leaning forward and putting his elbows on the glass desktop, "to make you think of her first. And only."

Betty shook her head. "It's just the way Wendy treats everybody."

"How's that?"

"Like she has a special edge on everything. Talent, looks, brains, even sex appeal, and that anyone who gets in her way had better watch out."

"That wouldn't make her a murderer necessarily." Kate shifted in her chair. Her back was beginning to ache. "Just a very ruthless woman."

"I didn't say that she was a murderer. All I said was that I wouldn't put it past her to make that tape."

Gallagher leaned back and shut his eyes. "If she isn't the murderer, why would she make the tape? That doesn't make a lot of sense."

"Now, you want me to make sense?" Betty's voice was agitated. "Yesterday I was scared spitless by a phone call and a poisoned cookie. This morning I wake up with the worst hangover I've had in years." Betty stuck out her hands. "See," she said, "I've got the whips and jingles."

Gallagher looked over the tops of his glasses and nodded.

"And now"—Betty's voice rose—"now you want me to solve your murder case by asking me whose voice is on the tape. When I answer, you say I don't make sense. Give me a break!" she shouted, and then burst into tears.

After they had quieted her down, Betty left. Kate wanted to get Gallagher's reactions to the woman and check them against her own, but she didn't have the opportunity. Joe Sousa must have been waiting nearby because he knocked on the glass door almost immediately.

"Y'all wanted to see me?" he said, slouching down in the chair so that his ponytail hung over the back of it. He stretched out his legs, crossing them at the ankles to show off his mahogany-colored tooled-leather boots.

"I answered all them questions 'bout that murder last week." He shook his head and studied his thumb nails. "Sad thing it was too. She was the sweetest little gal."

"We have just a few more questions, Mr. Sousa." Kate studied the man. As though to make up for the bald top of his head, he had grown a full, curly beard. He had also let the hair around the sides of his head grow long, then had pulled it all back into a ponytail, which he fastened with a long silver clasp inlaid with turquoise. He reminded her of someone whose hair was slowly oozing down from the crown of his head and had just reached the tops of his ears.

"In looking into your background," Kate read from her notebook, "we found out that you were born in Santa Clara, California, educated at Berkeley."

She eyed Sousa, who nodded his agreement. His smile froze when Kate added, "And we discovered that you are related to the alleged killer in the Holy Hill murder case, Tony Costa. Cousins, aren't you?"

"So what?"

Kate noted that the color drained from Sousa's face at about the same speed as the cowboy drawl from his speech. For a moment he looked as if he might cry.

"I knew somebody would find that out." Sousa squeezed his eyes shut. "That lousy creep. We're related, yeah, but he's much older than me. Growing up, I didn't really know him, except to know that he is a royal pain in the butt. Has been ever since he was a kid. Always picking fights, drinking too much. After he finally killed somebody, that guy in the bar, even though I was in Tahoe when it happened, I decided to move to Montana."

"May I ask why?"

Sousa's eyes shot open. "Why?"

"Apparently you were not involved." Kate shifted in her chair again, hoping for a more comfortable position. "Why would you want to leave town?"

"Have you ever lived in a small, closed community and been first cousin to a murderer?" Sousa stood and, turning his back to her, stared out toward the Bay. "Everyone starts talking to you differently. Never really about the murder, just around it. After something comes out in the paper, some people won't even look at you. Guys that you've known all your life start avoiding you, like maybe murder might be in your genes. Fathers wonder if their daughters should go out with you."

He turned to look at Kate. "I was distantly related to the guy he killed, too, but nobody remembers that. Anyway, I couldn't take it anymore."

With a heavy thud, Sousa sat back down in his chair. "So I decided to move out of town until it blew over. I would have done anything to make it just blow over."

His eyes looked imploringly at Kate. "You know what I mean?" When she didn't respond, he stared down at his thumbnail. "Wouldn't you know that I choose the time that the bastard is about ready to come up for trial to move back to the City? Just my rotten luck!"

Although she tried not to show it, Kate couldn't help feeling sorry for the man. "Why didn't you just stay in Montana?" she asked.

"I was having a tough time keeping a job. I missed the Bay Area and my family." Sousa shrugged. "And besides, I couldn't stand to keep up this cowboy lingo much longer." For the first time since he had come into Wayne's office, Joe Sousa smiled a crooked smile. "Have you any idea how tiresome 'y'all' can become?"

"Well, partner, what do you think?" Gallagher was the first to speak after Sousa left.

Kate stood up and paced the cubicle, hoping to get a little of the circulation back into her legs. "I don't know what to think." She stared out the window. The sky had become even darker with full, low-hanging clouds that threatened rain.

"Our friend Betty seems determined to place some

blame, any blame, on Wendy," she said, "and I can't help feeling kind of sorry for Sousa. Although he makes me wonder. If he's been lying about his background, even to putting on an accent, who knows what to believe."

"Sounds to me like the guy is damned frustrated." Gallagher fumbled through his jacket pockets for his cigar. "I don't blame him. You can't help who you're related to. Hell, I'd hate to be held responsible for what my brother-in-law does." He stuck the stub in the corner of his mouth, but did not light it. "Better this way for both of us." He pointed to the dead cigar, then continued, "The two of them swear that they were the first two into the studio and that they didn't notice any cookies on the news desk."

"That's because they were on Christina's chair, weren't they?" Kate paced the cubicle, flipping through her notebook until she found the entry. "When we questioned Ray Kerns, I believe, he attested to that. Here it is." She read from her notebook. "Quote, 'Christina picked up the plate of cookies and said, "Look what I found on the chair just before I went on."' Unquote." She flipped the notebook closed. "Denny, anyone could have surreptitiously slipped the plate onto a chair."

"Jeez, Katie-girl, will you sit down! You're driving me crazy. Bad enough we got surreptitious cookies, high-strung women, and a killer's relative, now you're pacing. What the hell is wrong?"

"The calves of my legs are cramping." Kate sat back down, stretched out her legs, and slowly moved her feet in circles. "And something else is bothering me, too, Denny."

"You having pains?" Gallagher's voice rose several notes.

"About the case, I mean. Something about the voice on the tape seems vaguely familiar." She pointed to the cassette Betty had given them. "Not the voice itself, but the cadence or something. I can't put my finger on it."

"Figures." Gallagher sounded frustrated. Picking up the phone receiver, he punched a series of numbers and succeeded in getting an outside line.

"The cookie report is back from the lab," he told her when he had hung up. "They analyzed all the ingredients. Nothing. Just plain stuff. Nothing you couldn't get at the local supermarket, except for the cyanide, of course."

"I guess it was too much to expect that there would be an unusual ingredient that can only be purchased at a specialty store."

Kate could sit no longer. She pushed herself up from the chair and started to pace again. "I wish I could place what it is that's familiar about that voice."

Gallagher watched her over the top of his glasses. "We've got to get a break in this case soon," he said. "Something or somebody's got to crack soon, goddammit, Katie-girl, before I do!"

—

"Aren't you afraid of a nosebleed?" Sister Eileen asked as Mary Helen wound the convent Nova higher and higher up the narrow road toward the top of Belvedere.

"Never mind the smart remarks," Mary Helen snapped. "Just make sure I'm clear of the embankment on your side."

"Have you a plan if we meet someone who is on his way down?" Eileen's brogue was beginning to thicken.

"From where I sit, you seem to be taking your half of the road right out of the middle."

Sister Mary Helen was too tense to answer. Why in the world would people choose to live up here, she wondered, to drive these hazardous roads every day and to pay such an exorbitant price for the dubious privilege?

When she walked into Christina Kelly's island home, she knew her answer. What an incredible view! The house itself leaned off a cliff with one entire wall of windows looking out onto San Francisco Bay. The Belvedere Cove was clear and a gray band of fog beyond Raccoon Strait blocked out Albany, Berkeley, and the Bay Bridge, making the island a sort of Shangri-la.

Gazing down on the roofs of elegant homes, the tops of oak and pine trees, tiny Mercedeses and Ferraris and a crest of boats berthed at the San Francisco Yacht Club, Mary Helen felt like Gulliver among the Lilliputians. Below her, a puff of sparrows flew between the branches of the trees and the wheeling sea gulls by the shore were mere specks.

Fascinated, she watched a miniature ferryboat cut its way through the slate-gray water past Angel Island, cottony in the fog. Near Corinthian Island, three sailboats braving the weather looked like children's toys skimming across a choppy pond.

"Such beauty outside." Eugenia Pappas stood behind her. "Such sadness inside. Come, sit. I have made you a light lunch."

Briskly, she led the Sisters past a staircase going, no doubt, down to the bedrooms, and into a dining room that shared the same spectacular view. The furniture, the rug, even the abstract art on the walls, were muted so that nothing distracted from the beauty outdoors. An antique wooden planter held the only color in the room: deep-red poinsettias apparently left from Christmas.

Mary Helen gulped. The table, set with elegant china, crystal, and linen napkins, was laden with food. She took her place next to a platter of delicate apricot-colored melon wrapped with prosciutto.

Unfolding her napkin, she eyed the feast: earthen-ware dishes of stuffed zucchini, tomatoes, baked then sprinkled with garlic and cheese, deep-crimson beet slices nestled in greens; a chafing dish brimming with golden croquettes. Mrs. Pappas passed a basket of crusty home-made rolls.

"If this is a light lunch, what must a heavy one be?" Eileen whispered when their hostess left the room to get the wine.

Mary Helen rolled her eyes and nodded in agree-ment.

"Sisters, it was good of you to come." Mrs. Pappas filled each glass without even asking. *"Siyian,"* she said, raising her own.

Remembering the winding road, Mary Helen smiled toward the head of the table and took a small sip. After a few silent minutes of food-passing, the nun's plates were heaping.

Oh, my aching diet, Sister Mary Helen thought, but quickly rationalized that to have refused Mrs. Pappas's hospitality would be not only rude but unchristian. With an air of resignation, she buttered her roll. After all, their hostess had gone to a great deal of trouble to prepare this meal. Years ago, Mary Helen had read somewhere, the *Reader's Digest*, maybe, that nature does her best to teach us to diet. The more we overeat, the harder she makes it for us to get close to the table!

Mrs. Pappas toyed with her melon. "This is bad business," she said, her cinnamon eyes as hard as polished stones. "My son warns me not to meddle in it. Is that the word, *meddle*?" She looked at Sister Eileen, who nodded.

"But, like I say to you before, Sisters, my Christina was killed. You were sent to help me avenge my daughter's death. My son, Teddy, tells me, 'Mama, you will only be hurt.' But my heart, it hurts now, so I say to my son, 'I must complete it.' "

"What do you mean, complete it?" Mary Helen asked. With this woman, the direct approach was undoubtedly best.

"I show you what I have." Mrs. Pappas pushed back from the table. "Then you must decide what to do with it."

The woman disappeared down the set of stairs, returning a moment later with a gray leather attaché case. "This contains my daughter's papers."

Laying the case on the end of the dining room table, she pushed on the two bright gold buttons and the locks clicked open. "She is, how you say? An investigative reporter. She was working on something to do with our sacred Greek icons."

Mrs. Pappas blessed herself, then twirled the open case toward Mary Helen. " 'Mama,' she said to me, maybe two, three weeks ago, 'Wouldn't it be funny if I uncovered one of my own relatives in these reports I do?'

" 'Uncovered? What do you mean uncovered?' I asked her. And she laughed. 'Just kidding, Mama,' she said. But I know my Christina. She is not kidding. She does not want to worry me. So, Sister, look." She stabbed her finger toward the case bulging with papers.

"I don't care who is the relative. I do not care about the disgrace. I do not care what Teddy say. Find him," she stated in a flat tone that Mary Helen could only label as ominous.

Putting down her fork, the old nun began to leaf through the contents of the attaché case. There were several Xerox copies of articles about stolen art—"hot art," it was called—one entitled "Confessions of an Art Cop," and another, "The Fine Art of Fraud."

Underneath them was a legal-size yellow pad filled with notes in what Mary Helen presumed was the dead woman's handwriting. On the bottom of the case were a number of religious magazines with paper clips marking articles on Byzantine art, icons, and iconographers. In a prominent place on the cover of each magazine were stamped in purple the words *Property of Mount St. Francis College, Hanna Memorial Library.*

Mary Helen's thoughts whirled like Shakespeare's "potter's wheel." Was this the reason Eileen had suddenly seemed to know so much about icons, Greek Orthodox practices, and customs? Had she been helping Christina to do research? One look at the sheepish expression on her friend's face told her that the answer to her question was a resounding "Of course."

"Tempus omnia revelat," Mary Helen quoted Erasmus, knowing full well that Eileen would understand the Latin. What she hadn't counted on was that Mrs. Pappas would too.

"Time reveals all," her hostess said aloud. "You are so correct, Sister. All will be revealed and you will be the one to do it. That is no doubt why God sent you to Channel Five on the day my daughter was murdered and then to pray over her dead body. God means you to reveal my Christina's murderer. Do you agree?"

Rather than answer, Mary Helen took another sip of wine. She had no idea what was on God's mind, let alone why He had allowed her to be in the studio when Christina Kelly died.

Certainly, He had not planned the anchorwoman's violent death. Yet, for reasons unknown to her, Christina had been killed and Mary Helen had been there when it happened. Was it Divine Providence or coincidence? Theologians of all faiths had been debating that point for centuries. And, quite frankly, it was one of the many questions she planned to ask God when she finally met Him face-to-face.

"I'll do the best I can, of course," Mary Helen said, "but your surest bet is to go to the police. Have you told them about these papers?"

Her jaw set firmly, Mrs. Pappas shook her head. A strand of gray-streaked hair slipped out of her twisted bun and curled around her flushed cheek. "They did not even ask me about my daughter's work. Only if she had known enemies. Foolishness! If an enemy is going to kill you, would he let himself be known?

"They say at the funeral that everyone loves my Christina." Impatiently, she pushed the piece of hair back from her face. "But"—her eyes, so like her daughter's, began to mist—"someone does not." As quickly as the hint of tears had come, it disappeared.

"The police ask me if she has boyfriends." The edges of her thin lips turned down as if the words tasted sour. "My daughter was a good woman, an honorable woman." Bursting into a volley of Greek that sounded to Mary

Helen like invectives, Mrs. Pappas disappeared into the kitchen.

"Why didn't you tell me you were helping Christina Kelly with her work?" Mary Helen hissed at Eileen.

"Because she told me it was confidential," Eileen shot back, "and confidential is confidential!"

"You were her researcher, not her confessor." She slammed down the top of the attaché case.

Eileen, never at a loss for words, narrowed her eyes and was just about to speak when Mrs. Pappas returned with a pot of coffee and a plate of twisted butter cookies dusted with powdered sugar.

Silently, the three women sipped their black coffee. Mary Helen bit into her cookie. Brushing the film of sugar from her navy blue suit jacket, she realized that she was getting pretty sick of cookies—both eating them and thinking about them.

At the moment, she didn't care if she ever ate another one, be it a sugar cookie, a butter cookie, a macaroon, a brownie, or Bernadette's oatmeal cookie, with or without raisins.

Raisins! An uneasy feeling skittered through her mind, just as it had earlier when she had met in her office with Bernadette Harney. What was it about raisins?

Who knew? Could something as simple as raisins be the key that would unlock the door? Could be, but at the moment, no matter how hard she tried, Mary Helen couldn't even put her finger on which door it was that needed to be opened.

—

The campus of Mount St. Francis was nearly deserted by the time Sisters Mary Helen and Eileen returned from Belvedere. The fog rolling in from the Bay had crept up the hill, swallowing the whole college in one wet gulp. The sound of a foghorn drifting in from the Gate bleated a mournful welcome.

"I had better check on the library before all of the staff leaves," Eileen said almost before Sister Mary Helen stopped the car.

"Wait. I'll go with you." Mary Helen fumbled for the attaché case, which Mrs. Pappas had insisted that she bring home. "I want to go through these magazine articles with you."

"I have already told you, at least four times on the Golden Gate Bridge alone, and several more times after that, that I know nothing about what Christina Kelly was investigating other than that she asked me, confidentially, to help her with some of the research. Which I did, confidentially." Eileen rolled her gray eyes to emphasize that point.

"Besides, shouldn't you check into your own office? No doubt Shirley has some important messages for you."

"Shirley's car is gone and whatever important messages she has will be just as important tomorrow. Can't we go over what Christina asked you to research? Perhaps you don't know what you don't know."

Mary Helen tried to sound as if she were throwing herself on Eileen's mercy without really groveling. Knowing her friend's stubborn streak as well as she did, she realized that to bulldoze the point was not going to work. Mary Helen pushed her glasses up the bridge of her nose and tried to look sincere.

Eileen studied her face, clearly not a bit fooled. "If you insist," she said finally.

And Mary Helen would have insisted had not Sister Anne burst into the convent garage.

"Thank God you're home," she said, opening the car door for Mary Helen. "Therese is in a rage. She signed out the Nova for four o'clock and you're late.

"Let me give Therese the keys." Anne waved her upturned palm in front of Mary Helen's nose.

Mary Helen checked her watch. It was only seven minutes after four.

"For heaven's sake," she said, setting her lips in a narrow line and following Anne into the convent. "I will give Therese the keys myself and apologize, of course."

By the time Mary Helen encountered her, Therese's rage had petered out into raised eyebrows and a huffy "Well, you are home at last!"

Another paper tiger, Mary Helen thought, listening to the back door slam. As soon as she heard the hum of the car engine, she grabbed Christina's attaché case and hurried out of the convent herself, bound for the Hanna Memorial Library and her friend Eileen.

As she made her way across the wide driveway, the hollow sound of an approaching motorcycle startled her. She squinted into the fog. She could see nothing. She could only hear it. She stood still, listening, straining to catch sight of a headlight.

"How-do?" she called out. If she couldn't see the motorcycle, then its driver, she knew, couldn't see her either. She fumbled with the attaché case, frozen to her spot, uncertain which way to move, ready to bolt when the cycle roared into view.

"How-do?" she called again. Her words ricocheted off the leafless trees. A sudden backfire made her start. Then a dim light swept the driveway, moving closer and closer. Poised to jump, Mary Helen put down the briefcase, covered her ears against the racket, and watched a gleaming black and silver Yamaha explode through the shifting fog.

"Hi, Sister." Revving the motor once or twice, Joe Sousa removed his Star Wars helmet. "You're the one I'm looking for," he said, shaking his head to free the ponytail, which had stuck in the collar of his cowboy shirt.

"You're looking for me?" Still slightly unnerved, Mary Helen tried to sound pleasant. "Whatever for?"

"They think it's me."

"Who thinks what is you?" The young man seemed to be talking in riddles.

Sousa's hazel eyes avoided her own. "The cops think I'm the one who murdered Chris."

"Did they say so?" Mary Helen was shocked. This fellow would be the last one she would suspect of killing the anchorwoman. He had only been with Channel 5 for a couple of weeks. What motive could he possibly have? Furthermore, it seemed almost un-American to point the finger at a John Wayne lookalike, even if he wore a ponytail.

"I know they think it's me." He was obviously agitated. "I know by the kind of questions they asked me."

"Don't be silly," Mary Helen watched his face carefully. His chin quivered and the curly beard undulated as if it had a life of its own. "Why in the world would the police think that?"

"Because I'm Tony Costa's cousin, that's why."

Tony Costa! The man's face flashed through her mind, surprising her with its vividness. Angry eyes glaring at her. The hard set of his chin.

Shaken, she studied Joe, remembering the low, menacing growl of his cousin's voice, the pungent odor of stale alcohol, and his mud-spattered clothes. Save for the color of his eyes, which still had not met hers, there was little resemblance between the two men.

Feet spread apart to balance the bike, Sousa stared out into the fog. Nervously, he revved the motor. The noise was deafening.

"Why in the world would Inspector Gallagher and Kate Murphy think that your being related to Tony Costa would make you apt to murder Christina? What could possibly be the connection?" Mary Helen shouted above the din.

Almost before the question had left her mouth, she knew the answer. Sousa's eyes met hers. From his uneasy glance, she knew that he, too, knew the answer. Her mouth dried out.

Not Christina Kelly, but she, Sister Mary Helen, was the intended victim. That is what the police thought. She was the victim and Sousa the murderer.

Ridiculous! She had not known until two days before she appeared that she would be on the noon news. And she might have refused Bernadette's request and never appeared. How could he have plotted her death? Surely, his being there was a pure coincidence. Unless, of course, he felt that fate had dealt him at least one lucky hand!

Mary Helen tried to shake that possibility from her mind, but it stuck like a scrap of paper gummed to the sole of a shoe. Her heart bumped so hard that she was sure he could hear it. She tightened her teeth, hoping to quell the fear, while the two stood in absolute silence.

Sousa balanced his helmet on one of the handles of his bike. Slowly, the man's right hand moved behind him. Mary Helen willed herself to stay calm as he fumbled in his back pocket for something.

What was it, she wondered. A gun? A knife? A piece of rope? Surely, if he was the murderer, he would have those things handy. But, of course, he wasn't. He just didn't seem the type—if there was such a thing as a murderer type.

"You don't think it was me, do you, Sister?" His voice was strained and the words came out slowly.

"Of course not, Mr. Sousa."

"Joe. Call me Joe," he said, pulling a clean white handkerchief from his back pocket.

"Of course not, Joe," Mary Helen said, hoping she didn't sound too relieved.

"I'd never hurt anyone, let alone a nun." He wiped his eyes and then, to Mary Helen's amazement, crumpled into sobs.

"Oh, Joe, don't." She put her hand on his shoulder. His leather jacket felt warm and pliable and beneath it she could feel him trembling. "You poor fellow. I'm sure that the police don't suspect you. And I certainly don't. Inspector Gallagher and Kate are probably frustrated because they can't get a handle on the case, so they are grasping at anything, anyone."

"I'm sorry, Sister." Joe took a deep breath. "I don't know what's the matter with me. It's just so damn frustrating."

Embarrassed, he turned away from her to wipe his face and blow his nose. "I just can't figure out why they'd pick on me. It's not fair."

For the first time he looked at her full-face. His hazel eyes sparked with raw anger. "It wasn't me! You do believe me, don't you?"

"Of course I do."

Savagely, Joe Sousa grabbed the handlebars of his Yamaha and revved the motor, again. Its roar tore through the quiet dusk. "Thank God for that!" His grin was tight as he put on his helmet and flipped the smoky goggles over his still angry eyes.

"See you later, Sister." He kicked the motorcycle into action, wheeled it in a circle, and sped down the hill.

Poor fellow, Mary Helen thought, watching the cameraman disappear into the thick fog. Imagine being accused of a crime just because you had a relative who was a criminal! Surely the fellow was innocent. No wonder he was upset, almost too upset. Yet he seemed so sincere.

"Who, in the name of all that is good and holy, was making all that racket?"

Startled, Mary Helen spun around. Because of the quickening dusk and the fog, she had not seen Eileen approaching.

"That was Joe Sousa, the cameraman," she said, "and you nearly scared the life out of me."

"Sorry, old dear." Eileen patted her arm. "Is that the one that you said spoke with a cowboy twang?"

Mary Helen nodded. His twang! It was gone. When they were speaking just now, it was gone. The realization gave her a sickening sensation. If Joe Sousa could so convincingly put on and take off an accent, what about an act? Was his sincerity nothing more than that—a convincing act?

Still clutching the attaché case, Sister Mary Helen

followed Eileen across the darkening campus toward the convent for evening prayers.

"Trust in the Lord," the familiar words of the Vesper psalm sprang into her mind. "He is our help and our shield. You who fear Him, trust in the Lord."

Mary Helen wasn't sure that she actually feared the Lord, but she surely trusted Him. And, at this moment, she was having trouble knowing just what to believe and who else to trust.

January 20
FRIDAY OF THE SECOND
WEEK OF ORDINARY TIME

The steady rain beating against Sister Mary Helen's bedroom window awakened her before her alarm clock did. She had slept fitfully and had been up several times during the night. Each time, her eyes had caught Christina Kelly's attaché case, which lay opened in the middle of her desk.

In the semidarkness, the lid of the case had cast long, dark shadows against the bedroom wall. Once Mary Helen imagined it as a tombstone. At another time during the long night the shadow resembled a small, narrow open casket. This morning, although the case looked like nothing more than an ordinary attaché case, she was determined to get rid of the thing as soon as possible.

Her eyes burned. She had read over the contents of the case several times. Although she had deliberately avoided looking at the clock, she felt sure it had been past midnight before she turned off her light.

Words such as *international crime, Interpol,* and *millions of dollars* had jumped at her from both the articles and Christina's scribbled notes.

She didn't comprehend totally everything that Christina had jotted down. Yet Mary Helen understood enough to realize that if she took this on, she was in way over her head. Art theft, unlike the garden variety of murder, was no simple crime of passion. It was a complicated network of fraud, forgery, and fences, with all the earmarks of organized crime. To her surprise, she had read in the research that art theft was the second largest international criminal activity, narcotics being the first.

Grim-faced narcotics bosses with dark, cruel eyes had peppered her dream, convincing her subconscious as well as her conscious mind that in this case, as Shakespeare was wont to say, "the better part of valor is discretion." Even in her bravest moment, she knew that she was no match for an art-swindling underworld czar. The very thought of meeting one turned her knees to spaghetti.

Nor would she go forward with her plan to pump Eileen. She didn't want to find out what her friend knew. As a matter of fact, the less the two of them knew about the shady world Christina Kelly was investigating, the better. Furthermore, she would take Kate Murphy's advice about not getting involved in police business and turn the entire gray leather case and its contents over to the young policewoman. And good riddance!

—

"Good morning, Sister," Shirley called cheerfully from the inner office. "I was just putting some notes on your desk. A few of the alums are finally beginning to get cracking on the St. Valentine's Day Tea. About time, too, if you ask me. It's less than a month away."

"You look as if you're dressed for the occasion already," Mary Helen said. She watched Shirley emerge from the room in a brilliant swirl of red and gold.

"This isn't for Valentine's Day." Shirley tapped her dangling earrings. "This is for Super Sunday!"

Mary Helen groaned. "Super Bowl Sunday! Of course! How could I have forgotten?" She propped her dripping umbrella in the corner of her office and, placing Christina's attaché case next to it, shook the rain from her coat.

"You must be the only living human being in the entire Bay Area who doesn't have Super Bowl fever," Shirley muttered, offering Sister Mary Helen a steaming cup of coffee and the morning *Chronicle*. "It's everywhere."

Shirley was right. The 49ers, their opponents, their coaches, their wives, the stadium, even the predicted weather for the day of the game, had dominated the TV for two weeks and today they covered most of the front section of the morning paper. *Gung hay fat choy,* the traditional greeting of San Francisco's upcoming Chinese New Year celebration, took a dim second place to the Super Bowl. National and world events with Christina Kelly's murder and the pending Costa trial were relegated to small articles on the back pages.

And that's what she would try to do too. Relegate Christina and Tony Costa to the back pages of her mind and turn whatever information she had to the proper authority.

After all, as had been pointed out to her often, her first duty was to Mount St. Francis College. Just as soon as she contacted Kate Murphy, she'd concentrate on this Valentine's Day Tea. And it was about time too. Tickets sales needed a boost. She must make a few calls, generate some more enthusiasm about the event, get someone to donate a Sweetheart Vacation as a raffle prize. What the alums needed was Valentine fever!

She would get to it right after she spoke to Kate Murphy. On second thought, she mused scanning the front section of the *Chronicle* again, at the moment the alums probably had all the "fever" they could handle. She'd best wait until Monday.

—

Kate Murphy recognized Sister Mary Helen's voice immediately. "What's up, Sister?" she asked before Mary Helen had a chance to ask her how she was. Kate was feeling so tired and so uncomfortable that she didn't even want to think about it, let alone discuss it.

"I'm calling about the Christina Kelly murder case," Mary Helen began.

"Why am I not surprised?" Kate fiddled with a 49er balloon that someone had stuck in the plant on the corner of her desk. "Didn't I ask you, Sister, to leave that to us?"

"I intend to."

Kate could tell, by the rather extended pause and the hint of coldness in the voice, that Sister Mary Helen was miffed.

"I didn't mean to offend you, Sister, but I do worry about you. I wouldn't want anything to happen to you."

"No offense taken." Mary Helen's tone was still a little crisp. "Nor would *I* want anything to happen to anyone, so that is why I'm asking you to pick up Christina Kelly's attaché case. I have it here at Mount St. Francis."

"Christina's attaché case! What case? We didn't find any case at her home. How the devil did you get it?"

"From her mother. We older women tend to have confidence in one another."

Touché, Kate thought, feeling her cheeks begin to burn.

"It's not that I don't have confidence in you, Sister. It's just that sometimes I am afraid that you might walk into something without realizing how dangerous it is. For example—" Kate was about to refresh the old nun's memory about her very recent and very risky encounter with Al Finn, the alleged murderer of her old friend Erma Duran, when Mary Helen cut her off.

"I appreciate your concern, Kate, which reminds me that Joe Sousa stopped by the college. He seems to think that you and Inspector Gallagher are afraid that he might be the murderer and that I might have been the intended victim."

Did Kate detect a glimmer of fear in the tone? "We are not ruling out any possibilities, Sister. This case seems to get more and more complicated. That's why we want you to be extra cautious and not put yourself in any unnecessary danger."

"Kate, let me assure you that no one wants to avoid danger more than I do."

Kate Murphy had heard that spiel too often to actually believe it. "Have you examined the contents of the case?" she asked.

"Of course I have. That's why I want you to pick it up. It contains Christina Kelly's research on the news story she was investigating. It's very complicated and very criminal, if you ask me. And it is definitely out of my depth. Shall I leave it for you at the switchboard?"

"Great!" Kate said, breathing a sigh of relief. At last, something was finally scaring the old girl! "Either Inspector Gallagher or I will pick it up as soon as one of us can get up to the college.

"And, Sister, leave the whole business to us, will you?" Kate added for good measure.

"Of course I will, dear," Mary Helen said.

And at the time she said it, she really meant it.

January 22
THIRD SUNDAY OF ORDINARY TIME
SUPER BOWL SUNDAY

Sister Anne had been planning the Mount St. Francis Convent's Super Bowl party for weeks. She had invited a number of Sisters from the other convents in the area, planned the menu, decorated the room, and persuaded Sister Therese to draw a chart for the football pool.

Thirty minutes before kickoff time, the Community Room was already crowded. The older nuns began to claim seats on the couches or in the rows of chairs that Anne had arranged in a semicircle around the television set. The younger ones, and the more agile among the old, found places on the floor where they could lean back against the arm of a chair or between two sets of knees.

The floor seats were far less comfortable, Sister Mary Helen noted, settling down in her chair. Yet they were a lot closer to the mounds of chips, the dip, and the heaping bowls of peanuts Anne had placed on the coffee table and the end tables around the large room.

In true holistic fashion, Anne had slipped some dipping vegetables and a bowl of twiggy-looking trail mix in among the fare. Mary Helen was not a bit surprised to see that all present were eating around the healthy snacks and getting right down to the junk food.

"May I get anyone anything to drink before the game starts?" Anne offered. Sister Mary Helen and several of the older nuns took her up on it.

"I hope they'll all pipe down before the lineup," old Sister Donata said in a deaf whisper that no one missed. In her prime, Donata had taught the grandmother of one of the team's linebackers, and so she followed the 'Niners religiously.

"They will have to be still for the national anthem. That comes before the lineup, doesn't it?" Sister Eulalia said to no one in particular. Eulalia was extremely patriotic and loved to sing "The Star-Spangled Banner" loudly, clearly, and one note behind everyone else.

Sister Cecilia stood at the door of the Community Room welcoming one and all to the college.

"You would think that she was running for office." There was so much activity in the room, Mary Helen didn't notice Sister Eileen settling into the chair next to hers until she spoke.

"How much are you planning to wager on our boys?" She opened her own coin purse and shook four quarters into her lap. "Here comes Therese."

"Pick your squares. Twenty-five cents a square. Hurry! Hurry! The good ones are going fast," Therese hawked away, shaking the tagboard chart in front of her as she sashayed around the room. Although she paused occasionally to explain the intricacies of Mount St. Francis's betting system to a neophyte, she was, for the most part, strictly business.

"She knows a lot more about a football pool than she does about a football game." Sister Anne was back with the tray of drinks and the 49er napkins. She stopped in front of Sister Mary Helen.

"And she enjoys it a great deal more, besides." Eileen reached over to get a drink too. "You seem to be in a bit of a fog this afternoon," she said when Anne had moved on. "Is that briefcase still on your mind? By now, Kate Murphy has it all figured out and she and that old teddy bear of a Gallagher are on their way to apprehending the murderer. And good riddance!" She patted Mary Helen's knee. "You did the right thing, you know."

"I'm sure that I did." Mary Helen took a sip of her diet cola. She would have preferred a cold beer, but she did have to pay some homage to her New Year's diet. Chances were, however, that she would more than make up for her abstemious behavior when the chili and sourdough bread were served at halftime.

"And you are right, Eileen. I am in a fog. I just cannot shake the feeling that something is missing. Even when Father Adams read the Gospel at Mass this morning, it was as if God was trying to tell me something. Do you remember how it started?"

"I can't even remember we had a morning, old dear. That is how I was feeling."

Mary Helen quoted the beginning verses of Saint Luke's gospel. " 'Many have undertaken to compile a narrative of the events which have been in our midst.' It is almost as if I have been trying since Friday to 'compile a narrative of the events' and that I am definitely missing something."

"You are going to miss something all right—your chance at a fortune—if you don't hurry up and get out your quarters!" Eileen pointed toward Therese, approaching them behind the waving tagboard.

Putting her glass on the floor next to the leg of her chair, Sister Mary Helen dug into her sweater pocket and found only tissue. She had been so distracted all day that she had forgotten to put any change in her pocket.

"Save my seat," she said. "I'll be right back."

As she rounded the corner, she heard the sound of chairs being pulled back and the slow, magestic strains of the band playing "The Star-Spangled Banner." Mercifully, her oversight had spared her from hearing Eulalia's one-note-late rendition of the national anthem.

Once in her bedroom, Sister Mary Helen quickly located eight quarters, her football pool limit. Since Christmas she had stored her small change in a blue, hand-painted pot from Portugal. One of the alumnae had given it to her. It was a lovely thing, but since she had no idea of its intended use, a money pot seemed as good a one as any.

While she was fishing out the last of her quarters, Bernadette Harney's round cookie tin caught her eye. Shirley had insisted that she take the cookies home with her on Friday. Mary Helen had set the tin on the edge of her desk next to the blue pot, determined to bring both the cookies and the money downstairs with her. In her state of mind, she had forgotten them both.

It was a good thing she had come back to her room. Having Bernadette Harney's cookies all to herself would have struck her diet a deadly blow.

As soon as she entered the Community Room, Eileen motioned her to her chair. "Hurry up, old dear," she called. "That cute fellow"—she pointed to a hunk of red and gold on the field—"returned the kickoff sixty yards. I think we are about to score."

All eyes were on the set; shoulders hunched forward; potato chips frozen midway to the mouths. Mary Helen hunched forward with the best of them. All the pressure was on the quarterback.

"Four, seven, hut-hut." The count was clear. The ball snapped. Weaving, dodging, twisting, the quarterback dropped back, raising the ball, slapping it down, raising it again, searching the field for a receiver.

The Community Room was tense, silent, except for Sister Donata's gentle snore. She saved her energy for the defense. The quarterback paused, rocked on the balls of his feet. With a quick turn he hurled the football, arching it and spinning it like a javelin through the air right into the grasping hands of the wide receiver. A perfect catch!

The room exploded into whoops and cheers. Donata sat up with a snort. "Touchdown!" Anne howled as the man plunged into the end zone.

"Quick, put your money on the 49ers." Eileen nudged Mary Helen, motioning her toward Therese, who was still working on her chart. "The team that scores the first touchdown in the Super Bowl always wins."

"How in the world do you know that?"

"I heard the announcer say it while you were out of the room."

During a time-out, Mary Helen placed her bets and put Bernadette Harney's cookies on the coffee table as far away from the trail mix as she could. While the opposition took three downs trying in vain to score, she watched several hands clear the first layer of the cookie tin.

"These are absolutely delicious." Marta, one of the visiting Sisters, raised the tin toward Mary Helen, who declined.

"What kind are they?" her companion asked.

"Oatmeal with raisins," Sister Marta answered with a half-full mouth.

"Ugh! I hate raisins."

I hate raisins. The three words echoed in Mary Helen's mind. Like the quarterback, she paused. Why did they sound so familiar? She rocked the words back and forth in her mind. Where had she heard them before? She searched the downfield of her memory, straining to recall. Then, swifter than the lightning flash of the quarterback's throw, she knew.

I hate raisins. Christina Kelly had said those very words moments before she died. The thought exploded as complete as a perfect catch. The cookie had not been intended for Christina at all. The killer had meant it for someone else, for someone who liked raisins. And who would know which person liked raisins? Touchdown! Daphne Wayne, of course.

Someone must ask her about it. When they did, they would know who the intended victim was and perhaps who the killer was too. Later in the afternoon, when everyone was too absorbed in the game to notice her absence, Sister Mary Helen went to the phone and dialed Kate Murphy's home number. A good quarterback is a team player, after all. A sudden roar from the Community Room startled her as she listened to the hollow ringing of the unanswered phone.

⏤

"Are you sure you feel like having this party, hon?" Jack Bassetti asked for the third time since noon. "It's not too late to call it off, you know. All I have to do is make a few phone calls. I told the guys something might happen. Here, let me take that."

Murder in Ordinary Time

"Jack, I am fine." Kate Murphy waddled toward the living room with a tray of salami and cheese. As they passed in the hallway, she kissed her husband on the cheek. "Don't worry, pal. I'm just fine. In fact, I haven't felt this good in weeks." And it was true, she hadn't.

Humming, Kate set down the tray on the coffee table. She fluffed the sofa pillows while she checked on what else they needed to put out before their guests arrived for the annual Murphy–Bassetti Super Bowl party. It looked as if everything was there.

"Is the beer on ice?" Kate called, sitting on the edge of the sofa to sample the spinach dip. But Jack had gone downstairs to get more logs for the fire.

Kate leaned back against the pillows and closed her eyes, although for once she wasn't tired. In fact, she was bursting with energy and she wasn't sure why. Maybe it was the excitement of the 49ers' chance to win the Super Bowl or the fun of throwing a party. They hadn't thrown many lately. More than likely, it was because she and Gallagher had finally had a breakthrough in the Christina Kelly murder case.

Their lieutenant had been ecstatic when they had brought in the Kelly woman's attaché case. Thank goodness Sister Mary Helen had notified them. Kate shuddered to think of what might have happened if the old nun had tried to take the investigation into her own hands. They were dealing with international crime here.

"He looks so smug you would think that he uncovered the information himself," Kate had said when Gallagher and she had left the Lieutenant's office.

"That look isn't smug, Katie-girl," Gallagher had answered, "it's the look of a guy who is measuring himself for a captain's suit!"

The slamming of car doors and the shouts from Geary Boulevard told Kate that their guests were arriving. Still full of unexplained pep, she lumbered to the door and threw it open. The baby kicked at the unexpected blast of cold air.

"Oh, my, Baby's dropped." Mrs. Gallagher was the first one up the front stairs. She kissed Kate on the forehead and patted her abdomen. "It won't be long now. How are you feeling?"

"Fine, really fine," Kate answered, letting in her partner, three sets of O'Connors—Kevin and Linda, Donnie and Mary, Brian and Kathy —Jack's partner, Bob Huegle, and his wife, Pat, Kate's two sisters-in-law with their current "significant others," and Ron Honore and his brand-new ladyfriend. Each pair carried in more goodies.

Kate was about to shut the front door when she spotted her mother-in-law hurrying down the block with a large covered pan.

"I know I'm not invited," Mrs. Bassetti said, drumming up the front steps. The January cold made her words come out in little puffs.

"You are always welcome, Loretta." Kate felt a sudden flush of affection for the round little woman. "It's just that we thought that you didn't like football."

"I don't." Mrs. Bassetti pushed the door shut with her foot. "Don't let the heat out. Who likes grown men throwing a ball, piling up one on top of the other, and being paid a fortune to do it?

"Holy Mother of God! My grandson dropped." Her soft cheeks flushed. "Jackie, where are you?"

"Ma!" Jack appeared in the entranceway before Kate

had the chance to ask her how she knew it was a boy. "What are you doing here?" he asked.

Kate could hear the roar of the television crowd and their own company as the game kicked off.

"I am here because I just made some artichoke frittata. Be careful! It's still hot." She handed the pan to her son. "I know with you both working and Kate pregnant . . . What kind of a man lets his pregnant wife work?" She swatted at the back of her son's head as he moved with the pan into the kitchen.

"I thought you might not have had time to make enough good food for your party, Kate. God knows Gina and Angela . . ." She rolled her brown eyes toward her two daughters, whom she spotted sitting on the same side of the living room. "They wouldn't think to bring you anything. Too much 'boyfriend' on their minds."

"But they did, Loretta." Kate took her mother-in-law's coat. "They both brought something."

"Thanks be to God! I may have raised somebody right, after all. Was it homemade?"

"Come in, Ma! Sit down. Let me get you an old-fashioned," Jack called from in front of the television set.

"Well, only for a minute." Mrs. Bassetti allowed herself to be coaxed into the living room. With a little moving around of the other guests, she found a seat next to Mrs. G. Kate could tell by their gestures and faces that they were both more interested in the position of her baby than the position of the team on the field.

With the tightness gone from her abdomen, Kate felt much better. She labored to and from the kitchen with refills of food. She cleared and washed the glasses and returned again with more goodies.

"Enough already, hon, sit down now," Jack told her finally. "You're wearing yourself and the rug out."

Kate wondered how he had seen her, since his eyes never seemed to have left the set.

"Watch this! Now, watch this." He pointed to the quarterback shifting and darting across the field, faking a start, finally slinging the football. Even the announcers were silent as it sailed through the air, wobbling slightly before it dropped into the hands of the waiting receiver.

Everyone in the room, even Mrs. Bassetti, burst into applause as the man plunged across the goal line.

"Way to go!" Honore shouted above the din, hugging his latest ladyfriend, who had just bitten into a piece of frittata.

Kate thought she heard the phone ringing, but, over the roar, it was hard to tell. She could go and check. But all of a sudden she was having quick, shooting pains in her legs. Furthermore, who in his or her right mind would call in the middle of the Super Bowl game, especially when the 49ers were winning?

If it was important, surely whoever it was would call back later; better yet, they could call back tomorrow.

JANUARY 23
MONDAY OF THE THIRD
WEEK OF ORDINARY TIME

On Monday morning when Kate Murphy walked into the Homicide Detail, past the Lieutenant's glassed-off cubicle, she could tell that he was still on a high. The silly grin on his face gave him away.

Two unfamiliar figures were in there with him. Although she could not be sure, from their sizes, haircuts, and the style of their tailored suits, Kate guessed they were federal agents of some sort.

Catcalls, boos, and hisses greeted her when she stepped into the larger room. It took her a surprised second to realize that she must have won the football pool.

"Eat your hearts out, suckers," she called. Taking the envelope from O'Connor's hand, Kate went to her desk to count its contents.

This is going to be some week, she thought, sorting out the bills into piles of ten and translating her winnings into adorable baby clothes and cuddly toys. Not only had she come into a windfall, but the Christina Kelly murder case had taken a new twist, Sister Mary Helen was in no real danger, she still felt full of pep, despite a few shooting pains in her legs, and there was enough food left over from the Super Bowl party that neither Jack nor she would need to cook for the rest of the week.

"Who are those pretty boys in there with the Lieutenant?" Gallagher asked, dropping down into the swivel chair behind the desk across from hers.

"It beats me, Denny. Somebodies from the FBI or Interpol or some agency like that. They've got that look about them, don't you think?" Kate scooped her take back into the envelope.

"Either that or they're a couple of models from Brooks Brothers." Gallagher cleared a space in the middle of his desk for his coffee and strawberry danish. "Want a bite?" he offered.

Kate refused. Somehow the sweet roll didn't appeal to her. What she really had was the urge for some warm home-baked yeast rolls. "From that self-satisfied gloat on the Lieutenant's face, you'd think he won this." She stuffed the envelope into her purse and tried to put the thought of food out of her mind. "If he gets any happier-looking, those guys are going to start wondering what's wrong with him."

Gallagher wagged his head. "Don't be too tough on the guy, Katie-girl. This is his big break, I guess. Hell, he'll get lots of press coverage, lots of attention from the brass. Be kicked upstairs, maybe. Poor devil!" Gallagher rummaged through his pocket for his cigar.

"What do you mean, poor devil? He wants it so bad he can taste it."

"That's exactly what I mean. I pity a guy who doesn't know when he's well off." Gallagher sat quietly for a few minutes, staring out the window, morosely studying the snailing traffic on the James Lick Freeway.

"Great party at your place yesterday," he said finally. "Even the wife enjoyed it. She got on famously with your mother-in-law. They were talking so hard about grandkids that they hardly saw the game. And some game it was! Our boys had me worried for a minute, but only for a minute." Having licked the last bit of jam from his fingers, Gallagher struck a match on the under corner of his desk and lit his cigar.

"Phew!" Kate waved the smoke away from her face. This morning the smell of her partner's cigar nauseated her.

"Sorry," Gallagher said, and to her surprise, stubbed it out. "You're feeling a little queasy, are you, Katie-girl? Maybe you should knock off for today."

"I'm okay. Actually, I'm feeling wonderful." Kate began to straighten up the top of her desk. "It's just that the smell got to me for a minute."

"Me too," O'Connor yelled from across the room.

Ignoring him, Gallagher went to the coffee urn for a refill.

"Where do you think we stand with this case?" Kate asked when he returned.

"Beats me." Gallagher sat down hard and motioned toward the Lieutenant's cubicle. "They'll tell us when they want us to know."

"And in the meantime?" Kate opened the bottom drawer of her desk and propped her feet up on it.

"In the meantime, let's catch up on this goddamn paperwork." Gallagher rolled a form into his typewriter.

"You know who the luckiest guys in the world are today?" he asked after they had been working for about forty minutes.

"Who?" Kate asked, eager for any distraction.

"The cops who drew parade duty. Front-row seats from behind the barricade for every damn one of them."

Kate had nearly forgotten that the victorious 49ers

were to be welcomed home by a spectacular noontime parade. The day was clear and crisp and so they should draw a large, noisy crowd of well-wishers; about 300,000, the Chief of Police had estimated. The parade was scheduled to start near the Ferry Building and slowly make its way down Market Street to the Civic Center, stopping business and snarling up the downtown traffic for a good hour or two.

Gallagher checked his watch. "Are you hungry yet?"

"Always," Kate said.

"What about we go to Fahey's Saloon for lunch?"

"Fahey's?" Kate was surprised. Sometimes on a Friday night she and Gallagher stopped by the friendly neighborhood saloon on their way home from work, but they had never been there for lunch. Kate was not even aware that Fahey's served lunch or that Snooky, the bartender, was a cook. Furthermore, it was clear across town.

Her partner must have anticipated her objections. "It's only out to 24th on Taraval, and everything down this way will be mobbed. Besides, Snooky has got himself a new wide-screened TV and I hear that he's serving hot roast beef sandwiches special for the occasion. My treat!" Gallagher looked so pleased with himself that Kate wouldn't have had the heart to turn him down, even if she wanted to, which she didn't.

"Shake a leg, girl, the team should be just about landing at Crissy Field." He reached out his hand and pulled her up from her chair.

"Crissy Field!" Kate was surprised. That was the airport the City reserved for special visiting dignitaries. She straightened up the paperwork that she had spread across her desk. "Just like the Pope and Queen Elizabeth," she said, putting the cover on her typewriter.

"None other!" Gallagher left his desk exactly as it was. "Don't fool around now, Katie-girl. We want to get a good seat."

Inspector Gallagher and Kate Murphy arrived at Fahey's Saloon in plenty of time to get the best seats in the house. Biting into their roast beef sandwiches, they watched as the mayor, the team owner, brandishing the Vince Lombardi trophy, and the head coach, all in the lead car, began the slow crawl up Market Street.

Red and gold balloons were everywhere. "Gold rushers" in red spandex tights waved gold-gilded pompoms. Men in business suits and women in dresses hung out of the windows of the tall office buildings throwing paper and tooting plastic horns.

Motorized cable cars carried the team members and their families. One jubilant lineman danced atop the car, ducking the overhead Muni wires with the same agility as he ducked his opponents. The blond quarterback rode with his blond wife and their towheaded children in a red vintage convertible behind the elflike 49er mascot, who was sporting a gigantic helmet.

As he passed, the crowd on one side of Market Street yelled, "Forty," while the crowd on the other side answered, "Niners." Uniformed patrolmen led the cheers on either side of the street.

"Crime must be on a rampage throughout the City," Snooky said, handing Gallagher and Kate each another half a sandwich, then refilling their coffee cups. "Every cop in town is either down there or"—he looked around the crowded room—"in here."

"Snooky has a point," Kate said to Gallagher as they watched the Channel 5 camera scan the barricades along the parade route. A policeman seemed to be standing about every twenty feet. In the parade itself, there were a dozen officers on horseback and a dozen or so more on motorcycles. Kate spotted the Chief of Police in full uniform. He was riding in an open car, just behind a balloon-festooned float, and was flanked by two of his deputies. All three men waved to the friendly, cheering crowd.

"The Lieutenant, poor old slob, must be the only guy still in the Hall of Justice," Gallagher muttered. He swallowed his last mouthful of roast beef. "I wonder how he and the federal boys are doing."

Kate wondered too. There was something about the case that just didn't settle properly. Like mental heartburn, she thought, chewing her sandwich slowly. According to the research in Christina Kelly's attaché case, the newswoman had been investigating a rather sophisticated ring of art smugglers. Would criminals of that stripe murder with a poisoned cookie? Wouldn't they use a more sophisticated and more certain method, such as a bomb or a hired assassin? She wiped the corner of her mouth with a paper napkin.

"I do too," Kate said aloud, glad that it was the Lieutenant's problem and not hers. She had no desire to wrestle with it. In fact, this was the first time that she had thought about the Lieutenant, the case, the federal officers, or the Hall of Justice since they had arrived at Fahey's.

—

On her way from the convent to her office, Sister Mary Helen passed by the college's long-abandoned incinerator. A black cat with a patch of white over one eye and a white front paw meowed at her from a hole in the charred brick. It was as if he were asking her what she was doing off the beaten path. Crazily, Mary Helen felt as if she owed him an explanation.

"The campus is crawling with girls. They're back from semester break," she said.

At the sound of her voice, the cat darted back into the rubble and out of sight.

"I know what you mean, kitty," she called after him, then hurried along the little-used path. Any day, except today, she would be happy to meet the students returning to Mount St. Francis. She enjoyed talking with them about their Christmases, or their ski trips, the 49ers' victory and parade, or even about their classes. But not this morning.

This morning, Sister Mary Helen was anxious to get to her office, start to deal with the plans for the upcoming alumnae St. Valentine's Day Tea, and then, get on the horn to Kate Murphy. She could hardly wait to tell Kate what she had remembered about the raisins.

She would have called Homicide the first thing this morning, but she had guessed she would be in for a long session with Kate and Inspector Gallagher. And she knew that time, tide, and the alumnae tea wait for no one.

Sister Mary Helen stopped to catch her breath by the small acacia tree. She shivered in its shade, then noticed that its fernlike branches were ablaze with clusters of bright yellow flowers. She had been so preoccupied with rushing to her office that she wasn't noticing much.

She had completely missed what a glorious day it was. Sometime during the night, polar air had swept in from the Bay and left the City clear and sparkling. The sky was an enamel blue, and the few clouds that were near the horizon looked more like a painter had wiped the white from his brush than like real clouds.

It was one of those days when both the Bay and the ocean were gray-green and flat, and when the natives exclaimed that "you can see all the way to the Farallons." The tiny group of islands lay thirty-two miles off the coast of San Francisco, deriving their name from the Spanish word for small, pointed islands.

Sister Mary Helen remembered reading somewhere that Juan Rodrıguez Cabrillo had discovered them in 1542 but had completely missed the Bay. Now, that's what I call a foggy day, she thought, letting herself in by the back door and hurrying down the steps to her basement office.

"How did you like the game?" Shirley, who was wearing her 49ers' championship T-shirt over a white turtleneck and a white flared skirt, had beat her to work.

Although this morning the game was probably the top conversation starter in most of San Francisco, it was the last thing on Sister Mary Helen's mind. She fumbled for a comment. "It was very interesting," she said, firmly determined not to waste time talking. She must get the particulars of the alumnae tea out of the way as quickly as possible, and then call Kate Murphy.

I only wish I could do it as quickly as that T-shirt company produced those championship shirts, she thought, riffling through her stack of messages.

As usual, Shirley caught her mood. The two set to work at a feverish pace and by eleven o'clock they had nearly everything in place.

"All we need to do now is boil the water," Shirley said. "And I need a coffee break. How about you?"

"You deserve one! Go ahead." Mary Helen picked up the telephone receiver. "I'll meet you in the cafeteria as soon as I finish this call."

"Are you sure you don't want me to make it for you?"

"Positive, thank you." Mary Helen waited until she heard the office door click before she dialed Homicide.

"She is out of the office?" Mary Helen repeated, unable to believe her ears. "Inspector Gallagher too?

"No message, thank you," she told the woman who had answered the phone. Frustrated, she hung up and stared at the nearly cleared top of her desk. Where in the world could they be? she wondered as she slowly left her office. She fully intended to follow Shirley across the campus for a coffee break.

A small Cessna buzzed overhead. Its hum mingled with the distracting buzzing in her own mind. What should she do? Wait for Kate to return? She and Inspector Gallagher were most likely up to their elbows in casework, what with Christina's attaché case and all. While she, on the other hand, had an absolutely free afternoon.

No doubt they would be delighted if she saved them the trouble of checking with Daphne Wayne as to who liked or didn't like raisins. After all, they were two very busy people. She could check and when she finally did reach them, she could give them some facts, rather than just her hunches.

Making a sharp left by the small sundial, Mary Helen detoured to the convent. *Grow old along with me,* the engraving on the dial read, *the best is yet to be.*

I hope you're right, Mr. Browning, Mary Helen thought, checking first to see if the convent Nova was available and then if Sister Eileen was also. The car was free. Eileen, however, was entrenched with several of the Senior Sisters in front of the television watching the

49ers' parade. She didn't even seem to notice Mary Helen in the doorway.

The parade crowd seemed mellow, and Mary Helen noticed that they cheered everyone including the Miller beer truck and a white stretch limo that accidentally rounded the corner.

"Hooray, whoever you are!" the crowd roared.

Eileen was so absorbed that Mary Helen didn't have the heart to pull her away. As a man, Zacchaeus-like, was shinning up a denuded tree on Market Street for a better look at the 49ers, she decided to go to Daphne Wayne's house by herself.

Standing in front of the Waynes' heavy oak front door, Sister Mary Helen was sure she could hear the lions roaring at Fleischhacker Zoo: the lions and little else. The Wayne home was very still. I should have called ahead, she thought, listening to the door chimes reverberate.

She was about to leave when she heard a faint scratching behind the door. The spy window swung back and Mary Helen stared straight into Daffy Wayne's eyes. The circles around them were so dark that they looked bruised.

"Oh, Sister, it's you."

From her tone of voice, Mary Helen was unable to tell if Daphne was happy or sad to see her. Whichever, she was polite. The door swung open. Perky Daffy Wayne, still in her bedroom slippers, looked as if she were suffering from a slow leak. Her shoulders drooped. Her face sagged. Without her makeup, you could see the deep lines that etched her forehead and around her eyes and pinched her small mouth. Even the woman's frosted hair looked deflated.

"Please, come in," she said, shuffling across the living room and into the yellow breakfast nook. Mary Helen followed.

"May I fix you a cup of tea?" Daphne asked. She sank into a chair like a tired runner.

"No, thank you. Nothing for me." Mary Helen tried to sound as if she hadn't noticed how wretched Daphne looked. "I don't mean to disturb you for long. I'd just like to ask you a question or two."

Sister Mary Helen watched Daphne's face become even paler. Moving her chair closer to the table, she kicked its leg. The sudden thud made Daphne jump.

"Sorry." Daphne averted her eyes. "It's my nerves."

"Are you all right? I think I dropped in at a bad time. Are you feeling ill or is there something wrong?"

"I'm fine, Sister, thank you. Everything is really fine. What is it you wanted to ask me about?" Daphne forced a thin smile, but in the warm, sunny room Sister Mary Helen was sure that she sensed fear in the other woman.

"It's about the cookie that Christine ate; the one that killed her. Yesterday, for some strange reason, something came back to me; something that Christina had said. After she bit into the cookie she said, 'Yuck! Raisins! I hate raisins.'" Mary Helen's eyes shifted toward her hostess.

Small beads of perspiration broke out on Daphne's forehead. She began to fumble with her glasses, finally letting them dangle from the chain.

"Are you sure you are all right?" Mary Helen asked again.

"Fine! What do you want of me?" Her voice quavered.

Although her own heart was thumping, Mary Helen tried to sound matter-of-fact. "It occurred to me that no one who knew that about Christina would try to poison her with a raisin cookie, so perhaps Christina was not the intended victim. Betty Hughes mentioned in passing that you've taken an interest in everyone at the station, prepared special treats for them, know what they like. And so I thought that perhaps"—Mary Helen was now weighing each word—"you could tell me who did like raisins. That way we would know, at least, who the intended victim might have been."

Like a shot, Daphne bolted from her chair, sending it clattering to the floor. The hollow bang echoed in the silent kitchen. Sucking in her breath, she moved toward the sideboard and pulled open a drawer.

Sister Mary Helen stared in disbelief as Daphne turned back, the kitchen shears clutched in her right hand. "Wendy loved raisins. She was allergic to chocolate, but she loved raisins. Wicked Wendy Hartgrave," she hissed.

The bright sunshine streaming into the room caught on the rim of Daphne's glasses, making her eyes glow gold. "She was the one who was supposed to be killed. She is the one who deserved to die for the way she's gone after my poor husband."

This can't possibly be happening, Mary Helen thought. With a sense of unreality, she stared at Daffy. It was like watching a drama on television.

With an unexpected lunge, Daphne moved back to the table. Breathing in short, rapid breaths, she stood over Mary Helen with her golden eyes glaring. Mary

Helen's mouth felt dry. She wasn't at all sure that she could control her voice. "Perhaps we should call Inspector Murphy," she said, her tone deliberately flat.

Daphne stumbled backward as though the words had been jabs. With a violent shudder, she raised the shears high above her head, the small muscles in her arm bulging.

Mary Helen's stomach buckled. She tightened her teeth, bracing herself for the blow. The vicious steel blades glinted in the sun. *"Anima Christi . . ."* The familiar words of the ancient prayer swirled under her fear. "In the hour of my death, call me. . . . Bid me come to Thee."

"Don't make things worse." Like a ventriloquist's dummy, she blurted out the words without even thinking. What should she do? Her mind was a blank. Hugging her arms around her own trembling body, she stared up into Daphne Wayne's gray, taut face.

Their eyes locked and, inexplicably, Mary Helen saw Daffy's change. They were no longer the eyes of a killer. They were bleak and dead. With a spasmodic jerk, Daphne dropped the shears on the shiny tabletop. The metal clattered.

"I did it," she said, her face suddenly blotchy. "I did it." Outside, a car door slammed. The agate eyes pleaded with Mary Helen. "Please, don't call the police yet. Just give me time to explain to Cheryl."

With unexpected force, she grabbed Mary Helen's upper arm. Even through her jacket, Mary Helen could feel the woman's fingernails digging into her flesh. "She's just a baby, really. And Doug. I want to call and tell Doug. Promise me, Sister. Please, promise me you won't call. Not yet. I'll do it myself as soon as I talk to Doug. I'll call and talk to that sweet Inspector Murphy." Daphne Wayne tried to smile, but her pale face was an unbearable picture of despair.

—

The Lieutenant was waiting for Kate Murphy when she arrived back at work.

"Gallagher with you?" A doleful expression had replaced the morning's silly grin. He rubbed the back of his hand across a stubbled chin that looked as if it needed shaving.

"He said he'd be up in a minute," she answered, wondering what this was all about.

The Lieutenant was about to growl out something when the glass door opened. Kate was relieved to see Gallagher.

"Glad you could join us, Denny." Apparently the Lieutenant's sarcasm was completely lost on Gallagher. He offered both Kate and his superior a doughnut from the bakery bag he was carrying.

"How can you eat another thing?" Kate made a face.

"Put that crap away and come in here, will ya?" the Lieutenant shouted. Only then did Gallagher seem to get the point.

"What's up, Lieutenant?" he asked after shutting the cubicle door behind them.

"Those damn feds, that's what's up. Interpol, to be exact. You saw those two guys who were in here this morning?"

"The pretty boys?" Gallagher asked, as if he didn't know.

The Lieutenant nodded, the nostrils of his flat nose flaring. "You got that right, Denny. Well, I spent the whole morning talking to them. And ten minutes ago, I get a call from the Chief. Seems like Interpol is going to take over our case. We're not equipped, they say, for this international business, like we didn't uncover it."

Did "we" include Sister Mary Helen? Kate wondered, but knew better than to ask.

"All we got to do is to feed them our information and keep out of their way. The goddamn nerve of them!" The Lieutenant slammed his knuckles into the back of his padded chair, raising a cloud of dust.

Kate covered her nose and mouth, more to hide her smile than to protect herself against the flying dirt. The poor Lieutenant! So much for the notoriety, the press coverage, and the promotion! One phone call and poof! it was all over.

"*Sic transit gloria mundi.*" When she was a student at Mount St. Francis, Kate had learned that phrase from Sister Eulalia, and sure enough, Sister Eulalia had been proven correct again. The glory of the world is passing.

"Don't tell the old man, but I am delighted the guys from Interpol are taking this case over," Kate said when she and Gallagher were back at their desks.

"How so?" her partner asked through a mouthful of doughnut. "And be careful who you're calling old. The guy is five years younger than me."

"Because one of these days, Denny, believe it or not, I am going to have this baby and go on maternity leave." Kate placed her hands on her abdomen. She could feel life. "And I'd really hate to leave you with this mess. When Sister Mary Helen turned in Christina Kelly's attaché case, the whole thing got so much more complicated, with suspected art theft and international smuggling. You know what I mean."

"I know what's bugging you, Katie-girl. You're afraid that I wouldn't be able to recognize a Greek icon if I met one."

"Not true, Denny. It's just that I hate leaving you with the whole nine yards."

"O'Connor could have filled in for you."

"Today, you just can't get to me, Denny. No matter what you say. Today, I feel as if I could take on the whole world."

"Oh, oh!" Gallagher ran his hand over his bald pate.

"What do you mean, 'oh, oh'?"

"Bad sign. That take-on-the-whole-world bit comes just before the labor pains." Gallagher rolled a report sheet into his typewriter and began to peck away with his two index fingers. "Mrs. G used to tear the house apart just before it was time. Nesting instincts! Clean stuff that wasn't even dirty. Sometimes, she didn't get the place all put back before the labor pains started."

He looked over his glasses at her. "You let me know, Katie-girl, when you feel the first twinge."

His solicitude made Kate feel warm and cozy inside and she wanted to cry. "You are sweet, Denny, to be so concerned about me." She blinked back the tears. "But the way I figure, I still have about a month to go."

"Sweet, hell!" He pecked a short, quick word on the typewriter. "I just want to make sure I get ahold of your husband. He started it, for chrissake, let him be here to finish it!"

About a half hour later, Kate's phone rang. "This really has been some day," she said, hanging up with a bang. "Do you know who that was, Denny?"

"What am I now, a mind reader?" Her partner looked at her over the front page of the *Chronicle*.

Kate was too excited with her news to spend time bantering. "That was Daphne Wayne."

"So?" Gallagher snapped over the page.

"So"—Kate couldn't help grinning—"she just confessed to the murder of Christina Kelly. Although she says that Christina was not her intended victim—Wendy Hartgrave was." She had Gallagher's attention now.

"What about all that art stuff and smuggling and Interpol?"

"It has nothing to do with the murder." Kate began to straighten up the top of her desk and reach for Jack's bulky sweater and her purse. "It is apparently just a coincidence."

"Well, I'll be damned! I'd give my eyeteeth, if I still had them, to see the look on the Lieutenant's face when he hears this one."

"You will," Kate said, walking splay-footed toward the glassed-off cubicle. "Mrs. Wayne wants us to bring her in. She has written up a confession and is waiting for us at her home."

"For us?"

"That's right. And get this." Kate narrowed her eyes at her partner, as though he were somehow to blame. "She doesn't want a black-and-white to pick her up. It might embarrass the family. And she doesn't want her husband to drive her down here, this is a direct quote: 'He's tired and he works so hard.' Sick!" Kate spat out the word. "Just plain sick!"

"My kind of gal." Gallagher dropped the newspaper to follow her. "I wonder if this Wayne lady gives lessons."

—

On the drive home from the Waynes' house, Sister Mary Helen pushed her free foot against the floorboard and held tight to the steering wheel of the Nova. She had to, to keep from trembling. She drove down Sunset Boulevard seeing nothing. Even the bright sunlight reflecting off the windows of the attached houses took on the color of skimmed milk. It was as though she were driving through the tail end of a dream, haunted by Cheryl's muffled sobs, Daphne's soft, apologetic tone of voice when she spoke to her husband, the brief call to Homicide.

At this very moment, Kate and Gallagher were on their way to the Wayne home. If I were in my right mind, I would be happy this is over, Mary Helen thought. But something in her mind was not right. She had lost her way. Not her way down the straight, wide boulevard, of course, but in her own mind. Something was amiss; something she ought to sort out. But not now. She needed time to do it; a little time and a little distance. But above all, she needed to be back at Mount St. Francis before the two policemen arrived, especially after Kate had given her specific orders to leave the murder business to them.

January 24
TUESDAY OF THE THIRD WEEK OF ORDINARY TIME FEAST OF SAINT FRANCIS DE SALES, BISHOP

Although she tried not to show it, all morning long Sister Mary Helen was distracted. She could not shake Daphne Wayne from her mind. What had Daphne said to Kate Murphy? What would happen now to poor Daffy? By her own admission, Daphne was a cold-blooded murderer, yet there was something so pathetic about her that Mary Helen could only feel the deepest pity for the woman.

Sister Eileen must have noticed that her mind was somewhere else. "We are semiretired, you know," she said when she set down her lunch tray on the table next to Mary Helen's place. "What is the use of being semiretired, old dear, if we don't play hooky once in a while?" Her bushy eyebrows rose in question.

Confound it! I'm more distracted than I imagined, Mary Helen thought, watching her friend remove a bowl of creamy potato soup from her tray and place it on the tabletop. When she'd passed through the cafeteria line, she hadn't even noticed the soup. And potato soup was one of her favorites.

"After lunch, would you be interested in a long walk along Ocean Beach?" Eileen asked, finally settling down to her meal. "The salt air will help you get the kinks out."

"What makes you think that I have any kinks?" Mary Helen asked, a bit put out that she was so transparent.

"Fifty years of experience in being your friend." Eileen scooped up a brimming spoonful of soup and grinned.

Before they began their walk, the two nuns paused on the sidewalk below the Cliff House to enjoy the view. The Seal Rocks were crowded with dirt-brown sea lions sunning themselves or barking at the gulls wheeling overhead. The sea gulls cawed wildly in reply.

Shielding her eyes, Mary Helen gazed out over the Pacific. Today the ocean was flat for as far as her eye could see, and blue; so blue that it was difficult to tell where water stopped and sky began. A miniature freighter inched along the horizon. Closer in, surfers in black wet suits rode small waves into the shore.

Without speaking, the two nuns started to amble down the walled sidewalk bordering Ocean Beach. They strode in tune with the rhythmic sound of the waves exploding against the sand and the brisk smell of the salt air.

"It just doesn't jibe," Mary Helen said finally. And even though Eileen didn't ask what didn't jibe—or maybe *because* she didn't—Mary Helen unloaded the whole story on her: Daphne Wayne, the kitchen shears, Daphne's confession, her concern for her family, staying with her until she had called Kate. As the two moved along, Mary Helen could feel the tension begin to leave her muscles. As she relaxed, her mind became clearer.

"What do you think?" she asked, making room for a pair of thin cyclists who whizzed by on their even thinner bikes. For the first time, she noticed that the color had left Eileen's usually ruddy face.

"I think that you are a very lucky woman to be alive," she said, "And furthermore, I think that the old saying is true."

"What saying?"

"That God takes care of fools, drunks, babies, and old nuns!"

"I'm not asking you what you think about me, Eileen." Mary Helen stopped by the wall to stare down, unseeing, at the graffiti and the dirty sand. "What do you think about the case?"

"Well, you are right about there being unanswered questions."

"See what I mean?" They walked for several minutes in silence. Since Mary Helen wasn't doing too well in the thinking department herself, she wanted to make sure Eileen had plenty of time. A grown man, barefoot and balancing on top of the wall like a tightrope artist, passed them. Sister Eileen said nothing. Mary Helen could stand it no longer.

"For example," she began as if she were giving a lecture, "how did the cookies get into the studio? To our knowledge, Daffy was not there that day. Besides—"

Eileen interrupted. "When the police questioned them, I am sure that neither her husband nor her daughter admitted to delivering anything for her, or she would have been arrested already."

"You're right," Mary Helen said, delighted that Eileen was helping out. At the moment, she needed all the help she could muster. "Furthermore, why would Daphne just trust to luck that Wendy would take the correct cookie? No one in her right mind would do that."

"From what you've told me, her right mind may be the real question." Eileen pulled up the collar of her Aran sweater around her ears. A wind had picked up, blowing the sand across the Great Highway and sending the windmill on the ocean edge of Golden Gate Park spinning.

"True." Mary Helen closed her eyes against the spray of sand. Automatically, the two turned their backs to the Pacific. A flock of pigeons descended on the asphalt parking spaces along the highway. Strutting, they began to feast on leftovers from the lunchtime crowd.

"Another thing." Mary Helen headed up the hill toward where they had parked the Nova. "She never once mentioned calling Betty Hughes or delivering a cookie to her home. Unless Betty just imagined it. That kind of trick doesn't seem like something a woman who is as eager to please others as Daphne Wayne is, would do."

"Then again, neither does committing murder, old dear," Eileen said, her brogue thickening. "Neither does committing murder."

―

"Hi ya, hon. Welcome home! Come in here and sit down. Put your feet up! Here, let me take your stuff." Jack Bassetti met his wife at the front door of their home on Geary Street.

"What the heck is wrong with you?" She struggled out of Jack's heavy sweater and lumbered after him into the living room. "And how did you happen to beat me home from work?"

Jack ignored her questions. "How are you feeling?" he asked. Concern clouded his hazel eyes as he gently kissed her forehead.

"Fine, just fine!" Kate sank into an easy chair and perched her swollen feet on the hassock. Closing her eyes, she let her head fall back against the soft headrest. The aroma of bubbling Italian pot roast filled the room and made her mouth water.

"You've even made dinner," she said, without opening her eyes. "Or at least you picked it up at your mother's. What in the world is going on?"

"Nothing, why?" Jack stood over her. "You just stay comfortable. I'll bring your dinner in on a tray. Shall I flip on the TV? The early news should be on."

"I've had enough news for one day, thank you." Reaching up, Kate squeezed her husband's hand.

"Yeah, I know."

"So, that's it!" Annoyed, Kate sat up in the chair. "That blabbermouth of a Gallagher called you, didn't he?"

"Well, I did run into him at the Hall."

"Run into him, hell! We rarely, if ever, run into you! He made a special trip over to Vice to tell you about my 'nesting instincts,' didn't he?" Kate didn't wait for his answer.

"This is ridiculous, I feel fine! I am perfectly capable of sitting at the table and eating like we usually do." She struggled to push herself up out of the chair, but couldn't get the leverage. "Help me!" she shouted, but Jack had disappeared into the kitchen. Exhausted, she sank back into the chair, closed her eyes, and listened to her husband preparing their dinner on trays.

After the two of them had finished every last morsel of Mrs. Bassetti's pot roast, Jack insisted on doing the dishes alone.

"What can I do to help?" Kate asked, still stuck in the same chair.

"Have I got the project for you!" Grabbing the arms of her easy chair, Jack leaned forward to kiss her, missing her mouth and landing on her nose. "It's name time!"

Straightening up, he handed her a stack of books. His latest purchase, *The Melting Pot Book of Baby Names*, was on top. Along with them was a copy of an old newspaper article he had found somewhere on naming a child.

Kate groaned. "More books?"

"This is getting serious." He ran his fingers through his thick, curly hair. "Our kid needs a name. And if Gallagher is to be believed, the kid needs one soon."

Kate shook her head.

"Read!" Jack shouted, and left her in the quiet room.

Kate read. She was astonished to discover that one couple let the obstetrician decide on the name. In some families, the article said, the father names the boys and the mother names the girls. One book suggested finding a name with rhythmic power; the more arresting the last name, the simpler the first name. Another advised avoiding newly popular names.

"Good news! You're thinking! You're twisting your hair." Jack's voice startled her. She hadn't heard him reenter the room.

He was right. She was so deeply absorbed that she didn't even realize she was twisting one thick piece of her auburn hair round and round her index finger, but it was not helping her decide on a baby's name.

"Listen to this." She read, " 'One couple took their baby's name from the graffiti on a rock near where they'd been sitting when they decided to have a child.' "

208

MURDER IN ORDINARY TIME

They were both laughing when Kate felt the first wave of pain. "Uh-oh, pal," she murmured, clutching her abdomen and waiting for the dull ache to subside. Jack stared at her in amazement, unable to speak.

Not four minutes went by before the second wave hit. Clenching her teeth, Kate grimaced at her husband. "I think it's time, Jack."

Sister Mary Helen left the Community Room early. The evening news was on the television and Wendy Hartgrave, who had taken Christina Kelly's place at the anchor desk, was relating the details of Daphne Wayne's arrest. Ray Kerns, San Francisco's most trusted anchorman, sat next to her, staring at her with his mud-brown eyes. His sincere face was expressionless. Mary Helen wondered what he was thinking. She had no doubts about Wendy Hartgrave's thoughts.

The woman's short red curly hair bounced as she read the details from the monitor. Her ice-blue eyes lit up at each sordid detail, as if she relished Daphne's misery. It was no wonder someone had wanted to murder her, Mary Helen thought, listening to Wendy flaunt the fact that she was the intended victim. Mary Helen could swear that the woman's uptilted chin was becoming more witchlike by the minute. She had seen enough.

"Why are you leaving?" Sister Anne whispered as Mary Helen threaded her way through the watching nuns and out of the room. "They'll probably mention something about you."

Do I need more of a reason? Mary Helen thought, pretending she hadn't heard the question. Age had its privileges and playing deaf was one of them. She was beginning to enjoy it.

Back in her bedroom she undressed quickly, plumped up her pillows, and settled in to enjoy her latest discovery, a San Francisco cabbie-detective named Ben Henry. Tonight she needed a good mystery; a make-believe tale in which the violence has a reason, the crime is always solved with the good guys winning and the bad guys getting caught.

She was just finishing chapter one when the convent phone rang.

"It's for you." Mary Helen recognized Sister Therese's hushed voice at her bedroom door. "Shall I tell your caller that you are indisposed?"

"Certainly not!" Mary Helen nudged her legs out of the bed. Indisposed indeed! She went down the hall, fuming. Whoever Therese said that to would not only think she was sick, but that she was someone right out of a Victorian novel.

"Hi, Sister." Despite the slight slur, Sister Mary Helen knew that it was Betty Hughes. "I'm celebrating," she said. "How about you?"

"In a way, yes," Mary Helen answered.

"I can hardly believe it was goofy Daffy. See, I told you somebody dropped off a poison cookie! Police identified her green Volks. More power to her, though. Too bad she didn't get Wendy after all. What a mess, huh? Good old philandering Wayne got his. His fair-haired days at Channel Five are over!"

As quickly as she could, Mary Helen terminated her conversation with Betty Hughes. Betty had begun to ramble and Mary Helen was tired. Listening to Betty criticize Wendy and gloat over the Waynes' fate didn't help anything. Besides, she had come to the phone so quickly that she had forgotten her slippers and now her feet were cold. She wanted to get back to her book. Furthermore, she still had nagging doubts about the outcome of this case. A victim and a murderer should match. One should fit into the other, like a key and a lock, she thought, padding down the hallway. Maybe after a good night's sleep, things would be clearer.

She hadn't even reached her bedroom door when the phone rang again.

"It's for you, Sister Mary Helen." Anne was panting. She must have taken the convent steps two at a time, probably during the commercial break. Mary Helen didn't even want to think about what the Sisters were watching on the television.

"Hello." Mary Helen recognized the Greek accent immediately. "The police. They call me today," Mrs. Pappas said, her words soft and ringing with sadness. "It was not my Christina, at all, they say, who was to be killed. But she was." The woman's voice choked.

"I am so sorry." Mary Helen waited for Mrs. Pappas to speak again, but all she heard was the low, muffled sound of a sob. "Are you all right?" As soon as the words left her mouth, Mary Helen regretted them. Of course she was not all right!

"Later. We will talk later. Pray for me!" Mrs. Pappas managed, then the phone went dead.

Carefully, Mary Helen replaced the receiver. Indeed she would pray; she would pray fervently that later, after the police had thoroughly investigated her daughter's findings on the theft of the sacred Greek art, the two of them wouldn't be talking about still more sad news for the poor woman.

Sister Mary Helen had just switched off her bedside lamp when the convent phone rang a third time. This time it was Joe Sousa.

"Hi, Sister," he said, his cowboy twang completely absent. "Did I disturb you?"

"No," Mary Helen fibbed. "What can I do for you, Joe?" she asked, glad that this trip she had remembered her bedroom slippers.

"I just wanted to congratulate you on helping to find Christina's killer."

Mary Helen felt her stomach turn over. "Was my name mentioned on the evening news too?"

"No, but Kerns mentioned your part in it to the rest of the crew during the commercial break. You are really something."

He paused, leaving her to wonder what.

"What I really called you about is my cousin Tony's trial."

Mary Helen sat down on the phone booth stool. Tony Costa's murder trial was what had led her into this mess in the first place. "What about it?" she asked, trying not to sound annoyed.

"There has been so much feeling about the case in the City as well as in the local Portuguese community in the Santa Clara Valley, that the venue has been moved to San Diego." Joe sounded as if he had been granted a reprieve. "There won't be as much publicity now as there would be if it were held here, so maybe I won't have to move again. I like my job at Channel Five, Sister, and I have a new steady girlfriend, so I do want to stay." He paused. "Am I keeping you from something?"

Sister Mary Helen couldn't bring herself to say, "Oh, no," and she was too polite to say, "Yes, you are."

Clearing her throat, she muttered, "I'm happy for you, Joe."

"Why I really called is to thank you for last Thursday. You remember? When I came to see you?"

"Certainly I remember, Joe." How could I forget? she wondered.

"Lots of people would have been scared, Sister. Me just appearing like that and so wrought up. But not you!"

Shows what *he* knows! Mary Helen thought, recalling her heart bumping so hard that she was afraid he might hear it.

"Yessir, Sister. You're something. I'll never forget how you said, 'Of course not, Joe,'" when I asked you if you thought it was me. I can't tell you what it meant to me."

Sister Mary Helen was glad that he couldn't. This ill-deserved praise was starting to make her uncomfortable. She probably should tell him the brutal truth: that for several long moments she had been scared witless. But what would be the point?

Joe went on singing her praises while Mary Helen tried to justify her silence now. Mercifully, she remembered that today was the Feast of Saint Francis de Sales. This gentle bishop was the soul of kindness. "You can catch more flies with a spoonful of honey than with a hundred barrels of vinegar," he used to say. Somehow his honey-and-vinegar theory fit in to her present situation. The kindest thing to say was simply nothing.

So Sister Mary Helen listened, resigned to Joe's unnecessary gratitude. She had to admit she was delighted when he hung up.

San Diego! The reality suddenly struck her. She shivered in the drafty phone booth. When in the name of heaven would the trial be held? She'd still have to appear, surely. What if it were at the same time as the alumnae tea? The tea committee would never understand. And just how long would she have to stay? Kate Murphy will know, she thought. She'd ask Kate.

Wide-awake now, Mary Helen started to dial Kate's home, then hesitated. If Kate even suspected that she had been with Daphne Wayne when the woman had confessed, after all Kate had said, she would surely have Mary Helen's head.

On the other hand, if Kate had had the slightest intimation, she would have called hours ago. Confidently, Mary Helen dialed.

"Hello?" The voice that answered was familiar, although Mary Helen couldn't place it right away. Had she dialed incorrectly? "Is this the Murphy–Bassetti residence?" she asked.

"Yes," the voice answered.

"May I speak to Kate?"

"She's not talking to anyone right now, except maybe the doctor." Loretta. That's who it was, Kate's mother-in-law, Loretta Bassetti.

"Loretta, this is Sister Mary Helen. Is Kate all right?"

"Fine and not so fine. She's at St. Mary's Hospital. From what Jackie says, she went into labor about an hour ago. But he's so rattled, I could hardly get a straight sentence out of him. You know that Jackie and her are doing all that Lamaze stuff, natural childbirth, you know what I mean? Husband in the room. I wouldn't have my husband, God rest him, near me when I was delivering. I had enough trouble. The delivery room is no place for a man, if you ask me. But I can't talk now, Sister. I've got to rush to St. Mary's with this crazy Lamaze bag, because my

214

dumb-cluck of a son, big man in the delivery room, was in such a hurry to get Kate to the hospital that he ran off and forgot to bring it with him. Could be worse, huh, Sister? Could be the other way around, I guess. Take the bag and forget the wife. You see what I mean about the delivery room? It is no place for a man!"

January 25
Wednesday of the Third Week of Ordinary Time
Feast of the Conversion of Saint Paul

 Sister Mary Helen buttoned up her Aran sweater and shoved her hands into its narrow pockets. I should have worn my knit hat and gloves, she thought, feeling the biting wind ruffle her short gray hair. Head down, she hurried across the deserted campus, eager for a cup of hot coffee.

A slit of daylight was beginning to show over the Oakland hills. Father Adams's short Mass was even shorter than usual this morning. He beat the dawn. No homily, that was why. Who could blame him? How could anyone improve on Paul's own account of a great light from the sky suddenly flashing all about him, forcing him to the ground? That must have been some sight!

She paused by the kitchen door just long enough to look up at the leaden sky over Mount St. Francis. This morning the sky created most of the view from the top of the hill since a gray bank of fog hid the City below. Braving the cold, she watched the wind push the clouds around until the entire sky looked bruised. Mary Helen shivered. Ugh! Don't tell me it's going to be another dreary, overcast day! As if to answer, the wind forced the heavy door from her hand and slammed it behind her with a loud bang.

"Sister Mary Helen? Telephone! Sister Mary Helen?" She was only two sips into her second cup of coffee when she heard her name on the loudspeaker.

Who in the world now? she wondered, making her way, coffee cup in hand, to the nearest phone.

"It's a boy. Seven pounds, eight ounces." Mrs. Bassetti's voice bubbled with pride. "My first grandchild!"

"Congratulations!" Mary Helen herself felt a ripple of pride. Nothing is quite so wonderful or so miraculous or so reassuring to the human race as the birth of a child. What had Carl Sandburg written? "A baby is God's opinion that life should go on."

"And how are Kate and Jack doing?" she asked.

"Kate is fine. Doing great. Jackie is a mess. Can't even talk straight. And would you believe, Sister? No name yet! I tell you, this is not right. No name for my grandson. What has he got? Two nuts for parents? Visiting hours start at noon. I'll pick you up at eleven-thirty sharp."

"Do you think that I should wait until tomorrow? Kate might need a chance to rest up," Mary Helen said. The only answer she received was the dull hum of the dial tone.

"This is a tow-away zone," Mary Helen said when Loretta Bassetti pulled the tires of her ancient blue Buick against the curb on Stanyan Street.

"So let them tow!" Mrs. Bassetti glanced at her wristwatch. "It's nearly twelve o'clock. I don't want to waste another second before I see my darling grandbaby!"

Sister Mary Helen followed the woman through a maze of hallways until Mrs. Bassetti pushed back a door to one of the maternity rooms. The two peeked in. Although the plugs and gadgets and the telltale smell of antiseptics gave away the fact that it was a hospital room, someone had gone to great pains to decorate the narrow room in soft, soothing peach and blue pastels and to make it appear as homelike as possible.

On one side of the room, Kate leaned back in the bed propped up against a mound of pillows. Close to her bedside, a rumpled-looking Jack snoozed in an over-stuffed chair. His left hand rested on his wife's knee.

Oblivious to his snores or to her visitors in the doorway, Kate, her face aglow, cradled a tiny, wriggling bundle in her arms. Tenderly she studied each small feature on the pink face, kissed the tiny alabaster fingers, and marveled at each minute toe.

Watching her, Mary Helen felt a lump forming in her own throat. She stood quietly, afraid to intrude. It was as if she had stumbled into a sacred moment and was an unexpected witness to a mother's secret love. Her own heart filled with a sense of wonder and joy as in that cameo she caught a glimpse of the enduring, overbrooding love of God.

"Let Nonnie see her baby boy." Mrs. Bassetti's cheerful voice broke the spell.

Startled, Jack jumped up from his chair, attempting

to tuck his shirt into his pants and smooth down his hair. "Oh, hi, Ma." His voice was groggy. "You here already?"

Ignoring him, Mrs. Bassetti headed straight for the bed, kissed Kate on the forehead, then began to coo at the baby, who slept peacefully. Gently, she ran her fingers over his fuzzy head.

"He is adorable. Absolutely adorable." She straightened up. "He looks exactly like you did, Jackie, when you were born." She beamed at her son.

"Ma, he looks like Winston Churchill."

Mrs. Bassetti gasped. "Shame on you! Imagine saying such a thing about your own child." She took another fond peek at the baby. "He is precious. An angel. Look at that sweet little face. What kind of a son have I raised that can't see that?"

Even though she scolded, it was clear that she, too, loved her child. And that he would always be her child regardless of how old he was. It was that mother love again, Mary Helen thought. What was that silly rhyme?

·Where yet was ever found a mother,
Who'd give her booby for another?

Mary Helen smiled down at Kate with her newborn child. In fact, she reflected, the whole series of events over the last three weeks was replete with mothers and their love for their children.

Bernadette Harney's love and concern for her daughter Danielle was really what had caused Mary Helen to be at Channel 5 in the first place. Mrs. Pappas's strong love for her daughter was what made her intent on finding the attaché case and having its contents investigated.

And Daphne Wayne's first thought in her own tragedy was for Cheryl. In her protective love she wanted to shelter her child from hurt. Poor sulky, sensitive Cheryl with the stringy blond hair, the pouty mouth, and the braces on her teeth that slurred her speech with sibilance.

Mary Helen frowned. Suddenly, a thought had come to her "like a full-blown rose," as Keats had said. Of course! That was it! Mary Helen was as stunned as if she, like Saint Paul, had been thrown to the ground, a great light flashing from the sky. How had she missed it? It had been there all the time. She could hardly wait until the visit was over. In fact, Mary Helen was so concerned with getting out of St. Mary's Hospital and over to the Wayne home that she scarcely heard Mrs. Bassetti shout, "Sweet Mother of God! What do you mean, you still have no name for this precious baby? Listen to your mother, Jackie, and listen to me good. You get a name for the baby and you get one fast!"

―

"Well, that's over with," Jack said, watching the heavy door of the room close behind his mother and Sister Mary Helen. "I was dreading it."

"She seemed to like him." Kate looked up, wondering what he meant.

"Like him? She was crazy about him. And who wouldn't be? Who could resist that face?"

Heads touching, Kate and Jack gazed down at the baby's small, round face, still pink and scrunched up, yet perfectly formed.

"I wonder what he's thinking about?" Jack tried to force his broad finger into the baby's clenched fist. "He's really got a grip, Kate. Look at that!"

"Why were you dreading your mother's visit?" From

the expression on his face, Kate could tell that Jack was so absorbed with his son that he'd already forgotten that he'd said it. "That's what you you said when she left. You said, 'I was dreading it.' Why?"

"Oh, that. Watch his mouth, Kate. See. Look. He's moving it like he wants to say something. Did you ever see anything like it?"

Kate sighed. Good Lord, she thought. Her Jack was going to turn out to be one of those doting fathers who thinks everything his kids do is wonderful!

"He probably wants to eat," she said. "Or maybe he is having a little gas pain."

"I don't think so, Kate. Look at him. See how he grabs my finger? I'll bet he realizes we're his parents and he wants to say hi." He beamed at her.

"Don't say that to anyone but me, okay, pal?" With her free hand, Kate rubbed her husband's unshaved cheek.

"Why not?"

"Because, for an intelligent man, Jack, you are beginning to sound like the village idiot. Now, why were you dreading your mother's visit?"

Sinking back into the chair, Jack drummed his fingers on the arm rests. "The name thing. I knew she'd have fits that we haven't chosen one yet. Actually, I was afraid that she would have plenty more to say than she did. I was kind of glad that the nun was with her. Maybe the religious presence toned her down."

"Your mother? It probably only made her feel more convinced that God was on her side." Kate pushed a stray piece of hair back from her forehead. "And, as much as I hate to admit it, she is right. We need to name our son."

"Any ideas?"

"Now that I've seen him, Jack, I know that I want him to have a special name. One that's special for me anyway. Maybe the name of someone I love very much so that every time I say it, I feel warm inside."

"Great idea! How about Michael?"

"Michael?" Kate was puzzled. Michael who? What on earth made Jack think that Michael was the name of someone that she loved very much?

"After your father, Mick Murphy."

Leaning her head back against the mound of pillows, Kate closed her eyes. "Jack." She enunciated each word. "My father's name was not Michael. We have been together for all these years. We have had a child together. And you don't even know what my father's name was? To quote Dennis Gallagher, 'He must be rolling over in his grave.'"

Opening her eyes, she watched a dumbfounded expression spread across her husband's face. "Everyone always called him 'Mick,' hon, so I just assumed—"

"It was a nickname, Jack. He got it as a kid, probably because he looked so Irish."

"What was his real name?"

"Patrick! Patrick Emmet Murphy!"

"Well, I'll be damned!"

A soft whimper from the baby broke the silence. "I hope your son didn't hear you," Kate said, rocking the baby back and forth. "He'll begin to wonder what else his daddy doesn't know about his mommy."

Standing up, Jack leaned over the bed, his face close to hers. "I'll tell him"—she could feel his warm breath as he spoke—"that I know everything I need to know to love his mommy with all my heart." He covered her lips with his, his hands gently caressing her. "And that I want to show her just how much before the nurse—" An angry wail interrupted Jack's sentence.

"I think that your son wants to eat!" Kate smiled down at the baby's face, which was quickly growing red. As if on cue, the nurse entered pushing a cart of baby bottles.

Straightening up quickly, Jack reached for his jacket and ran his fingers through his hair. "You better feed him," he said, "while I go out and scout up some cold champagne and a couple of glasses. Tonight we parents are going to celebrate, Kate, and I'm going to give you some idea of how much I love you. Besides, tonight we are going to decide on a name."

"What name do you want?"

Jack shrugged. "Any one that makes you feel warm when you say it is okay with me. So, be thinking, hon, 'cause I'll be right back."

Sister Mary Helen was nearing the Lakeshore turnoff on Sunset Boulevard before she really started to think about what she was doing. And when she did think about it, she tried not to be too logical, knowing full well that if she allowed herself to think logically, she would turn right around and head back to Mount St. Francis College.

The morning paper had reported Daphne Wayne's bail as $500,000. "A king's ransom," to quote Sister Therese. Surely, the family would have arranged for it immediately, Mary Helen reasoned as she pulled up in front of the two-story house, which had most likely served as collateral. Its white weather cock twirled in the steady breeze off Lake Merced.

Set back on a manicured lawn, the house looked so proper, so upstanding, so neat and clean, painted an understated blue, trimmed in gleaming white that shone through the dull fog like . . .

"Whited sepulchres"—Jesus' harsh words flashed through Mary Helen's mind—"which indeed appear beautiful outward, but are within full of dead men's bones."

An unnatural silence hung over the neighborhood. Except for a pair of joggers trotting by on the exercise path across from the house, the whole block was deserted. Not a child playing, not a dog or even a cat were visible on the long block. All was still, so still that the crunch of the joggers' feet echoed in the distance.

Sister Mary Helen studied the house in search of any sign of life, but found none. The Levolors on the front window were shut tight. The shades in the upstairs bedrooms were still drawn. The driveway was empty of cars. Even the leaves on the rosebushes closed in on one another as if they, too, were hiding some horrible secret.

Despite appearances and a feeling of foreboding, she decided to ring the front door bell, just in case. The chimes resounded through the silent house. Once, twice. Still no answer.

Raising the lion's-head knocker, she banged it against the oak door. To her surprise, the door opened a crack. She peeked in.

"How-do, Daphne? Are you there?" Cautiously, Mary Helen stepped into the entryway. She shivered. The living room was as dark and as cold as a house in mourning, undisturbed by even the familiar hum of the heater or the buzz of a refrigerator.

A silent funeral, she thought, listening to the stillness. The only sound she did hear was an odd, hollow, slapping noise coming from the direction of the kitchen. "How-do, Daphne? Is that you?" she called a little louder, wondering just what she would say if it was, or, for that matter, what she would say if it wasn't Daphne after all.

Mary Helen stopped in the doorway of the chick-yellow breakfast nook. Even in there the blinds were drawn, shutting out the view of the lake and shutting in all the misery.

Peering into the dim kitchen, she saw Daphne. Her shoulders sagging, Daphne Wayne stood over a mixing bowl. Her marble eyes glowed. Fascinated, Mary Helen watched from the doorway. Both of Daphne's hands were in the large glass bowl. With a vengeance, she pummeled . . . something. Turning it, punching it with her fists, slapping it, finally squeezing it until snakes of red meat oozed out through her clenched fingers.

"Dinner," she said in an absent voice. Obviously, she was aware of another's presence. "Meat loaf."

Mary Helen watched the woman press the ground beef into a lump, then slam it with her fist. Save for the hollow pounding sound, the house was still deadly silent. Mary Helen eased into the kitchen. In its dimness, the organdy curtains seemed to droop. Even the smiling bills of the ceramic ducks looked grim.

"Why, Daphne? Why did you lie to me?" Mary Helen's voice was hushed. She had not taken the time to plan what to say, nor how to approach the subject. Before she thought, the words had slipped out. "Why?" she repeated.

Without looking up from the mixing bowl, Daphne turned the ground meat over again. Clutching it in one hand, she patted the beef into a neat, square loaf and placed it back in the bowl.

"They'll be hungry," she said, her eyes still avoiding Mary Helen's face. With a practiced move, she pulled a baking tray from the cupboard. "My poor family needs a good dinner. Everything looks better after a good meal." Daphne mouthed the words like a robot programmed to sound cheerful, upbeat. But they came out flat. Like a soda that's lost its bubbles, Mary Helen thought.

Filled with compassion, the old nun crossed the kitchen floor and put her arm around Daphne's thin shoulders. "I shouldn't have asked why. I know why you lied. And I know who really killed Wendy."

For the first time their eyes met. Mary Helen was shocked by Daphne's vacant stare. It was as if the awful reality had clouded those clear marble eyes. Had taken away their luster.

"I didn't lie, Sister. It was my fault. I did it. Really, I did." This time her voice was lifeless. "And actually, if I had to do it all over again, I would." She shook off Mary Helen's arm and wiped her soiled hands on her dainty yellow apron. "Yes, I would."

"Mommy, stop it! Stop it this minute!"

Beside her, Mary Helen felt Daphne's body stiffen, then give a violent shudder. Both women turned toward the back door. In it stood a crimson-faced Cheryl.

Pushing her blond hair back from her eyes, Cheryl gave the door such a violent slam that the glass window panes rattled. "Stop it! I said. Tell the truth." Her brown eyes were no longer doelike but blazing. She clenched her

226

fists. "Tell the truth, Mommy," her voice caught, "or I will."

"Pumpkin, no!" The words were barely a whisper.

"Don't call me that, Mommy," Cheryl shouted savagely. "I am not a child." Her cleft chin tilted up in defiance. "No, Mommy, I am not a child. I am not your little girl. I am not a pumpkin. What I am is a murderess." She exploded in a high-pitched giggle. "A pumpkin murderess, and I am glad."

"Goddammit! Now what?" Douglas Wayne stood at the kitchen door, his head down like an angry bull. "I told you I wanted this house kept quiet. Goddammit, I mean it." He glared at his daughter. His eyes smoldered. "Come with me, Cheryl." He put out one broad hand.

Glaring back at her father, Cheryl edged toward the corner of the kitchen. "I don't want him near me, Mommy. I don't want that pig to touch me. I did it and I'm going to tell everyone why."

For the first time, Wayne noticed Sister Mary Helen. His eyes shifted toward her.

"She knows," Cheryl taunted him. She crouched in the corner, next to the stove. "But she doesn't know why. And I am going to tell her why." Viciously, she pushed the hair back from her eyes. "I am going to tell her that you and Wicked Wendy were lovers. Yes! And I could hear Mommy crying at night." Covering her ears with her hands, she stared at her father. Hatred in her eyes, she jutted out her chin. "I couldn't stand it anymore. So I—"

Before she could go on, Wayne lunged for her. Dodging her father's grasp, Cheryl swept the metal grates from the stovetop. They crashed onto the linoleum.

"Goddamn you." His thick fingers reached for her.

She cringed. "When I catch you, I'll beat the hell out of you."

"But you can't change what I did!" Cheryl shrieked, kicking and wriggling to avoid his grasp.

He caught hold of her hair with one hand, and yanked her toward the middle of the kitchen. Her face pinched with pain, she twisted, struggling to get loose. "Stop it, Cheryl!" He grabbed her arm with his free hand and gave her a hard shake. Her head snapped back. "Stop it!" he shouted.

Cheryl seemed to calm down. Turning her face away from him, she sniffled and brushed away a tear. Still holding her firmly with one hand, Wayne untangled his fingers from her stringy hair. "Stop now, will you? Please, pumpkin."

At the sound of the name, Cheryl's head jerked around. Slowly she raised her eyes to his. With a look of contempt, she pulled herself up to her full height and spat in her father's face.

The kitchen was deadly quiet. Mary Helen watched, horrified. It was like a scene from a nightmare with time standing still. Wayne drew back his broad, thick hand and slapped Cheryl once across the face. She tumbled backward.

"You goddamn brat!" he bellowed, moving toward her. "I told your mother all you needed was a good beating and this time you're going to get it." He raised his hand to slap her again.

Beside her, Mary Helen felt Daphne spring to life. "Enough!" she shouted, her rage exploding. "Enough!" From behind, she grabbed her husband's full head of hair in her meat-spattered hands and jerked his head backward. "Enough, I said! You are not going to hit her or me ever again."

Momentarily startled, Wayne turned on his wife. "What the hell?" When he realized who it was, he took a menacing step toward her. "And who is going to stop me? You?" His eyes narrowed into slits. "All this is your fault, you know," he sneered. "Daffy's a perfect name for you. Everything you do gets all screwed up. You're a joke. You can't do anything right . . . not make me happy, not raise the boys right, not keep the house clean, not even control your own daughter."

With savage speed, he backhanded Daphne, sending her sprawling against the sideboard. An angry welt rose on her cheek. His eyes like flint and with no more concern than if he had swatted a fly, he turned his full rage on his daughter. Instinctively, Mary Helen grabbed his forearm. He spun toward her, eyes blazing. With a quick twist, he pulled free. "I guess I'm going to have to teach you a lesson, Cheryl," he said. Slowly, he doubled up his broad fist. "I don't want you to turn out like your mother, now, do I? Never be able to do anything right."

Stupefied, Sister Mary Helen watched Daphne Wayne raise the mixing bowl. Closing her eyes, Daffy flung it like a missile across her cute kitchen. Direct hit! Obviously, there is something she can do right, Mary Helen thought. Douglas Wayne crumpled to the floor, his blow-dried, carefully styled hair oozing with stringy red meat.

"You can call your inspector now," Daphne Wayne whispered, cradling her sobbing child in her arms.

—

Still shaking, Sister Mary Helen sat in the yellow breakfast nook drinking a cup of hot tea. She had pulled up the shades to let in the light. Streaks of apricot swept the sky as the sun set behind the dark clouds. Daphne sat silently beside her. Cheryl had sunk down onto the kitchen floor, pulling her knees up under her chin. From somewhere she could hear the mumble of Douglas Wayne's voice. He must be talking on the telephone. In the distance, Mary Helen made out the shriek of a siren. In a few seconds, Inspector Gallagher would arrive at the house.

Poor man! Although they'd had their differences, she didn't envy him his task. Some cases are solved like an intellectual puzzle, she had read in one of her mysteries, others by emotion and imagination. This case would defy both. Christina's murder would only be solved by unraveling the complicated and incomprehensible bond of love between a mother and her child.

—

"Anybody home?" The door of the maternity room cracked open, sending a sliver of light into the darkened room.

Kate Murphy blinked her eyes and stretched, then checked the luminous dial of the clock on her nightstand. Five-thirty! She must have dozed off.

"Come in, Denny." Reaching up, she switched on the lamp. Soft shadows filled the small, cozy room.

"Jeez, Katie-girl, if you had your eyes shut and your hands folded, I'd swear to God you'd been laid out." Gallagher pointed to the flower arrangements and blooming plants that filled the room. "It smells like McAvoy and O'Hara's in here."

He leaned over and gave her a buss on the cheek. His stubbly beard scratching against her face felt reassuring. "Where do you want these?"

"Oh, how sweet!" Kate reached for the arrangement of Cecile Brunner roses in Gallagher's outstretched hand.

"Who the hell ever heard of putting flowers in a baby diaper?" He shrugged. "But that's what the guy in the florist shop told me was 'in.' Far as I can remember them, flowers are not what was ever in any of my kids' diapers."

Wrinkling up her freckled nose, Kate put the ceramic diaper-shaped vase with its dainty bouquet of roses and baby breath on the nightstand. "It's good to see you, Denny." She reached over and squeezed his hand. "I miss you already."

"I'd have been here sooner, Katie-girl, but all hell broke loose right after Jack called the detail to say you'd had a boy. He was so high you could have heard him without the phone. How are you feeling, kiddo?"

Kate felt fine and she could tell by the look on her partner's face that something big had happened. Something he was so eager to tell her that he hadn't even gone home after work. He had come right to the hospital. "What do you mean, 'all hell broke loose'?"

"Your pal, Sister Mary Helen." Gallagher sat down in the easy chair alongside her bed, tugging at his jacket and trouser legs until he was comfortable. Like a mother bird snuggling into her nest for a long sit, Kate thought, watching his antics.

"What about her?" she asked.

"That nun is going to be the death of me yet," he said when he was finally settled.

"She was here around noontime with my mother-in-law."

"Then she must have hotfooted it right over to the Wayne house."

"Whatever for?" Kate adjusted her pillows and sat up in the bed.

"Because she had a bee in her bonnet. That's what for. She figured the Wayne woman didn't do it after all and was covering up for somebody. Probably for that skinny kid of hers. So instead of calling us, like I told you to tell her—"

"Cheryl?" Kate interrupted what she figured would end in the usual tirade.

"None other and, hot damn, Kate, she was right."

Kate was really puzzled now. "Why in the world would Cheryl want to kill Christina Kelly?"

"Not Christina." Gallagher loosened his tie. "Daphne gave us the correct scoop on the intended victim. It was Wendy. From what I gathered this afternoon, the kid was really distraught about dear old dad having an affair with Wendy and hurting the mother."

Kate cringed. "You don't mean physically?"

"Mostly emotionally, but, yeah, physically too. Anyway, she'd had enough. The daughter, I mean. She's a high-strung son of a gun—"

"Daughter of a gun," Kate corrected.

"That, too, and damn smart. A chemistry major, actually, the teacher's trusted lab assistant, I come to find out. So she lifts herself a little potassium cyanide from the school lab. Looks as innocent as salt. Then she keeps it hoping she can think of a way to use it on Wendy. When, bingo! An idea made in heaven.

"The mother suggests that she bake some cookies to

take to the studio the day she was going there to spend some time with daddy dearest. Remember? That was why she was at the studio that day."

Kate remembered. And she remembered thinking at the time how sad it was that a girl of nineteen had no relationship with her father and hoping that Jack would be close to their child.

"As I was saying," Gallagher continued, "she slipped one poisoned cookie into the batch. Then she stuck the whole plate on what she thought was Wendy's chair behind the news desk."

"But it wasn't Wendy's chair."

Gallagher leaned forward and unlaced his shoes. "Do you mind? My feet are killing me."

Kate shook her head. "Feel free." She chuckled. "The flowers will kill the odor. Go on, Denny."

"Very funny, Katie-girl. Anyway, you're right. It wasn't Wendy's chair. Usually it was, but because Christina was going to interview Sister Mary Helen, Betty Hughes had them switch chairs."

Kate wriggled in the bed. "Even so, it doesn't make much sense. How could she be sure only Wendy ate the right—or should I say, wrong—cookie?"

"The kid had listened to her mother ranting about how selfish Wendy was and how much Wendy liked raisin cookies. You know how kids are. Or at least you will. Little pitchers with big ears, like they say. Anyway, she listens and hears the mother say how Wendy was allergic to chocolate. So she puts two and two together. She figured that if Wendy shared the plate at all, she'd be sure to take the raisin cookie for herself and leave the chocolate chip ones alone."

"I still say it doesn't make much sense."

"Nobody said the kid had much sense, just that she was smart. There's a big difference, you know."

Kate nodded. "But there are so many loose ends. For example, Betty Hughes. Why threaten Betty Hughes?"

Kicking back in the easy chair, Gallagher ran his hand over his bald pate. "Give me a chance. It's been one helluva long day. I'm getting to that." He fumbled in his jacket pocket until he found his cigar stub. "Do you mind?" he asked.

"I don't, but the hospital does. Hurry up, Denny, you've got me going."

With a resigned shrug, Gallagher put the stub back into his pocket. "Betty Hughes. Well, the kid has the plate of cookies in that backpack of hers and she slips the plate of cookies onto the chair when she passes behind the set coming into the studio just before the show. Betty hollered to go in front of the desk. Cheryl was afraid that since Betty was the floor manager, she would remember. Little did she know that Betty doesn't remember saying it at all. Maybe Betty gets on the sauce a little early some days to calm her nerves."

"Why did Cheryl threaten Sister Mary Helen?"

"She saw Betty and the nun talking at the Kelly funeral. Betty was into her cups, so Cheryl wasn't really sure what she was saying or how much stock Sister Mary Helen was putting in it. In the end, it was the tape that did her in."

"How so?"

"Your friend Mary Helen remembered what it was about the tape that bothered her."

"Thank goodness," Kate said. "Something about the sound, the cadence, something that I can't put my finger on, has been driving me crazy too. What was it?"

"The hissing sound. She figured out it was—"

"Braces!" Kate finished the sentence for him. "Of course, that's what it was. The sound created by a mouth full of braces. And her mother figured it out long before any of us, and came forward to take the blame."

"She had more of the facts." Denny brought his easy chair to an upright position. "But enough about murder, Katie-girl. I want to see this kid that Jack has been raving about."

"And everything I said is true." Jack Bassetti pushed open the maternity room door. "It's just about feeding time, too."

He leaned over the bassinet in the corner of the room and handed Kate the tiny, wiggling bundle. With a small noise, like the cry of a newborn kitten, the baby announced to all that he was hungry.

"Jeez, he's right here in the room?" Gallagher huffed. "Nothing's the way it used to be. Not even having babies. In my day, they were all behind glass where they belong."

Lifting back one corner of the blanket, Kate gazed at the round pink face with its button nose. His eyelids, still closed, were nearly transparent, like delicate pieces of alabaster. She marveled afresh at his perfect ears, the wisps of curly blond hair. The rosebud mouth opened and twisted, telling her without words that he was ready for dinner.

Gazing down at him, Kate wondered if she would really be able to leave this precious baby in six months to go back to work. He shifted in her arms, full of the life that she had given him; her own dear miracle. With a rush of love, she understood why a mother wants to protect the child of her womb. Right or wrong, Kate understood the feeling that caused Daphne Wayne to lie to protect her child. It was that tremendously strong bond called mother love. Holding her own child close, she understood it very well.

FEBRUARY 5
FIFTH AND LAST SUNDAY IN ORDINARY TIME

Sister Mary Helen let the heavy bronze door of the convent chapel close behind her. It was empty, thank God, save for the single flickering red flame in the sanctuary lamp that told her she was not alone. Her God was here.

Genuflecting, she slipped into a back pew, happy to sit for a few moments in the semidarkness and think. On this cold wet Sunday afternoon, the steam heaters gave a friendly hiss and turned the chapel into a warm, comfortable haven. The familiar aroma of incense mingled with the scent of burning wax lingered from the morning's liturgy.

Before Mass, Father Adams had reminded the congregation that this was the Fifth and last Sunday of Ordinary Time. In his homily he had warned them that Ash Wednesday and the penitential season of Lent would begin this very week.

Lent, already! Mary Helen shifted in the pew. I am still picking up stray Christmas tree needles and pieces of tinsel from the carpet in my office. Next thing you know, it will be a mess with Easter grass!

No, it doesn't seem possible. Although it is just as well, she thought, resigning herself to the inevitable quick passage of time. And, in a more practical vein, she checked to see if the buttons on her clean white blouse pouched. Come this Wednesday, I'll have no excuse not to diet, and what's more, since it is Lent, I can call it fasting. Much more respectable!

Nonetheless, this year the Season of Ordinary Time was unusually short and, in Mary Helen's opinion, anything but ordinary. The events of the last few weeks ran through her mind like cards being shuffled, all dovetailing into one another and stacking up: her unexpected invitation to appear on television; Christina Kelly's death; stumbling on the theft of valuable Greek icons; Daphne's confession; and uncovering Cheryl as the real murderer. In the midst of it all was the birth of a baby boy.

Strange, she mused, drinking in the deep silence of the chapel, how all the events somehow hinged on a mother's love for her child. And even stranger, how God works in the lives of His children. Some of them good, some warped, some selfish, yet He loves each one of them with His own unconditional love. "Can a mother forget her infant, be without tenderness for the child of her womb? Even should she forget, I will never forget you," He promised. She was counting on it.

The winter sun set the stained-glass windows along the chapel's west wall aflame, spilling their brilliant colors over the wooden pews. Mary Helen checked her wristwatch. Two o'clock. Soon the others would start to arrive for the baptism of Baby Bassetti.

Kate and Jack wanted their child baptized here and Father Adams had readily agreed. Mary Helen was glad. To her way of thinking, St. Francis Chapel had all too few baptisms. She found it thrilling to see new life and revel in it. The fact that a child is born means that God Himself has spoken. His creative power working through Kate and Jack had invited a special person into existence. This baby is a special little person, she thought, whatever they decide to call him.

Sister Mary Helen closed her eyes hoping for a few more moments of peace to recollect herself, but it was too late. Behind the sanctuary, the sacristy door shut with a soft thump. She heard the rustling of Sister Anne moving through the cupboards collecting the holy water, the chrism, the linen cloth, the candle, all the things needed to administer the Sacrament. Before long, the guests would arrive and the festivities would begin.

"Oh, there you are, at last. I have been searching high and low for you." Eileen slid into the pew next to Mary Helen. "Did you have the opportunity to read this morning's *Chronicle*?"

Mary Helen shook her head.

"There is a big spread about Interpol uncovering a ring of importers smuggling valuable Greek icons." She waited for Mary Helen to respond. When she didn't, Eileen rushed on. "They gave some credit to the cooperation of the San Francisco Police Department. But honestly, Mary Helen, they didn't even mention you."

Thank God, Mary Helen thought.

"You don't seem surprised about the story breaking." Eileen raised her eyebrows.

"I'm not," Mary Helen whispered, remembering the sadness in Mrs. Pappas's voice when she had called yesterday evening. It was as if her spirit had been broken, and all the fire that love and hate kindled was burned out, leaving her heart with only cold, empty ashes of sadness.

"Christina's mother telephoned me," she said.

"She must have been very upset."

"That's the understatement of the year! Although she was glad that none of her close relatives were involved. Just a distant cousin. She was distressed enough about that. She told me she felt ashamed that any member of her family was involved in so disgraceful a crime as stealing sacred images."

"She shouldn't. That poor woman has been through enough. Thanks be to God, you can't be responsible for what your relatives do," Eileen said with conviction. "Every family has its hooligans."

Mary Helen nodded, remembering poor Joe Sousa. She hoped that he had finally settled down to his job and his girlfriend now that Tony Sousa's trial and all the publicity about it had been moved to San Diego.

"What else did Mrs. Pappas have to say?"

"Only that policemen were swarming all over Valencia Street. Do you remember that small Greek import shop next to the Cathedral of the Annunciation?"

"The one with those barrels and straw wine-casks in the window? What was its motto?"

" 'Home of the largest selection of imported Greek food and wine in the entire Bay Area.' " Mary Helen cleared her throat.

"Right you are, old dear! How in the name of heaven did you remember that?"

"Mrs. Pappas told me when she called. She said that no one realized how large their selection really was. It seems that they were importing more than wine and cheese. Their contacts in Greece, which included this cousin of hers, had smuggled several valuable icons in the straw."

"Did her son know? Was that why he didn't want his mother to get involved?"

"I think Teddy may have suspected and he knew that his mother would feel responsible, somehow. He was trying to spare her any more grief." That mother–child bond again, Mary Helen mused, with a twinge of guilt that she herself had been suspicious of Ted.

Both nuns sat quietly for a moment. Sister Anne switched on the sanctuary lights, illuminating the marble altar and sending shadows across the large crucifix that hung over it.

Sister Eileen leaned toward her. "By the way, did Therese ever find you for the phone?"

Mary Helen rolled her eyes. "Indeed she did. And it was a good thing too. The call was from the new controller at Channel Five. The station has decided to give me the ten-thousand-dollar reward they had offered for information leading to the arrest of Christina Kelly's murderer."

"Will they be announcing it soon?"

"It will be on the evening news tonight. Frankly, Eileen, it couldn't have come at a better time. I've done precious little to promote the St. Valentine's Day Tea ticket sales, so the money will ensure the tea's success."

"That is a bit of luck," Eileen said.

The two nuns smiled at one another, knowing full well that by tomorrow morning the phone in the alumnae office would be ringing nonstop, and that the St. Valentine's Day Tea would be jam-packed with alums who wanted nothing more than to talk to Sister Mary Helen about her latest adventure.

"Other than that, how are you doing this morning, old dear?" Eileen's gray eyes opened wide.

"Just fine, why?"

"I thought that you might be a bit nervous, what with being the godmother and all."

Mary Helen shoved her bifocals up the bridge of her nose and studied her friend in disbelief. "Why in the name of all that is good and holy, would I be nervous? God knows I've been to enough baptisms, Eileen, that I know exactly what to do."

"I was not worrying about your forgetting the rubrics, Mary Helen. What I am worrying about is your meeting the godfather."

"Umph!" Mary Helen responded. Although she was reluctant to admit it, in all honesty she was a bit nervous about that herself. The last time she had seen Inspector Dennis Gallagher, he was nearly breathing fire, insisting that she stay out of Homicide business and ranting about how she could have gotten herself, or somebody else, killed.

"Inspector Gallagher is a sensible man," she whispered to Eileen with more conviction than she felt. "Surely he will have calmed down by now."

Eileen rolled her eyes. "We will see," she said, "and soon. I think they are here."

The jumble of voices and the sound of laughter wafted from the vestibule into the quiet chapel. Someone pulled back the heavy door. The Bassettis, the Murphys, and a battalion of friends arrived to witness the baptism of a son. Godfather Gallagher brought up the rear.

He raised two fingers in a V when he saw Sister Mary Helen. "Peace," he said with a sheepish grin.

"Peace be to you, too, Inspector." She smiled. "Now see, Eileen," she whispered to her friend, "you fretted in vain. The man is just fine."

"Don't be swallowing gudgeons 'ere they're catched,

nor counting chicken 'ere they're hatched," Eileen said with a sniff that Mary Helen chose to ignore.

"You know what to do, don't you, S'ter?" Gallagher asked.

"Absolutely." Mary Helen squeezed his arm and watched his face flush. "All you need to do is follow me, Inspector."

"Figures," he muttered, taking his place beside her in the first pew.

"I suppose you read the *Chron* this morning," he whispered.

Mary Helen just smiled. No sense explaining that Christina Kelly's mother had called. At this point, she figured, the less said, the better.

"Thanks to you, both Kate and I are getting a commendation." The color in his face deepened. "I just wanted to say that I appreciate what you did."

"You are very welcome." Mary Helen tried not to gloat. "To my way of thinking, you both deserve it."

"No offense, S'ter." Gallagher bent closer to her. "I appreciate what you did, but some one of these bright days you are liable to get yourself hurt. So, in the future, I think it would be for the best if you stuck to your business and let the police stick to—"

As if divinely sent, Father Adams entered the sanctuary before Gallagher could finish his sentence. Mary Helen breathed a sigh of relief. She was in no mood to listen to a lecture by Inspector Gallagher. Today was a day of celebration. Furthermore, they still had the party at Mrs. Bassetti's after the baptism to get through together. If they started this early, it could prove to be a very long day.

When all the guests were settled in their places in the front pews, Jack and Kate brought the baby to the font.

"What name do you give your child?" the priest asked, beginning the Rite of Infant Baptism.

"John Patrick," they said in unison.

Mrs. Bassetti gasped.

"After the two men I love most deeply, my husband and my father." Kate's voice was clear and certain. Jack beamed.

"What do you ask of God's Church for John Patrick?"

"Faith," his parents answered, again in unison.

"It is your duty to bring John Patrick up to keep God's commandments as Christ taught us, by loving God and our neighbor. Do you clearly understand what you are undertaking?"

John and Kate answered, "We do."

"And the godparents?" The priest looked inquiringly toward Inspector Gallagher and Sister Mary Helen.

The Odd Couple, Mary Helen thought, leaving the front pew and walking with Gallagher into the sanctuary. They took their places across from Jack and Kate.

Father Adams's eyes bulged. "Are you two going to be the godparents?" he asked in a stage whisper.

"We are." To their mutual surprise, they answered in unison.

The priest read aloud from the Rite. "Are you ready to help Jack and Kate in their duty as Christian parents?"

"Both of us got to help them? Together?" Gallagher's face reddened.

"That won't be so hard, Inspector. We have had a great deal of experience working together." Mary Helen smiled sweetly up at Gallagher. "And this time, I can legitimately make it my business."

Not that that has ever stopped me before, she thought, bowing her head piously.

Father Adams cleared his throat. "I said, Are you ready to help Jack and Kate in their duty as Christian parents?"

"We are," the godparents proclaimed aloud.

Mary Helen isn't positive who it was, but to this day she swears she heard somebody mumble, "Heaven help them!"